The lean male figure silhouetted by the sunlight

reminded Dusty of all the cowboys she had known in her life, all the rough-hewn men who rode the sagebrush hills and prodded cattle.

His hat was tilted low on his shadowed brow. One booted foot was cocked over the other. Lean, hard-muscled thighs were covered with worn denim seasoned by long hours in the saddle.

The man in the barn doorway, like all the cowboys Dusty had known, carried a naturalness about him. Jake Valiteros was in his element here. From the top of his work-softened hat to the tips of his scuffed boots, he was a cowboy, born and bred.

And Dusty was drawn to him, like steel to a magnet....

Dear Reader,

Welcome to Silhouette **Special Edition**...welcome to romance.

Fall is in full swing and so are some of your favorite authors, who have some delightful and romantic stories in store.

Our THAT SPECIAL WOMAN! title for the month is *Babies on Board*, by Gina Ferris. On a dangerous assignment, an independent heroine becomes an instant mom to three orphans in need of her help.

Also in store for you in October is the beginning of LOVE LETTERS, an exciting new series from Lisa Jackson. These emotional stories have a hint of mystery, as well...and it all begins in *A Is for Always*.

Rounding out the month are *Bachelor Dad* by Carole Halston, *An Interrupted Marriage* by Laurey Bright and *Hesitant Hero* by Christina Dair. Sandra Moore makes her Silhouette debut with her book, *High Country Cowboy*, as **Special Edition**'s PREMIERE author.

I hope you enjoy this book, and all of the stories to come!

Sincerely,

Tara Gavin
Senior Editor
Silhouette Books

Please address questions and book requests to:
Silhouette Reader Service
U.S.: 3010 Walden Ave., P.O. Box 1325, Buffalo, NY 14269
Canadian: P.O. Box 609, Fort Erie, Ont. L2A 5X3

SANDRA MOORE

HIGH COUNTRY COWBOY

SPECIAL EDITION®

Published by Silhouette Books
America's Publisher of Contemporary Romance

Thanks to Jeanne Rees Danks, who went on her first cattle
drive at age five, for all the information and for sharing her
stories of childhood on a ranch, especially the stories about
her father, "Oley" Rees.

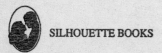 SILHOUETTE BOOKS

ISBN 0-373-09918-5

HIGH COUNTRY COWBOY

Copyright © 1994 by Sandra Moore

SANDRA MOORE

moved from Texas to Wyoming to be closer to the mountains. Summer means hiking, and autumn, camping. "During the long cold winters," she says, "I slide down ski slopes until I have squeezed all the winter out of spring."

A Letter from the Author

Dear Reader,

For over twenty years I encouraged teenagers to appreciate the English language—both as writers and readers. A thankless job, but the material and the students dazzled. And all the time, as I struggled to bring into focus the blinding brilliance of language, I yearned to write for myself, to play with words and meaning on my own terms.

I needed a message, some compelling reason to leave the umbrella of the classroom and splash into the puddles of my own stories.

A little over ten years ago, I began reading romance novels—secretly and in the dark and always purely for pleasure. Gradually, like the slow drip of summer rain, I understood what I needed to say.

Recently I heard someone on the radio observe that women are disappointed in men. Yes, I thought, but the real problem is not the disappointment but the expectation: Women expect too little of men and get what they expect. What if women began to expect more, to expect the best? Could men live up to our ideals?

Romance novels help us define the ideal. They tell us stories that explore the strength and passion of a woman's heart. I want to be a part of that. I want to tell those stories of remarkable women and the men who meet their challenge.

This story of Dusty and Jake is my first effort. I offer it to you with nervous anticipation and great hope.

Sincerely,

Sandra Moore

Prologue

AUCTION!

Dusty Macleod slammed her truck to a complete stop at the turnoff to her ranch. The dreaded word blinked at her from the top of a flapping handbill, tacked precariously to the corner fence post.

"What the hell?"

Big letters proclaimed:

AUCTION, MACLEOD RANCH,
BIG PINEY, WYOMING

She scowled at the words in slightly smaller print: today's date, Saturday, April 13; a list of machinery that had claimed long sweaty hours of her life; two bulls she knew by name rather than the crisply formal description on the notice...

She turned onto the double-track road that led to the ranch house, dust spinning out behind her. Her truck bounced over the dried ruts where heavy-duty tires had slogged through the mud of melting snow. The road led her straight as an arrow over the roll of a hill and down toward a dry creek bed and back up again toward the rise where the white frame house stood with the other buildings of a ranch's headquarters: a small dark red barn, corrals, shed.

Alien ranch trucks crowded into the open space between barn and house. They were parked helter-skelter, crammed into a snarled semicircle, violating the pristine order her father laboriously maintained. In the eye of the semicircle stood the hay wagon stripped of its winter load of feed. Instead of hay bales, a stranger stood on its bare boards, shouting at the people standing around him.

At the entrance to the ranch yard, Dusty stumbled out of her truck, grabbing the open door for support. That man on the hay wagon was an auctioneer; she could figure that out easily enough. Those people standing around the trucks, neighbors from nearby ranches, had the look of prospective buyers. She felt as if someone had clobbered her when she wasn't looking.

No one seemed to notice as she approached the edge of the crowd. The broad-brimmed hats and felt caps were turned toward the auctioneer. There were a few women sprinkled throughout the group, barely distinguishable from the men, everyone dressed in worn jeans and quilted vests or jackets in the brisk wind.

The auctioneer was gesturing toward the hay baler. The big machine sat in uncomfortable silence by the barn. It was a good baler. Dusty's father, Blackie Macleod, took care of his machinery. His machinery and his horses. Especially his horses.

Icy fingers gripped her insides, as if the wind had invaded her body. Wrapping her wool-lined jacket closer around her ribs, she made her way along the edges of the parked vehicles. Several people waved as she passed within their line of sight, their smiles tight and their eyes worried.

A man and a woman stepped out from the cab of their truck to speak to her.

The woman, her aunt, Ruth Taylor, enfolded her in a big hug. "You come from Laramie for a visit, Dusty?" she asked.

"That was the idea," Dusty answered, her eyes seeking the western horizon for the familiar mountains of the Wyoming Range. "Ruth," Dusty said huskily, her gaze returning to her aunt's face, "what's happened to my ranch?"

"That fool Blackie." Ruth's full mouth twitched derisively. Dusty admired her aunt's weathered face, lines around eyes and mouth from the hours Ruth spent in wind and sun doing the work she loved. Dusty remembered her mother's face had looked the same, as if it had been carved by the sharp Wyoming wind.

"Now, Ruth," her husband, Ed, cautioned. His kind face took on a concerned pucker. Where the weather had tautened Ruth's face, it had puffed and creased Ed's so that, with his sweeping moustache, he looked like a diminutive Santa Claus.

"Don't 'now Ruth' me," she returned. "Dusty deserves to hear the truth. It's her inheritance he frittered away. He sure didn't put up much fight to keep it. My poor sister is probably whirling in her grave."

"Did Blackie sell the ranch?" Dusty whispered, looking frantically from Ruth to Ed. Ed ducked his head and studied the ground.

"I bet he didn't say a word to you," Ruth said, squinting at her. Dusty shook her head. "That fool. He'd rather be wrapped in barbed wire than talk to anybody." She squeezed Dusty's shoulder consolingly. "Yes, honey, Blackie sold the ranch."

Dusty stared out into the open sagebrush. She rested her gaze on the fenceless hills, reminding herself that some things are beyond owning. Then she shook away the thought. The homelessness was too new; it wasn't persuaded by reason.

"Who bought it?"

Ruth scowled uneasily at Dusty before she answered. "Jake Valiteros," she said finally.

"Oh, I see."

Dusty knew Jake Valiteros. Of course, she did. There was hardly a rancher along the Wyoming Range she didn't know. The Valiteros place was one over from the ranch that had always belonged to her family. Most small ranchers helped one another out in this hard country; their survival depended on it. But the Valiteros spread was big enough not to need anybody. It had been too big to join the rest of the neighbors when they had gotten together for drifting cattle or branding or any number of things. In fact, it was big enough to swallow up its neighbors.

Ruth crossed her arms and tucked her chin in her chest. "It's this way, honey. Jake 'Lord Almighty' Valiteros has been after your property since his daddy died and left him nothing but greed. First, he got Hooter's ranch to the south of you, but I guess you know about that. That had to be almost ten years ago. Then a year or so ago, he picked up that little piece of property of T.J.'s to the north. Poor ol' T.J., he couldn't do anything to help himself. He's been wandering around here looking like the angel of death ever since."

"I didn't know," Dusty said. She had probably been too busy at the university to notice, she thought grimly. "Did T.J. lose his cabin?" T.J. was almost like family. He was the last remnant of a pioneer clan that had barely clung to survival, and he had worked for her father, now and again, for as long as she could remember.

"Oh, no, not the cabin," Ruth said, shaking her head. "He's still holed up in that box canyon of his. I don't suppose Valiteros or anybody else has any use for that run-down place. But you can be sure, Valiteros has been after every piece of property that borders Big Piney Creek." She paused and drew in a long breath. "Well, now he's got it all. I just hope he's satisfied, but I doubt it. The rest of us will probably have to put up mounted guards to keep him off our places."

"To be fair," Ed offered, "Blackie seems to think Jake has some pretty good ideas."

"Now, how would you know?" Ruth asked, disgusted. "Blackie hasn't let on to you any more than he has to me."

"No," Ed said, chuckling, "I guess he hasn't."

"And it's sure Jake Valiteros hasn't spoken to you in years." She frowned at Ed's smile. "You're the wrong sex."

"Ruth," Ed admonished, shooting a look of alarm in Dusty's direction.

"Oh, you fool," Ruth scoffed. "She's twenty-five years old, old enough to know the facts of life. And forewarned is forearmed." Ruth nodded curtly. Then she said to Dusty, "Valiteros ran off one wife, like his daddy ran off his mama. Now he cats around here, taking every female he can, married or not. You'd think he's ugly enough to keep them at a distance, but there's no telling what a little money can do to make a woman think a man is handsome as sin."

"Ugly?" Dusty asked, too stunned to follow everything Ruth said. She didn't remember thinking Jake Valiteros was ugly, but then she had been looking at his horse. The only place Dusty remembered seeing Jake was at rodeos. He was a calf roper, and she had admired his horse. It was lean and confident, and it had spirit. Being Blackie's offspring, Dusty knew about horses.

"Well, more like used," said Ruth, and Ed shook his head. Ruth squeezed Dusty's shoulder again, her hand reassuring in its strength. "I checked in the Big Piney library to be sure they had that master's thesis of yours, like you asked me," she said softly.

In spite of Ruth's unusually soft voice, Dusty was startled by the mention of her thesis. She thought about the last three years she had spent working and preparing for it, to the exclusion of everything else, even the ranch. For a year and a half, she had traveled all over the state, tramping out to pastures to talk to ranchers, poking her nose into county courthouses and libraries. Finally, the last six months or so, she had spent writing, compiling all the research, working late into the night and at it again early the next morning. She had barely stopped long enough to come home for Christmas, and she hadn't stayed long then. No, until about a month ago, the thesis had been her whole world. But since she'd left campus she hadn't given the thesis one small thought.

"I was so proud of you when I read about all those pioneer ranching families," Ruth was saying, "especially what you had to say about ours. Just thinking about what those people did to survive makes me shudder."

Dusty smiled wanly. It was hard to picture her aunt shuddering at anything. "I'm glad you read what I wrote. I really enjoyed interviewing the descendants of Wyoming's pioneer families." She grinned at her aunt's weathered face. "I even enjoyed talking to you." Her expression became solemn, and she looked up at the mountains. "This country must have been terrifying to the first people who brought cattle here. They came from such different backgrounds."

"Humph," Ruth snorted. "Background didn't matter once they started ranching around here. All that matters here is the dust and the cold and no water and the damn mountains."

Dusty didn't even flinch at her aunt's expletive. She had long ago become accustomed to such language from both men and women. Usually, only those things that commanded most respect received the benefit of curses. The *damn* mountains, the *damn* cattle, the *damn* horses, but most of all the *damn* weather.

"It's for sure Valiteros wasn't in your master's thesis." Ruth nodded curtly. "The Valiteros bunch were latecomers. Jake's daddy never wanted anything that some-body hadn't tamed first."

Dusty pulled her coat tighter and ducked her head. When she looked up, she glanced toward the spot by the barn where Blackie leaned against a fence and watched the auctioneer. From where she stood with Ed and Ruth, she couldn't see a hint of tension in her father. He might have been watching somebody else's belongings being sold one by one.

Dusty didn't see the worried looks Ed and Ruth exchanged. "Honey," Ruth said, "you're not upset about what Blackie did, are you? Why, you've hardly been around here at all since Mac died—" Ruth's voice halted at the sharp look Dusty gave her.

Mac. Even three years later, Dusty had to fight back the tears. Her big brother and her best friend. A patch of black ice had sent his truck spinning off the road three years ago this spring.

"Well, you know," Ruth said softly, "we thought there wouldn't be much to come back to. I mean, after Mac died, you stayed right there in Laramie at the university, and you'd already graduated from college and everything."

"No, I didn't come home then." Dusty had holed up in Laramie with her grief. She had absorbed herself in a master's degree in history and tried to forget Blackie's silent grieving, the wordless pain in her father's eyes, a pain that never healed. First her mother's death and then Mac's.

"We just got a good price on that hay baler of Blackie's," Ed was saying. "Several of us put in together to buy it. I used to rent it from Blackie, anyway, so I was real anxious to get it. Too bad Blackie don't come along with it to do the mechanic work."

Ruth's mouth puckered with worry, but she kept quiet. Dusty was grateful for Ruth's silence. Her aunt couldn't help her anyway. Everything had been lost before Dusty had even been considered.

Ed moved closer and placed his worn hand on Dusty's shoulder. "I see you haven't lost your timing, Dusty. You waited 'til calving was over to come home. I remember how you used to hate it."

She tried to smile. "You're right about that. Calving never was one of my favorite things."

Ed grinned at her. "I had a time this year. Never seen so many green heifers. I pulled calves until my bones ached. We missed Blackie's help."

Dusty felt herself jerk. "Blackie didn't help you this year?"

"Why, no. Blackie was too busy working Jake's first-time cows."

Dusty's eyes widened in shock. "Blackie's working for Jake Valiteros?"

"Sure he is. Jake's too smart to pass up a good hand like Blackie. Especially with his horses. I guess Valiteros wants the best-kept horses on the upper Green River."

Dusty turned away without another word and, moving slowly and jerkily, was almost around the semicircle of vehicles before she saw the man standing with her father. Jake Valiteros. He and Blackie were leaning against the corral fence by the side of the barn. She stepped back behind a pickup to study the contrast the two of them made. Even though he wasn't more than six feet himself, Jake Valiteros towered above her father.

Blackie's hunch-shouldered posture added to the contrast. He hooked his thumbs in the front pockets of his jeans and cast his gaze at the ground in front of his bowlegged stance. Or at the toes of his boots, always a favorite target of Blackie's gaze.

Jake Valiteros, younger and less worn by time, leaned against the wide boards of the fence, one boot heel propped on the rail behind him. His fleece-lined jacket hung open, allowing him to hook both thumbs on a fancy belt buckle. Except for the expensive jacket, he was dressed no differently from any of the men standing around the yard. Even the belt buckle was no bigger or more ornate than those worn by most of the cowboys. Although his black hat had a perfect crease in the crown with leather braid at its base, it was stained with the sweat of a working man.

His face, shaded by the wide brim of his hat, held no expression at all. It might as well have been chipped out of stone. Despite Ruth's assessment, Dusty didn't think he was ugly. He had a stern, unhandsome face, clean-shaven but weathered by sun and wind into ridges that ran from cheekbone to jawline. His eyes were narrowed as if habitually protecting his sight from the constant sun and the fierceness of the dust-laden wind.

His face reminded Dusty of a good many of the men who rode the land beneath the Wyoming Range. It was shutdown and boarded-up, like an abandoned line shack high on summer pasture. It gave away nothing, no thought or emotion. She remembered what her aunt had said about his reputation with women. Of course, she knew not to believe gossip around here, but she could understand why some women would enjoy the challenge. The stern-faced cowboy emanated power, banked-down power that could explode at any second. He looked dangerous, like a low-hanging cloud, dark with barely suppressed energy, ready to strike out in an angry bolt of lightning.

She had seen his power in action at rodeos when she was no more than a kid in high school. He had ridden a big buckskin, a quick-moving horse that bested the most uncooperative of calves. She had admired the way the horse and rider worked together, equally matched in skill and strength. She had hung on the arena fence, too awed to have sense enough to step back. Mac had grabbed her and hauled her down.

As she watched now, the air seemed to sizzle around him, the way it does right before a mountain storm. A portly cowboy, making his way from the front to the back of the crowd, neared her father and Jake Valiteros, before glancing self-consciously at them and veering away. Blackie nodded at the cowboy, but his silent companion showed no acknowledgment at all.

"Hello, Dad," she said, stepping in front of the two.

Blackie Macleod looked up slowly. "What you doing here?" he said in his hushed voice, his mouth barely moving under his bushy moustache.

"I think that's my line, Dad." Dusty's eyes flashed.

Blackie moved his thumbs to the back pockets of his jeans and considered the upturned toe of his boot. He said finally, "I decided to sell the place. Jake here give me a good offer."

Jake Valiteros eased away from the fence and inspected her from head to foot. Only the eyes moved in his stone face.

"When did this happen?" Dusty's stance didn't slacken.

Blackie shrugged and continued the close observation of his boot.

"Your name's Dusty, isn't it?" Jake interjected in a voice like rough gravel. He stared at her with his narrowed eyes, his face furrowed in a habitual scowl.

"Yes, that's my name." Dusty shifted to face her adversary squarely. She had to look up to stare him in the eye, but she wouldn't back down. "I'm Dusty Macleod of the former Macleod Ranch, your neighbor to the northwest."

"Well, Dusty Macleod," he said, the straight line of his mouth twitching once, "where have you been for the past seven months? I bought this ranch last fall."

Dusty almost crumpled, as if someone had given her a blow to the midsection.

Blackie looked up sideways at Jake. "I never told her I'd sold the ranch. She was away at school and I—"

He was interrupted by the auctioneer, who shouted Blackie's name across the crowd. Blackie gave Dusty a sheepish look, clearly grateful to leave whatever he was going to say unsaid. He ambled off to help the auctioneer with the bulls he was planning to sell.

"I'm sorry Blackie didn't tell you," Jake said, a little less harshly than before. "I can see it would be a shock to walk in on it like you did."

"You could say that."

"But you have to see the ranch is Blackie's to sell," Jake said, looking out over the sagebrush hills. "After your brother died, there didn't seem much reason to keep it together."

"Is that what Blackie told you?"

"Well, no," admitted Jake, bringing his gaze back to her. "I just assumed..."

"I guess I don't look like much of a reason to you." She tossed her head back and fixed him with a green-eyed glare. "You probably think because I'm a woman I don't have any claim on the ranch."

"No, I..." His voice trailed off as he stared at her. He had been thinking of her as a child, not a woman. But now that she mentioned it, he was suddenly aware of her unusually green eyes, her tawny mane of hair, and, letting his gaze take it all in, the nicely rounded way she filled out her jeans. One side of his mouth kicked up in a grin.

The grin made her madder. He was laughing at her. "Regardless of how I look to you, I thought I was coming home in a few weeks to run a ranch. Until a few minutes ago, when I found out you'd talked Blackie into selling out, my life was all set."

"Now wait a minute." He looked around, checking the stares of some curious onlookers with a stare of his own. Damn, he thought, I don't need a hot-tempered female to start tongues wagging at my expense. Then, an image flashed in his head, returning his attention to the woman standing in front of him. The image was a picture of a good-looking woman in the Big Piney newspaper a few weeks back. Something about the story of ranching families. Yeah, that was it. The original ranchers in Wyoming. The picture made her look sophisticated, very cool. The woman who was glaring at him now looked more like a spitting bobcat.

"Blackie should've told you about our business deal," he said, admiring the view in spite of himself, "but that's not my problem. Just for the record, I didn't talk him into anything. I just came around today to give him my support."

"No, you wait a minute," she retorted. "I just remembered something my brother told me years ago." Mac had told her about running into Jake Valiteros in a bar. Valiteros wanted Mac to talk Blackie into selling. He said he'd make Mac manager. Mac laughed about the offer. He said cows were ornery enough without belonging to somebody else. "You've been trying to get this place for a long time. You tried to get my brother to sell out. He told me about it."

"This ranch is on some prime creek bottom. Naturally I was interested."

"I know all about our creek bottom. I've worked this ranch since I was old enough to ride. I know every inch of what you made off with."

Jake glanced again at the accusing stares aimed at him. "Let's move over by the house out of earshot."

He reached out to take Dusty's sleeve, but she jerked it out of his grasp. For some reason, one he didn't want to examine too closely, her reaction irritated him, sending him stomping off toward the house.

Dusty, suddenly aware of the interested eyes of her neighbors, reluctantly followed Jake to the narrow front porch.

Jake propped one booted foot on the second porch step, taking off his hat and slapping it against his knee. He doubted the wisdom of going on with this discussion. He was sure he would regret it later, but her eyes spit green fire and, just for a second back there, when he told her he had bought the ranch last fall, that fire had softened. Her eyes had looked vulnerable, the color of new aspen leaves.

"Look," he said, trying to be reasonable, "I admit I've been interested in buying this place for a long time, but I didn't make Blackie sell it."

"That's something I wouldn't know, Valiteros," she said, storming up to him until her boots were against the bottom step. Even bent over his propped-up knee, he was taller than she was. She looked at his stern face and felt her breath catch at the power of him. The absence of his black hat hadn't softened his expression. His hair, she noticed incongruously, was only slightly darker than the dust color of her own.

She forced down the weakness he made her feel. "Just what were you willing to do to get your hands on this property?"

Jake roused at her angry words. Had she been a man, he might have made the disagreement physical, but when his grim face was only inches from hers, the green fire from her eyes arrested his forward motion. He watched, fascinated, as the fire mellowed to that aspen green again.

His stare burned her, searing into her with its intensity. Something inside her curled, like a slender branch in the heat of a campfire. She knew she should protect herself, look away, even run, but she couldn't move from that spellbinding stare.

Jake settled back on his heels. "Listen to me a minute." He had to clear his throat before he could go on. "You know what they say about ranchers in the high country. We live poor and we die rich. We put everything we have into land and livestock, every penny we can scrape up. We live on nothing so we can pour it all into the ranch. Then a rancher dies and his heirs sell everything, and get rich."

Dusty sighed. None of what he said was new to her. She put herself through college because she knew whatever money Blackie had went back into the ranch. Her family had always had enough to get by—but just enough.

"Think about it. Maybe Blackie wanted to see some of that money himself—before he died."

Jake didn't really believe Blackie wanted the money for himself. No, Jake suspected Blackie wanted to get the best deal he could for his daughter. He probably thought that, being a woman, she would be hard-pressed to get top dollar when she tried to sell the ranch. Jake was sure the belligerent young woman scowling at the dirt in front of the steps wouldn't listen to that argument.

Dusty shrugged and stuck her thumbs in her hip pockets, looking at her boots and unconsciously imitated her father. She turned from the long, lean man who loomed between her and the steps of the house she had lived in with her mother and Mac and her father. She looked out toward the willows marking the creek bottom.

"Anyway, like I said before, the ranch was his, to do with as he pleased," Jake went on, watching her. "He should've told you before he sold it, but he didn't have to."

"Blackie never was one to tell anybody anything." Her voice was choked with the tears she refused to shed in front of the man who had bought her dreams. She kept her back to him. "What about the house? Is Blackie still living here?"

Jake felt ill at ease. He could tell by her rigid back that she was holding herself together by force of will. "Yeah," he said quietly, "he kept the house. He also kept the barn and the corrals. He holds the deed on fifty acres, including the buildings and the land between them and the creek." He thought to himself that he sounded like a damn lawyer.

"Well, that's something, anyway."

"Blackie's working for me. He's taking care of my horses."

She whirled to face him. "The horses. Did Blackie sell you our horses?"

"No," Jake said quickly. "Blackie would never give up his horses."

"That's a relief." She sighed. She knew there were only a few horses left after Mac died, but they were important. "I guess I'll still have enough gear to get work on some other ranch around here."

"What?" Jake asked incredulously. "You expect to hire out as a ranch hand? Little slip of a girl like you?"

An angry flush crawled up her neck to her cheeks. "You don't think I can handle it, do you?" she said. "You don't know anything about me, Mr. Jake Valiteros. I can work circles around a man any day. Ranch work is the only kind of work I've ever wanted to do, and I'll do it right here, too, in the Green River Valley." She swept an arm upward in the direction of the red peaks of the Wyoming Range that formed the western boundary for every ranch for miles around. "Look at those mountains. I was born right here within sight of those mountains. They belong to no one and nobody, and they'll outlast us all. They'll be here when your big ranch has blown away on the wind." She stopped and dared him with a hard look. "And just as certain as those mountains, I'm staying here. You can buy my ranch and my livestock, but you can't buy me away from those mountains. You can't buy me out or run me out. Those mountains are my birthright. They're in my blood. I belong here. Remember that." She turned abruptly on her boot heels and stomped around the side of the house.

"Damn," he said to himself, raking his hand through his hair and replacing his hat. Jake watched the forlorn figure making her way toward the creek. She was hunched up in her jacket, her head bowed. Her hair glinted golden in the sunshine. She looked frail and vulnerable. Jake wasn't accustomed to wavering about anything, but the sight of her tugged at him.

I'm a damn fool, he thought. She's about as helpless as a bobcat.

Chapter One

At dawn, over a month after the auction, Dusty pulled on leather gloves in the laundry room that served the ranch house as back entrance and mudroom. As she stretched her hands into the well-used leather of her work gloves, she smiled and remembered the fond welcome her father had given her last night.

She had dragged herself stiffly from the cab of her truck to greet Blackie, who waited for her on the front porch—after a long month of silence. The horrible day of the auction, she had hurried back to the university, unable to stay at the ranch, needing time to become accustomed to the loss. Last night, Blackie had surprised her by opening his arms and pulling her close in a bear hug. There, with her head resting on his tough old shoulder, he had whispered a stumbled explanation about the ranch.

He couldn't find the words, he had said. He tried to tell her when she was home at Christmas, but he just didn't know how. So he told himself he'd wait until she finished her master's in the spring. Then he figured she'd already have her plans set up with that professor she was so crazy about. Dusty winced at remembering her father mention Charlie. Dr. Charles Bradford Benson, assistant professor of History, specializing in the settlement of the West. Blackie had thought she would marry Charlie and settle down in some university somewhere. Good ol' Charlie thought the same thing. They were both wrong.

As she finished tugging on her gloves, her glance caught another pair, still on the shelf where hers had been. They were lying, palms up, unclaimed.

They were Mac's gloves. Her big brother. Yesterday, Blackie had said he thought she didn't want the ranch without Mac. After all, since Mac's death, she hadn't been home much, just Christmas and haying in the summer. She had to admit it hurt to work the ranch without Mac. Before he died, nothing at the university held her interest. Every spare minute had been taken up with schemes to get back to the ranch and the horses again.

She reached out to trace the curl long use had left in the fingers of Mac's gloves. The palms were stained a dark rich brown, and cuts roughed up the leather. She picked up one in her own glove and smiled at the difference in size. Her build was small and wiry like Blackie's, but Mac had been tall and big-boned like their mother.

Their mother died when Dusty was ten years old and Mac barely fourteen. Their big, laughing mother. The long two-hour drive to the nearest hospital in Jackson came too late to save her. Ironic that a woman so full of life could die from something no deadlier than pneumonia.

After she was gone, all the words seemed to leave Blackie. But not Mac. Like his mother, he kept up a constant stream of chatter, drawing the young Dusty behind him all over the ranch. Blackie, ever-patient, taught the two of them as if they were an unbreakable set. He grinned at Mac's chatter and winked at Dusty when she caught him at it. Mac had been the glue that held the family together.

She liked the idea of keeping Mac's gloves on the shelf with hers and her father's. Some things didn't need putting away in a sealed box after a death.

On the back stoop, she looked toward the horizon and the Wyoming Range. In the soft light of dawn, the rising sun tinted the entire sky, including the rugged peaks of the west. She rested her eyes on the pale violet caught in the snow patches above the timberline.

Blackie's horse strolled out of the barn with a smiling Blackie in the saddle. He led Dusty's horse by the reins.

"I thought you might decide to give us a hand with the branding," he said.

"I thought I might," she agreed.

She took the reins from Blackie and drew her fingers through the mare's silky black forelock. Early Snow nickered softly and tossed her head, welcoming Dusty with appropriate enthusiasm. Blackie's stallion nudged her with his gray muzzle, as if to get her attention for himself. Dusty laughed into her father's grin.

The Appaloosa mare was a beautiful complement to her father's stallion. Early Snow had a black head and forelegs and a large patch of snow white across her rump. The black spread into the white in large black flakes. Blackie's horse, True Blue, was a stout blue-gray, his spots a deep charcoal across his muscled rump.

Dusty swung easily into her saddle, relishing its smooth familiarity. She breathed deeply. The soft squeak of the leather promised a day of hard work, just what she needed. Dusty urged Early Snow forward, bringing her even with True Blue. They walked the horses into the pasture, taking their time in the dewy freshness of the day. She knew without asking that no one would rush things today. It was Saturday. The hands had one bit of work to do, branding a couple hundred calves, and then they could celebrate the end of the workweek. Of course, there would be chores on Sunday, but no big jobs. The individual work schedules, where everyone did assigned tasks, wouldn't begin again until Monday.

"Wait a minute, Dusty," Blackie said, halting his horse.

She pulled the mare around so she could face him. "What is it, Pop?"

He chuckled at the "Pop." Dusty had picked up that name from her brother. Mac used to call their parents "Mop and Pop" to get a rise out of their mother. Then Blackie's eyes softened as he looked at her and Dusty knew he was seeing her mother. Dusty had her mother's long thin nose that would be sprinkled with freckles after today's sun got to it. And the mouth with the full bottom lip.

"Well, Blackie, did you want to say something to me?"

"I was just thinking you look like your mother."

"You stopped me to tell me I look like my mother?" She grinned at him. "After you gave me her name, I had to look like her. That's the only way I could justify being stuck with such a silly name. Mac started calling me Dusty to keep from cracking up every time he said my name."

He ducked his head sheepishly. "Nobody liked that name. Just me and your grandfather. We liked it."

"You liked it because it belonged to her. I can't imagine what his excuse was."

"He was an old-fashioned man. He figured Vera May sounded like a girl should sound. He never quite got used to the way Vera liked to work the cattle." He looked at Dusty thoughtfully, as if he was trying to size her up.

"I guess I'm like your grandfather in a lot of ways," he said. "I always wondered what would've happened if Vera had a chance to know something besides ranching." He paused. "Your mother was a smart woman, Dusty. She'd be real proud of your education. I thought about her the whole time I read that thesis of yours." His voice was even softer than usual.

"So you thought I wouldn't want to come back to the ranch after I'd been out in the big world?"

"Something like that."

"Oh, Pop," she chided. "I'm your daughter, too. I might leave the cattle, but I could never leave the mountains." She scowled. "Charlie took a job with a college on the high plains of West Texas."

"Plains, huh?" Blackie's mouth curved into his familiar half smile under the moustache. "No mountains. Guess that means goodbye Charlie."

"Yep!"

He squinted to look out over the rise of land toward the mountains. "This country is changing, Dusty. The life we know, have known for almost a hundred years, is going away. It's like it's blowing away on the wind. Too much grazing in the high country. Not enough water. Not enough land to go around." He brought his gaze back to his daughter. "I'm not sure how much longer it can last, how much longer the ranchers can count on using public land for grazing. It won't be too long before the small rancher will be squeezed out of this country. He just won't have enough land to run his cattle on." He didn't say he had been afraid, before he sold out, that their ranch wouldn't pay much longer. But the thought hung in the air.

Dusty gazed out over the pasture along the creek. In the distance, she could see several cowboys working cattle, herding them together, chasing idle cows and their calves into one loose herd. It was a familiar scene. Would the mountains themselves be able to recognize this high country without the cattle and the horses and the cowboys?

"Well, I gotta say I spent a lot of time thinking on the problem." Dusty smiled at that, and Blackie smiled back. It was a long-standing joke between them. When she fussed about his lack of conversation, he blamed his silence on a habit of constant thinking.

"I got some ideas," he said. "I think you need to specialize in some part of ranch work. If you're the best at something, there'll be a place for you."

"What specialty did you have in mind?"

"Well," he drawled, grinning, "what about breeding the best cow horses?"

"You mean Appaloosas?"

His grin twitched under his moustache, and he kicked his horse into motion. "We'll talk about that later. Right now we better lend a hand to these boys here."

"Hey," she shouted after him. He stopped to look back. "I'm not going to let you raise Appaloosas without me."

He sketched a silent salute with his finger against the brim of his hat and urged his horse into an easy lope.

Dusty followed at a slower pace, letting herself enjoy the morning. She looked behind her toward the eastern horizon where the sky was breaking open with the cold fire of the dawn. She turned her horse and leaned forward on the saddle horn to let it all wash over her.

On the horizon, drenched in sunrise, the Wind River Range pierced the sky in a long line of ragged peaks. Their snowy crests stretched for a hundred miles, south to north. They were mighty and mysterious mountains, a constant lure for a mountain lover like Dusty. The Wind River Range on the far eastern horizon and the Wyoming Range to the west marked the boundaries of her world. Spread between the two ranges lay the wide Green River Valley.

Between Dusty and the eastern mountains, behind the rolling sagebrush hills, the Green River divided the basin in a long slender line that trailed through the desert. All along its banks grew the lush green of willows and cottonwood. Ranches backed up to it, drinking nourishment from its rushing water, and all the creeks, like Big Piney Creek that ran behind her, emptied into it. It was an old and fabled river. The first white men in the basin, the mountain men, trapped their beaver on the Green and held their annual

rendezvous along its banks. Later, travelers on the Oregon
Trail ferried their wagons across it.

How could a girl like Dusty, born and raised in this wide
valley, not nourish a love of history? Western history was all
around her, touchable, enduring.

Dusty's great-grandparents, her mother's grandparents,
had made their way into the Green River Valley from Ne-
braska. They came as far as Green River City to the south
by train before loading up on wagons to travel north and
look for land—land for cattle. For Dusty, history was a living thing, a daily encounter. Smiling, she rode her horse into
the sagebrush land claimed by her great-grandparents.

The straggly herd of protesting cows stirred up the dust
into billowing clouds around them. Out of habit, Dusty
checked the sky for possible weather. She could see the range
needed moisture; it always did. The only time a rancher
didn't pray for moisture, rain or snow, was when the hay
was lying in the field ready to be baled. Then rain could ruin
the feed supply for the coming winter. But the rest of the
year was too dry. Not enough water to go around and not
enough to encourage the tender shoots of grass in the late
spring of the mountains.

Only a handful of men worked the cattle. Dusty looked
over each one cautiously, preparing herself to encounter the
stony face of Jake Valiteros. Two hands, older cowboys who
looked vaguely familiar, slapped their hard-worn chaps with
rope coils and shouted their guttural urging to the cows. The
foreman, a man Dusty recognized as Hooter Calhoun, rode
at the head of the herd, pointing the lead in the right direction. Hooter's son Ollie scampered his horse this way and
that at the opposite end of the slow-moving cattle.

Across the herd of milling cattle, a rider lurched up out
of the willows. He wore a broad-brimmed black hat that hid
his face as he concentrated on moving a reluctant cow and
calf toward the herd. Dusty's breath caught in her suddenly dry throat. Only Jake Valiteros would ride that big

yellow buckskin, a true aristocrat of a cow horse, the horse she remembered from the Big Piney rodeo. That horse moved the balking cow with confidence and sharp-eyed intelligence. There was no wasted motion and no false moves. Man and horse worked in unison, a practiced unit.

When the cow and calf faded into the herd, Jake sat back in his saddle and surveyed the rest of the cattle. His gaze trailed over the backs of the animals until it slammed into Dusty sitting motionless on Early Snow. His body rigid in the saddle, he stared at her as if she were an unwelcome omen sent to threaten his domain. She stared back, unaware of the dust billowing around her or the bawling cattle.

"Hey, Dusty," Ollie shouted, riding up beside her. "When did you get home?"

She jumped as if he'd scared her. Fortunately, he was too busy controlling his horse to notice. She smiled at his exuberance. Although he had been only a couple of grades behind her in the Big Piney school, he still had the excitable manner of a little boy.

"Last night."

"You planning to spend the summer here?"

"I'm planning to spend the rest of my life here," she said, smiling wryly.

Ollie's mouth fell open, and then he broke into a wide grin. "You don't say. I thought you were a professor or something over in Laramie."

"Hardly." She laughed. "I was working on my master's degree in history, but I finished that this spring."

"Don't tell me you came back to brand some poor little calves." Ollie sat nonchalantly in his saddle as if he had all day to chat.

Dusty stood up in her stirrups to watch the cows at the back of the herd stop to munch on some grass sprouts. Just then, a bass roar erupted from the other side of the herd.

"Uh, Ollie . . ." She nodded toward the back of the herd. "I don't think we're going to have any calves to brand if you don't get back to your job."

"Oh, damn," Ollie exclaimed, looking sheepishly at Jake across the way. "I won't have a job, either." He took off at a run and shouted over his shoulder, "Come on, Dusty . . . Help me."

Her glance followed Ollie's toward the glowering figure on the other side of the slow-moving cattle. She was alarmed to find he wasn't watching Ollie's departure. Instead, the man on the buckskin stared at her, a fixed stare that she couldn't begin to fathom. The horse shifted under him, obviously anxious to chastise a few more cattle into line. Dusty wasn't able to move until Jake gave in to his horse's impatience and moved himself. Then she nudged her horse into a trot and followed after Ollie.

Soon Dusty was laughing out loud at the pure pleasure of being back in the saddle and punching cattle. Dusty and Early Snow chased down the wanderers with steady patience. Like she was trained, the sturdy mare made sure every cow and calf had joined the herd before she relented.

One white-faced calf cut his big brown eyes at her and bolted. Like a miniature rodeo bull, he bucked toward some cottonwoods near the fence. His mama stood still and bawled at him with no effect whatsoever. Dusty moved toward him and he broke into a run. She chased and hassled him in and around the cottonwoods until she finally got herself between him and the fence. Then she was able to turn him back to the herd.

When the calf was trotting meekly beside his mama, Early Snow retreated, and Dusty looked up to see the man in the black hat on the yellow horse turned in her direction. She barely had time to realize he had been watching her before he turned his attention back to the cattle.

Dusty leaned forward and stroked Early Snow's neck, "Good girl," she crooned.

Blackie rode his handsome gray horse up beside hers. He grinned at her under his moustache. "Dusty, you remember Sadie the Sow?" he asked. Dusty laughed. Of course, she remembered that old cow. Who could forget Sadie? "Well, looks like we're missing her, as usual."

"Say no more, Pop. I can find Sadie for you."

Dusty turned Early Snow back the way they had come to look for Sadie. She knew just where she would find the cow. And sure enough there she was, knee-deep in the mud of a spring. The cow's habit of preferring one particular mud spot over any other place in the pasture had earned her the name of Sadie the Sow. She enjoyed mud more than any pig Dusty had ever known. Of course, Dusty hadn't known many pigs, since Blackie could tolerate only cows and horses on his ranch—and he wasn't too fond of cows.

A black calf with a clean white face scampered toward Sadie as Dusty approached. He bobbed up and down like a seesaw, but Sadie did no more than switch her tail.

"Well, Sadie," Dusty said to the indifferent cow, "I see you got yourself another fine calf. If you didn't do such a good job of earning your keep, nobody'd fool with you, lazy as you are."

Dusty walked Early Snow toward the balky cow until Sadie got the idea she'd better move or get stomped on. Reluctantly, she shifted in the mud and gave Dusty a put-upon look before she moved out of the horse's way. Dusty stayed right behind her, urging her on every step of the way. The calf frolicked first on one side of his mama and then on the other. He seemed to think the trip to the holding pen was some kind of game.

Dusty let the cow take a well-worn path by the creek. She knew Sadie would be discouraged if she had to dodge sagebrush or gopher holes. Besides, the gurgling of the creek and the yellow warblers in the willows made perfect music for a slow ride. Across the creek, two antelope does stood up in the cup of a hill. Their white sides glowed in the clear morning light.

"Hey, ladies," Dusty said softly. "Let's see some babies out there. It's about time for you to put the nursery in operation."

Pronghorn antelope dropped their babies in late spring. Beautiful babies, Dusty thought. But then, unlike cattle, antelope were beautiful when they grew up. Calves were cute, but they grew to be as ugly as their mamas. The antelope does that watched her cautiously were all grown-up and still beautiful. Their deep brown eyes stared at her from under the longest eyelashes in the animal kingdom.

Dusty looked back at Sadie's muddy rear end and shook her head. No wonder Blackie wanted out of the cow business. No animal had a right to be as ugly as a cow. Or have as many foul habits.

"The only good thing I can say about you, Sadie, is you picked a great place to live. A high country ranch is cow heaven." Early Snow's ears twitched appreciatively, and Dusty laughed, a clear free sound that seemed to reassure the antelope does. She watched them fondly as they lay back down in the protection of the hill.

By the time Dusty's little procession caught up with the herd, the cattle were being urged into a holding pen. The pen was constructed of portable fencing sections in a corner of the pasture that bordered the acres still owned by Blackie. Dusty shouted and pushed at Sadie until she joined the other cows.

The hands were unloading the branding apparatus from the back of a pickup pulled up beside the fence. While the cows milled about in the holding pen, Hooter started up the fire in a steel barrel brazier. He put his practiced eye to work getting the fire and the branding irons to the right pitch of glowing red. Dusty noticed her father and Jake were the only ones still mounted. They concentrated on the cattle in the pen, quietly riding back and forth outside the fence while they did a count.

Dusty dismounted and tied up her horse to the fence by the side of the others. Leaning against the fence beside Ollie, she considered the toes of her boots, as her father was in the habit of doing, and relaxed for a few minutes. At least she tried to relax. Confoundedly, the back of her neck prickled at the nearness of the man on the yellow horse. She tried not to notice when he looked her way from time to time.

"Dad didn't tell me you and Blackie were both working for Jake," Ollie said.

Dusty jerked nervously at the comment. Then she silently cursed herself for reacting so strangely. She forced her shoulders back into a slump.

"We're not," she said. "At least I'm not." She cut her eyes at Ollie. "I just thought I'd help out today. You don't think Hooter will mind, do you?"

"Are you kidding?" Ollie exclaimed. "He'd be a fool to turn down a good hand at a branding." He grinned at her. "Especially when the hand is free. Why, he'd have a mutiny on his hands from Carl and Jeep there. Those two old cowboys want to get this over with as soon as they can. I bet they have an appointment with a case of beer this afternoon."

Dusty laughed. "I wouldn't be surprised."

Her sudden laughter stopped the buckskin. She looked up self-consciously to meet a narrow-eyed stare. For a moment, she was sure that Jake was going to raise some objections even if Hooter didn't. Then the stare moved to Ollie before moving back to the cattle.

She dragged in a long breath. Ollie was watching his father and didn't pay any attention to Jake's disapproving look. "Are you a regular hand now?" she asked him.

"Naw," answered Ollie. "Just for the summer. I usually work at the ski hill in Jackson during the winter."

Dusty grinned at him. "Still a ski bum?"

"Yep, and proud of it." He chuckled. "'Course, that means I need something to keep me during the summer. I'm lucky to have this ranch to fall back on." Ollie's face became serious. "Jake's been real good to us. Dad's his foreman and Mom does a little housekeeping at Jake's new house. And, on top of the work, we live in what used to be the main ranch house." He shook his head. "Down right luxurious for a ranch family."

"You live in the main house?" Dusty said, startled.

"Yeah. Can you beat that? Jake said he wanted Dad to be at ranch headquarters, so he turns over the big house to Mom and Dad and builds himself a log house way on the other side of the creek. Mom thinks she died and went to heaven."

"Maybe Valiteros didn't want to live that close to the real work."

Ollie looked at her, his forehead puckered in puzzlement. "Naw, Dusty, that's not it. Nobody does more of the ranch work than Jake. Not even Dad. Most guys who ranch the high country can't afford to sit behind a desk and let somebody else do the work. Oh, some rich guys up here fly in and out in their own planes and sit around in fancy houses. But they're just owners. They're not ranchers. Jake's the real thing."

Dusty grinned at his obvious hero worship, but Ollie didn't see. He was too busy watching Jake check out his rope. Jake twirled the rope a couple of times and looped it over a fence post, pulling it tight. Dusty knew he was getting ready to lasso calves for the branding.

"Looks to me like he's more cowboy than rancher," she observed. "He just doesn't want his hired hands to have all the fun."

Ollie nodded. "Well, I guess he's just about the best cowboy I ever saw."

"Better than Hooter?" Dusty teased.

"Yeah," Ollie answered with a devilish look. "Maybe even better than Blackie."

She gaped at him. "That I don't believe."

Dusty and Ollie both straightened up and moved away from the fence as if from a signal. It was time to brand calves. They joined Carl and Jeep who stood in front of the holding pen, waiting for the first calf. Hooter stuck a clipboard under his arm, for the record keeping, and examined the red-hot brands. Blackie tested the hypodermic needle for the inoculations. The pinchers for the castration of the bull calves stuck out of his back pocket.

Inside the holding pen, Jake and his big buckskin moved skillfully into position between a calf and its mama. As quickly and effortlessly as a breath of wind, Jake looped a rope around the neck of the skittish calf. Then the horse took over, stepping gracefully backward until the rope was taut. The calf bucked and fought, but Jake and his horse dragged it inexorably to the waiting cowboy.

Standing at the calf's head, Carl grabbed the rope and gently flipped the calf on its side before releasing the noose around its neck. Then, with Carl holding down the calf's neck and front leg, Jeep pulled back its hind leg. Hooter stepped up with the hot brand and Blackie injected the vaccines. Since the calf was male, Blackie pulled out the pair of large metal pinchers to do the castrating.

When they were all finished with the calf, Carl and Jeep released his legs and let the bawling calf loose. The new "steer" made a dash for the pasture, limping from the brand and tossing its head in fright. Ollie and Dusty stood between the calf and the opening to the holding pen, just in case it wanted to rejoin its mama. Branded calves had to be kept separated from the unbranded ones. Besides, a newly branded calf, exhausted from the trauma of branding, might lie down in the holding pen and get stomped by the other cattle.

Only a few seconds later, Dusty reached for the rope of her first calf. She laughed out loud at its baleful expression. Its ears were back and its eyes were rolling.

Before the calf knew what hit it, Dusty grabbed the taut rope around its neck with her right hand. When her left hand grabbed its flank, the calf gave a predictable little jump. She used the jump to get her knee under it, picking it up and putting it on the ground on its right side. Ollie used the calf's jump to grab its left hind leg, which he pulled back and held secure once the calf was on the ground.

Dusty freed the rope around the animal's neck before grasping the front leg with her right hand to put the calf off balance. With her knee on the calf's neck and her left hand still on its flank, she cleared the way for the brander and the vaccinator. When Hooter gave the word, she turned the calf's head toward the open pasture and let it loose. The whole procedure took only minutes. It was a process she had done hundreds of times before.

Only when the calf had scampered away into the pasture did she realize she had an audience. Carl and Jeep stood off to the side squinting first at her and then at Jake. Jake and his buckskin stood motionless in the opening to the holding pen. He hadn't moved an inch since Dusty released the rope from the calf's neck. Instead of lassoing another calf, he had watched her, watched every practiced move she made. The silence hung around the man on the horse like the dust in the air.

"She's purty good for a girl," Jeep said around his plug of tobacco. "Ain't she, boss?"

Jutting out her chin defiantly, Dusty looked up at the man on the horse. Jake didn't acknowledge Jeep's comment or Dusty's expression. He pulled in the limp rope, studying it as he coiled it in readiness for the next calf. Then he turned the buckskin back to the job in the holding pen.

The crew had been working for about an hour when a bawling, bucking calf almost got away from Dusty. Ollie ran over to give her a hand while the others stood by and laughed at them. Between laughing and grabbing for calf parts, Dusty and Ollie were barely able to contain the calf. The crew moved in quickly to get their business done. When they were finished, Ollie moved off the calf before Dusty, leaving her to release it. The calf gave her one final kick before running off a short distance to glare back at her.

The kick sent her sailing backward, knocked off her hat and landed her in the dirt on her bottom. She was laughing so hard, she collapsed, sprawling in the dirt. Ollie, laughing with her like the rest of the crew, offered her a hand up.

But no one was laughing hard enough to drown out the sharp voice that boomed her name. She sat up quickly, taking a swipe at the remains of the tears of laughter on her face, and peered up in the direction of the voice.

Jake glared at her. He was not laughing.

"Okay, that's enough. No more calf wrestling for you." His voice had the edge of flint. "Hooter," he twisted in the saddle to yell at his foreman. "Get her out of there. We don't need any hurt little girls to fool with."

"Who're you calling a little girl?" Outraged, she took Ollie's hand and leapt to her feet. "I'll have you know it'll take a lot more than one of your durn calves to hurt me."

Jake's eyes widened at the fiery anger in her voice.

"Aw, Jake, Dusty grew up throwin' calves," offered Hooter. "Besides she's working for free. We're not paying her nothing."

Jake flinched at the amazed looks on the faces of his hands. Obviously, they were having a hard time understanding his objections. He shifted uncomfortably in his saddle.

"So you're working my cows for free, huh?" he scowled at her.

"Don't take it as a favor to you," she snapped at him. "I just like the company, at least *most* of the company."

Blackie covered his moustache and coughed. Ollie laughed out loud, but he smothered the laughter when Jake glared at him.

"See to it that you stay clear of flying hooves from now on. Hooter," he called over his shoulder, "give her something else to do. Something a little less physical." He scowled at her one more time before he turned his horse toward the holding pen.

Hooter came up beside her and grinned. "I got the perfect job for you in the frame of mind you're in. You take over Blackie's job."

Dusty didn't catch on until Hooter handed her the pinchers they used to do the castrating of the bull calves. Blackie chuckled appreciatively, and Ollie slapped her on the back.

She grinned at Hooter. "Yep," she said, "I'll be real good at this."

Jake turned his horse in the opening to see what was going on. Dusty stood in the middle of the grinning hands and cocked her head in his direction. She sashayed toward his horse, swaying her jean-clad hips, until she was almost touching his foot in the stirrup. Then she reached her right hand up even with his belt and snapped the pinchers loudly. The hands laughed when Jake moved uneasily in his saddle.

"Okay," he barked, working his mouth to keep from grinning, "you made your point. I think I'll just get out of the way of those things you're holding there."

"Watch out, boss," Jeep teased. "She looks like she's awful good with them things."

"Yep, she's good, all right," Blackie grinned. "It makes the hair on the back of your neck crawl to see her use 'em."

Dusty stood to one side, affecting a smug look and polishing the pinchers with the sleeve of her flannel shirt. She shied a look at Jake from under the brim of her hat.

"Yeah," she said, lowering her voice in an affected masculine growl, "no bull's safe around here."

Jake grinned back at her, his stony face relaxing. It was obvious his anger was misplaced. No one else seemed to be at all surprised at having Dusty Macleod work beside them at a branding. He shook out his rope and resumed his snaring of the calves.

The work moved smoothly, and it wasn't long before the crew was branding the last calf. Just to make sure there were no more calves hiding in the cows, Jake cut out a few cows at a time, releasing them into the pasture to trot off in search of their young. The crew stood back when the newly released mamas came through the gate. No sense getting in the way of a determined mother.

When the last cow had been released, Ollie grabbed Dusty and waltzed her around. She twirled from Ollie to Jeep to Carl, waltzing with each one. Jake leaned forward in his saddle and watched. Standing to one side, Blackie grinned at his irrepressible daughter, but no one seemed to notice that Jake wasn't smiling. In fact, anyone who glanced his way might think he looked envious.

"Hey, Dusty," Ollie yelled from his perch on the fence, "how about dancing with all of us in Big Piney tonight?"

"Good idea," offered Carl, who had just finished giving Dusty a fancy whirl. "They're gonna have a live band at the Waterhole tonight. I might even teach you a thing or two about cowboy dancing." Dusty laughed at the weathered cowboy as he did a few solo steps.

"Can't think of anything I'd rather do," answered Dusty. She knew the Waterhole. It was a popular gathering place on Saturday nights. Sometimes the dance floor was as crowded as the bar.

Blackie mounted his horse and swung toward his daughter. "Well, if you got your social calendar all fixed up, I'll just mosey on home and make us some lunch. I'd like to get up in the mountains this afternoon. Check on the summer grass."

Hooter laughed, "Ain't no grass up there yet, Blackie."

"He's got mountain fever, Hooter," Dusty said, smiling up at her father. "He can't wait to ride a horse on a mountainside. After a long winter, his mountain-man blood starts itching."

"That's all right, daughter," Blackie said over his shoulder as he rode away. "I'll see how long you last before you get up there, too."

Chapter Two

The rest of the cowboys packed up the truck with the branding equipment before mounting their horses to ride back to ranch headquarters. Dusty waved to them and walked over to the corral fence where she had tied Early Snow. Jake broke the quiet study that had captured him and nudged his horse to follow Dusty.

She paused with her hand on her saddle horn to squint up at him. "You want something?"

He made a dry sound that might have been a laugh. His gaze took in the picture she made, standing by her horse with her hat in her hand. Wisps of her blond hair, loosened by the day's hard work, floated around her face.

"You worked hard today," he said.

"So?"

Lord, she didn't give an inch. "So I was thinking you might want a job on the ranch. I can see you're a good hand."

She laughed shortly, a sound far from her easy laughter with the cowboys. "Yeah, I'm a good hand," she said, swinging up into her saddle. "That's why I don't need any charity from you."

"You won't get any charity on this ranch," he snapped. "I offered you a job because I could see you know ranch work, not for any other reason."

"Well, if that's the case, I'll just have to think about your offer." Her expression eased, softening the eyes that regarded him curiously, squinting slightly as a cloud slid away from the sun. Sunlight fire caught in her hair and gave it the glint of molten gold. To his disgust, he was disappointed when she clapped her hat on her head, hiding that glorious halo of hair.

"That's a good horse you have there," she said, pleasure lighting her eyes as she looked at the horse. "What do you call him?"

"His name's Ol' Yeller."

She grinned. "For the dog?"

He grinned back. "Sort of. The name just seemed appropriate."

She laughed, a clear light sound. "I can see it might be. Right color." She didn't notice how still his face became when she laughed. The grin left his thin mouth and crept into his eyes.

He had been struck by her laugh all morning long, stopped dead by the sparkling sound of it more than once. She liked to laugh, and, dammit, he liked listening to the sound of her laughing. How could a confoundedly quiet man like Blackie be the father of a woman with a laugh like hers? Come to think of it, what would a decent man like Blackie say about the decidedly carnal thoughts her laugh provoked? Maybe Blackie wouldn't appreciate his friend lusting after his daughter.

"I guess Blackie taught you a lot about horses," he said.

"Yeah, Blackie's the best there is with horses, all right," she said wistfully. "Mac used to tease him because he cared more about his horses than he did us. Blackie would just grin and say that horses were less trouble and—" she grinned mischievously, wrinkling her nose "—they smelled better."

He chuckled and nodded toward the dark green slopes on the horizon. "What will Blackie do up in the mountains this afternoon?"

"Blackie never could resist mountain riding," Dusty said, her eyes sparkling. "He'll probably ride up one of the creek drainages."

Propping an elbow on his saddle horn, he leaned toward her, reins flipping idly between his long fingers. "Why, Dusty?" he said, his low voice making a rumble of her name.

She saw his thin mouth lift slightly in a half smile and his eyes burned into hers. She felt as defenseless as a newborn antelope fawn caught in the gleaming speculation of a coyote's eyes. She wondered how it would feel to fit her mouth against his, to smell horse and sweat and mountain air.

"Wh-what?" she stammered breathlessly, realizing he expected some coherent answer.

"Why will Blackie ride up a creek drainage?" he repeated, his grin twitching ever so slightly.

"Oh." She shrugged and dragged her eyes away from his to focus on Lander Peak, just as a cloud drifted over it, dulling the snow patches.

Unconsciously, she licked her dry lips, and the seductive movement drew Jake's attention to her full bottom lip. His hand closed tightly around his reins.

Keeping her gaze on the bare rocks of the peak, she said softly, "He enjoys the mountains more than anything. He'll probably stick to the south-facing slopes where most of the snow has melted. He'll follow some game trails and keep an eye out for any newborn fawns, maybe elk calves. Blackie's at home in the mountains. His world's mountains and horses."

Something about the cold dull light on the cloud-shrouded peak sent a chill through her. She shivered, aware of the danger so close, threatening her from the back of a gorgeous buckskin. What did he want? He already had her ranch.

She turned to Jake, her gaze steady, her chin lifted. "You need to relax, boss. Why don't you come to the Waterhole tonight?"

"I might do that," he answered, his mouth a straight line of displeasure, as he settled into his saddle.

She smiled coolly, giving him a cowboy's salute with a gloved finger against the brim of her hat before riding off toward home and lunch with Blackie.

The next morning she woke late, poking her head out of the covers to check the weather. Sunlight glowed on the curtains. No sign of last night's storm. Quietly she listened for morning noises.

Silence. No sound of Blackie moving around in the house. Nothing. Sunday morning silence filled the house, glistening in the air, like the sunlight.

Maybe Blackie's in the barn, she thought, as she dressed. Stuffing her work shirt into her jeans, she headed outside, her boots making a hollow echo through the house.

The barn was filled with more Sunday-morning quiet. The horses in the corral came to the open door and looked at Dusty expectantly. She put feed in the empty troughs in the stalls and moved out of the way to let the animals get to it. They all seemed especially eager to be fed. Mac's sorrel gelding, Sunny Boy, pushed his way to the trough. Yesterday, Blackie had planned to get back in time to exercise Sunny. The horse was a rodeo roping horse and, like any athlete, needed regular training.

Where was Blackie? His horse wasn't there. Would he go for a ride without feeding the other horses first? Worried, she watched the horses as they munched their rolled oats. Her own mare was the only horse to pause long enough in her eating to lift her head and look at Dusty. The others consumed the feed greedily.

Dusty ran back to the house and headed straight for Blackie's room. She banged open the door, suddenly frantic with worry. The room was untouched; the silence rang in her ears. The spread neatly covered the bed, faded images of moose and elk and bear in the print. Sunlight streamed through the open curtains of the window, dust motes dancing idly in the shafts of light. The dresser was bare, a framed picture the only ornament. From inside the simple silver frame, her mother smiled out at her. Behind her mother's chair stood a solemn young Mac. Dusty herself was the child on her mother's lap.

In the kitchen, Dusty found the remains of yesterday's lunch in the refrigerator. Blackie had planned to eat that for supper. Dusty's uneasiness increased.

She stepped out the back door, pausing uncertainly on the top step. Nothing moved. A haze of moisture from last night's storm obscured the mountains. The storm had been a fierce one, sweeping down from the mountains and blasting the valley with wind-driven snow. It was late for spring snow, but the weather in the mountains was always unpredictable. As Jake had warned her before she left the Waterhole, her drive home had been unusually treacherous.

Could Blackie have been caught in last night's storm? Surely he would have headed toward home when he saw the clouds approaching. But, he wouldn't be the first experienced mountain man to be a victim of an unexpected storm, she thought anxiously. He could be in trouble up in the mountains right now.

She ran for the phone just inside the living room and fumbled with the phone book, straining to focus on the number. She misdialed the first time, looked up the number again and redialed.

"Valiteros," the gruff voice said in her ear.

"Jake," she said, almost giddy with relief. "Thank goodness."

"Dusty? What's wrong? Are you all right?"

"It's Blackie. I don't know where he is." She regained some of her control, but she didn't question her having called Jake for help—instead of the sheriff or one of Blackie's friends. "I haven't seen him since he left for the mountains yesterday afternoon. And his horse is gone."

"Stay put. I'll be right there."

The phone clicked in her ear when he hung up. She clutched the receiver to her chest and rested her forehead against the cool door frame. Jake was on his way. She cursed herself for feeling so relieved. Who was Jake Valiteros, anyway? At lunch yesterday, after the branding, Blackie had made a point of telling Dusty that Jake was "a good man." In Blackie's terms, that meant Jake was a good rancher. Ollie had a bad case of hero worship; that was obvious. But at the auction, Ruth hadn't bothered to hide her sneer when she talked about Jake Valiteros. She said he was greedy, land hungry. She didn't seem to be the only person in the valley who didn't trust him.

At the Waterhole last night, Jake sat alone.

Dusty had been leaning against a post between the bar and the dance floor and trying to catch her breath. She had just begged off dancing again with Carl. It was hard to see why Carl needed a partner at all because he seemed to do most of his fancy steps by himself. Bemused, she gazed out at the hazy yellow light that bathed the dancers on the crowded wooden floor. They stomped and twirled, shaking the building and her leaning post.

Then her idle gaze collided with Jake's pointed stare. He was seated at a table against the wall, his chair tipped back and his hat pulled low on his forehead. His eyes burned under the brim of his hat, his stare almost predatory.

Ollie leaned toward her and said loudly, "Hey! Where did you go?"

She shuddered involuntarily and focused on Ollie. "What?"

He laughed and shouted back, "I said, where did you go? Do you want to dance?"

She smiled and shook her head, "No, thanks. Too tired."

Ollie rolled his eyes at her. "You're getting old." He danced unsteadily toward another partner. As he and his partner launched into a vigorous swing step, Dusty kept her eyes on them, careful to avoid looking in Jake's direction. All the same, she was aware of how alone he looked, seated at the small round table by the wall.

Every other table was crowded with more chairs than available space. Returning dancers quickly faded into clumps of people, drinking their beer and shouting their laughter. Groups quickly formed and reformed, including anyone who walked up with the easy familiarity of long acquaintance. Only Jake sat alone. In spite of the deadliness of his stare, his isolation pricked at her. Occasionally, someone glanced at him, but no one approached him. No one spoke to him. No one sat beside him. Still, she knew everyone in the place recorded his every move, as she did. Probably everyone observed that he was staring at her.

Then there was what Blackie had said after lunch about Jake, that business about Jake being a "good man." Maybe Blackie felt the need for a son, since Mac's death, and he had settled on Jake. But his choice was disturbing. He had taught her never to confront a wild animal, to watch it carefully and keep her distance. Even antelope does had sharp hooves. A predator like Jake was best avoided entirely.

When the band dropped from western swing into a slow tune, Dusty felt Jake's presence before she saw him. There

was a cold prickling up her nape before she cut her eyes to
see him standing close enough behind her to move the wisps
of her hair with his breath. He was so close that she could
see the tiny creases radiating from his eyes. His gaze scraped
over her. They took in her hair, pulled back in one long
braid, her high forehead, her long narrow nose and firm
chin. He brushed his knuckles across the freckles on her
high cheekbones.

His hand took hers and lifted it. He studied its slenderness, lying in the hard roughness of his. Then, without a
word, he pulled her gently toward the dance floor. She felt
his right arm slide around the small of her back. It settled
on the slope of her hips, bringing her close against the heat
and lean strength of his body. His left hand encircled her
hand and pulled it into their bodies, holding her palm on his
chest. She stared at the brown column of his throat and felt
the sheltering brim of his hat brush her hair. All around
them, couples danced and laughed and teased one another.
Dusty and Jake swayed softly to the plaintive sounds of the
music, as if they were alone on a quiet island in a storm-
tossed sea.

"Is Dusty your real name?" he had asked.

"What?" Trying to make sense of his low rumble, she
stirred in his arms, but he stopped the movement with the
steel clamp of his arm.

"Is Dusty your real name?" he repeated, his voice no
more than a rough whisper.

"N-no, it's a nickname," she mumbled, startled by her
own breathlessness. "My brother Mac gave it to me."

"Because of your hair?" he asked, and she felt a kiss in
the strands above her ear.

"Yes, because of the color," she said, trying to shake the
dreaminess. "Mac said I had natural camouflage for the
high country. He teased me about getting lost anytime the
wind blew up." His laugh was a low rumble brushing against
her ear.

Because it sounded rusty from lack of use, his laugh curled up inside her and she smiled. She moved her free hand over the wide shoulder, and his arm moved against her back. Each touch of his rancher's body felt like home, so familiar and strangely safe. Outside the wind blew around the corners of the wooden building. But inside a western fiddle whined a mellow tune, and a cowboy's strong arms held her close.

The music stopped and Jake pulled back, looking deeply into her eyes. The question that burned in the flint blue of his eyes held her fascinated, unable to move or speak. All around them, dancers shuffled off the dance floor and headed for half-finished beers and deserted companions. In a corner by the bar, band members put down instruments for a well-deserved break. Jake and Dusty stood, frozen in place, staring at each other.

Someone left through the door on the far side of the dance floor. The wind caught the flimsy wood and slammed it against the side of the building. The loud noise and the cold swirl of wind from the open door snapped them out of their reverie. They looked toward the door, startled. In the opening, horizontal snow streamed past the inky darkness. Already the ground was covered in white. A freak May snowstorm wreaked its havoc on the high country. Dusty shivered.

"It's okay," Jake said softly, pulling her back into the shelter of his body. "It's only Wyoming weather."

She smiled into his shoulder and wondered at herself. What had happened to the misgivings she had felt just a few minutes ago? Why did it feel so good to be held in his arms? He walked her to her leaning post, holding her close to his side.

"How are you getting home?" he asked.

"I have my truck."

He nodded in the direction of the side door. "Bad storm. Spring snow makes driving dangerous."

"I know," she said, shivering suddenly. A spring storm had caused Mac's accident. She lifted her chin. "I'm used to taking care of myself. Storm or no storm."

Jake raised an eyebrow. "Are you now?" One corner of his mouth twitched. "Well, see that you do a good job taking care of yourself." Dusty saw the hint of a smile, and her nostrils flared in angry reaction. "Don't stay too late." He tapped her nose with a long finger.

He had walked away without a backward glance. Gritting her teeth, she had watched him weave through the tables in the bar on his way to the front door. And now he was on his way here—to her house—because she had called for help.

She waited on the front porch for him, watching his truck rush toward her and screech to a halt in front of the house. He slammed the door of his vehicle as he leapt out and ran up the steps. She clutched her arms with both hands when he paused on the top step. His gaze assessed her, taking in the self-protectiveness of her posture. A flash of irritation flickered around his eyes at the invisible curtain she dropped between them.

"I can't think where he could be," she said, her voice whispery with anxiety. She cast her gaze down at the porch floor in front of her.

"Could he be visiting friends?" He tried to keep the irritation out of his voice, but when she flinched, he realized he hadn't been successful. He tried again. "Your aunt and uncle, maybe."

"You mean Ruth and Ed?" To his relief, she looked at him again. But her anxiety was almost tangible. "No, I don't think so. He'd leave a note." She led him inside the house. "I don't think he came back from the mountains yesterday. He didn't eat his supper and the horses hadn't been fed."

"I sent Hooter with Carl and Jeep to look for him."

He was so close behind her that she jumped, and stepped away from him. "They won't know where to look," she said.

"You mentioned he'd go up a creek drainage. Hooter thinks he probably went up either Big Piney Creek or Bull Creek."

She nodded thoughtfully. "That makes sense, I guess."

He closed the gap she had put between them and cupped her shoulder with his hand. She seemed so fragile under his hand. He tried to sound reassuring. "Hooter said Blackie probably got caught in the storm and spent the night sitting by a fire on the mountainside." He tipped her chin up with his finger, his rough finger relishing the softness of her skin. "He might wait for the morning sun to melt the snow for his trip down. He's probably on his way home now."

She shifted uncomfortably and stuck her hands into her back pockets. "I'll make some coffee." She escaped into the kitchen.

Shrugging out of his jacket, Jake glanced around the small living room. Now that he was here, he felt useless. He didn't like just sitting around. He took off his hat and threw it on the sagging sofa. Maybe he could look around, see if he could find anything helpful. "Uh, Dusty," he called out, "where's Blackie's bedroom?"

"It's the middle one."

In the hallway a door on his right was open to a masculine bedroom, the rodeo ribbons and outdated football calendar on the wall obviously belonging to a young man. Probably Mac's room. The door straight ahead had to be the middle bedroom.

He looked inside Blackie's room. The sparseness of the room told him he wouldn't find anything there, but he went in, anyway. The only decoration in the whole room was a picture on the dresser. Jake stared at the composed woman in the picture. She bore a remarkable resemblance to Dusty, although he realized Dusty was undoubtedly the child on her lap. He lightly touched the face of the happy little girl with the proud brother looking over his mother's shoulder. Jake had been a brother like that once. He shook off the memory, filled as it was with regret and loss, a little sister's life snuffed out when she wasn't much older than Dusty in the picture. And his own mother, unlike the sweet-faced woman in the picture, running away from him and his father and the looming mountains she feared and hated.

The top dresser drawer stuck out, a contrast to the neat tightness of those beneath it. More pictures peeked out at him from inside the shallow drawer. His curiosity piqued, he eased the drawer out a fraction more. A jumbled pile of snapshots took up almost half the space. Dusty's mother was the center of every picture he picked up. "Damn, what's he want with all these pictures?" Jake mumbled, sifting through the photographs. The same woman laughed in every picture, except for one. A young Blackie was in that one. The two of them were horseback, holding hands between their mounts and looking solemnly into each other's eyes.

Jake thought wryly that he didn't know much about that kind of feeling for a woman, the kind of feeling that made a man keep a drawerful of snapshots. He thought about the young woman he had married after his father died. She hadn't lasted a year in the wretched loneliness of ranch life before she headed straight back to the city she came from, stopping by a divorce court on the way. He hadn't missed her and he hadn't collected pictures. If he had—he snorted at the thought—she wouldn't have been laughing in any of them.

Back in the kitchen, Dusty was pouring him a cup of coffee. He took it from her. "I looked around Blackie's room.... I guess the woman in the picture is your mother."

"Yeah." Dusty stared out the window over the sink and sipped slowly from her cup. After lunch yesterday, Blackie had talked about her mother. He had sat at the kitchen table and sipped whiskey from a shot glass and talked. Dusty had listened, amazed because Blackie never drank and Blackie never talked, but yesterday he had cut his arm in the barn after the branding. The bottle of whiskey, dust-covered from lack of use, sat on the counter while she'd helped him bandage the cut. Later, he'd sipped the whiskey and said Vera was beautiful like the mountains were beautiful. "You look like your mother," he had repeated.

Jake sat at the table and studied the steam rising off the coffee. "When did she die?"

Dusty looked around at him. Most people in the valley wouldn't have to ask that. It was curious how little he knew about her family and, she admitted, how little she knew about his. "About fifteen years ago."

His eyes flashed a question before he said, "Long time."

She shrugged, "I guess. I talked to Ed on the phone just now. He hasn't seen Blackie. Ruth was at church."

"Ruth's your mother's sister?"

"Yes."

"Thought so. I see the family resemblance," he said, looking at her.

She grinned. "I hope you're not talking about personality."

He grinned back. "I had noticed a similar testiness."

"Humph." She scowled and dropped into the chair opposite him across the small table.

"What was your mother's name?"

"Vera." She laughed, a bright sound in the stillness of the room. "Vera May."

"Why the laugh?"

"Oh, a family joke." She bit back another laugh. When Jake raised an eyebrow at her, she relented, "I was named for my mother. My name is Vera May, too." Jake grinned at the absurdity of such a frilly name for a woman like Dusty. "Yeah, funny, isn't it? I always thought Blackie named me that to get back at his own parents for naming him Angus."

"Angus? In the middle of cow country?" Jake laughed out loud. Black Angus cattle were a favorite breed in the high country. "Was that Mac's name, too?" Dusty nodded ruefully and Jake shook his head. "No wonder everybody calls him Blackie. Didn't your mother have a nickname like the rest of the family?"

"Sometimes Blackie called her Jade." Dusty's voice was suddenly husky. "He said her eyes were the color of Wyoming jade."

He stared at her head, bowed over her coffee cup. So her mother had green eyes—the color of jade, according to Blackie. He understood how Blackie felt about Vera's eyes, because he had fallen under the spell of Dusty's. He wondered at himself. Maybe I'm getting lonely, he thought. Maybe the emptiness of that big house, sitting by itself up on the bluff, is getting to me.

"You don't have any family?"

He started at the suddenness of the question. Clearing his throat, he said, "Not anymore."

"Oh," she said, looking away in confusion, but not before something that looked a lot like pain flashed in Jake's flint-hard eyes.

"My mother died a couple of years ago," he said into his coffee. "Not that she was much family. She lived in Salt Lake City." He paused to force his mind from the horror that had sent his mother there. His little sister, lively Penny, robbed of life before she lived it. "My father died a long time ago," he added, his voice low, "right after I graduated from college."

"A long time ago?" She tried to smile. "Are you such an old man?"

He cleared his throat. "Older than you, freckle nose."

She rubbed her nose self-consciously. "Don't let the freckles fool you. They could be age spots, you know."

He grinned. "I doubt it." One long finger traced the brim of his cup. "I'm thirty-eight, Dusty."

She closed her hand in a fist on the table. "I didn't mean to pry."

Reaching across the table, he took her hand between both of his. "I know you're worried, Dusty. But remember Blackie has lived in the high country all his life. He might have been caught in the storm, but it probably wasn't the first time something like that happened to him." He stroked her hand, his fingers rasping warmly against her softer ones. "He knows how to keep warm and wait for a chance to come down. And you know he's not lost. He'll be okay."

She looked at his hand, a cowboy's hand, capable of strength and tenderness. Yesterday he had leapt from the back of his horse to grab a terrified calf about to get itself trampled in a knot of clumsy cows. He had brushed against the dangerous bulk of the cows as if he were immune to the ordinary frailty of bones and flesh.

"What if he was injured?" she asked, suddenly alarmed.

"Then Hooter will find him." He knew the odds were against that. One man would be hard to find in the bigness of the high country. Of course, Dusty knew that, too.

They sat in silence and sipped their coffee. He kept one hand on hers and tried not to think about how good it felt to sit with her at the kitchen table, how good it had felt last night to hold her against him while they danced. He had watched her dancing with Carl and admired the swaying movement of her rounded hips in her black jeans. And the sound of her merry laugh. How could someone so small and so full of laughter fit so perfectly in his hard arms?

Long minutes later, she refilled their cups, and he took his coffee cup out the back door. He wasn't sure why. Maybe he'd check the barn.

Dusty followed him, not wanting to lose the surprising gentleness of his company. When she opened the screen door to step outside, Jake was staring at something down by the creek. Her gaze followed his.

Ollie and his father were riding up out of the fresh green leaves of the willows. Behind them was a sheepherder on his pony, leading another horse. It was Blackie's horse, True Blue, plodding behind the herder's horse. Something was draped across the saddle.

Dusty's coffee cup slipped out of her hand and rolled off the top step onto the ground.

Chapter Three

When Jake and Hooter lifted Blackie from the horse's back to carry him inside, she panicked. She ran to her bedroom, unable to watch Blackie's awful helplessness. Not Blackie. He never allowed anyone to do anything for him. He had taught Dusty to face any challenge the ranch required, the way he did. At fourteen, she shot a cow that couldn't make it through calving. At sixteen, she pulled a dead foal from the body of a favorite mare. She never shrank from what had to be done.

But she couldn't watch her father's dead body being lifted from his horse. "No! Please!" she whispered frantically, burying her face in the soft chenille of her bedspread.

In her mind she saw Blackie as he'd appeared yesterday, riding away from her toward the slow-moving herd of cattle. He sat True Blue comfortably, a man in his natural setting, with that half smile under his bushy moustache. "You look a lot like your mother," he had said.

Yesterday she had come into the house to discover Blackie rinsing the cut on his arm in the kitchen sink. Blood mixed with water ran off his arm onto the white porcelain. He said he had cut himself on the feeding trough when he was working around the barn after the branding. But Blackie never had accidents. One of the certainties of her childhood was absolute trust in Blackie's ability to avoid problems, both for himself and for his family.

Everyone in the happy family who had lived in this house—her mother, Mac, now Blackie—all dead. Mac's truck had slid on a patch of black ice and rolled, over and over, down a steep embankment. Her brother Mac, her fun-loving brother, whose room down the hall still remembered all the things he enjoyed—his horse Sunny Boy, the rodeos, the calf roping. His best rope hung coiled on the wall, his chaps were in the closet, his worn boots collapsed in the corner. All still there—but no Mac.

Cold shivered over her in spite of the sunshine outside her window. She pulled at the bedspread to wrap it around herself, and she remembered the cold blue silence of the ride to Jackson behind the ambulance that carried her sick mother, ten-year-old Dusty crammed between Blackie and Mac in the cab of the ranch pickup. They trailed the ambulance on the icy, winding road and watched the flashing lights silently screaming red and blue into the piercing winter stillness.

And the cold emptiness of the house when they returned from Jackson—without Vera. All the next morning, Dusty had stood at the front window and watched grizzled old T.J. move around the barn and corrals, his battered black hat wagging from side to side. He had moved the way she felt inside, heavy and slow and full of dread. He had come to take care of the animals because he knew Blackie wouldn't be able to do it. Blackie, who never failed his animals, had been as empty as the house. After Mac's death, she had walked into another emptiness, when she drove across the vast Wyoming openness from Laramie to the ranch. Now, again, the awful emptiness broke open inside her, as she huddled inside the bedspread.

Heavy footsteps tramped through the house from the kitchen to the hall to Blackie's room. She clenched cold fingers tightly over her ears, trying to force the sound out of her head. But, despite her tight fingers, she heard. The thudding footsteps came out of Blackie's room and echoed hollowly toward the front door.

Finally, she pushed herself wearily off the bed, dragging the sleeves of a jacket over her arms. At Blackie's room, she gripped the doorframe and stared at the still body. She felt Jake moving behind her in the narrow hallway.

"I'm all right," she said, answering his silent question, and clamping her teeth shut to stop their unbidden chattering.

"Here." Jake pulled her hand toward him and placed the shot glass in it. "Drink this."

"What is it?" She looked dumbly at the amber liquid filling the glass.

"It's some whiskey. That's all I could find."

"Blackie doesn't keep much liquor." The memory of Blackie, sitting at the kitchen table and sipping this very whiskey, was an icy pain in her chest. "Just whiskey."

"I figured that out," Jake growled. "I found this in the bottom cabinet behind the mixing bowls."

"That's where he keeps it." She herself put it back there yesterday, when Blackie and True Blue had disappeared from sight in the willows by the creek, on their way into the mountains. "He pours it on the fruitcake Ruth sends us for Christmas. He thinks the whiskey..." Her voice trailed off and her hand gripped the small glass, her knuckles white, bloodless.

"Drink it," Jake said gently. He didn't like the paleness of her face, the coldness of her hand when she took the glass.

The whiskey tasted rotten. It burned on the way down. Dusty coughed and gasped, her face wrinkling into a distasteful frown. Jake smiled with grim satisfaction at that small show of life.

"This stuff could kill sagebrush," she said, staring at the empty glass.

He grinned. "Want some more?"

She didn't answer, but she moved away from the door toward the small living room with its worn sofa. In the middle of the room, she stopped and looked around as if she didn't know where she was.

Behind her, Jake said, "Sit down, Dusty. Before you fall down. We have to wait for the sheriff. It'll be a while before he and Doc Brophy can get out from town."

"The sheriff and Doc?" she said numbly.

"We don't know what killed him, Dusty. The sheriff has to come out to ask questions. He wanted to bring Doc to have a look before we move him again." Jake sighed and poured himself a shot of whiskey from the bottle he had left on the coffee table. "The sheriff'll bring the ambulance to take the body into town."

She flinched at the reference to Blackie's body. Then she consciously stiffened her back, holding herself up straight on the soft cushions of the sofa. "Who's sheriff now? Is Dan Reed still sheriff?"

"Yeah. Dan's still sheriff." Jake sat beside her to sip his whiskey. He was careful not to touch her; she looked as though she might break if he did. "He's been sheriff so long, some folks are talking about deeding him the job."

Jake relaxed into the sofa and stretched out his legs in front of him. He sipped the whiskey and studied her still profile. Her hair caught the stubborn sun rays that filtered in through the windows, gilding it with the molten shimmer he had admired yesterday before she hid it under her hat. God, she was something to look at, sitting there with her shoulders squared, ready to face anything, even death.

Dusty was everything the daughter of Blackie Macleod should be, as strong and resilient as the high country itself. As he studied her, Jake pondered what it must have been like to have a father like Blackie. Until Jake started negotiating with Blackie about the sale of the ranch, he hadn't realized what he had missed from his own father. Somehow, Blackie's silence had seemed approving, prompting Jake to pour out all his plans for the ranch. Jake's only reward was Blackie's half smile that had been satisfyingly eloquent. Blackie had worked himself into Jake's life in a way no other man ever had.

Dusty wrapped herself in stillness, and Jake watched her, unable to look away. Perhaps it was because she appeared so strong and capable that she tugged at him. Perhaps he couldn't stand the thought of seeing her defeated by anything. She had lost her ranch and now her father. Would she blame him for Blackie's death, as she blamed him for stealing her ranch?

Finally, the wail of the ambulance siren shattered the silence. Feet shuffled around on the front porch. The men there, the sheepherder and Hooter and Ollie, got up to meet the sheriff's car and the ambulance as they drove into the front yard.

Dusty blinked and stood up. Jake followed her outside. When she paused on the front steps, turning as if to run back inside the house, Jake reached out to clutch her slender fingers in his broad hand. He squeezed her hand hard, forcing her eyes to look into his. He watched the fierce green of her eyes soften under the reassurance of his steady gaze. At last she turned to meet the cluster of people gathered in the yard, but she didn't let go of Jake's hand.

"Hooter, send somebody inside with Doc Brophy," the sheriff was saying as Jake and Dusty joined them. "The rest of you folks wait outside here while Doc gets his business done."

The sheriff looked at Jake and Dusty, his assessing gaze dropping to take in their joined hands. Then he stared hard at Jake, his squinty eyes making slits in his face. "Morning, Dusty," he said, but he looked at Jake. After a thoughtful pause, he broke his stare and said to the awkwardly silent group, "I'll go in to check on Doc and then I'll be right out to talk to the rest of you."

He paused on the front steps and turned around to ask Jake, "How did you get yourself involved in what's going on here?"

"Blackie works for me."

The sheriff cocked his head thoughtfully. "I heard that in town. Does that mean his business is your business, even on his day off?"

Jake stiffened. "Cowboys don't have days off." His voice rumbled in the stretched silence. Both his hands covered Dusty's protectively. "Dusty called me this morning when she couldn't find Blackie."

"You don't say," the sheriff mused out loud. "What made you think Jake would know where Blackie was?" he asked Dusty.

"I d-don't..." Dusty mumbled, her hand groping for the reassuring warmth of Jake's grip.

"She didn't think I knew where Blackie was," Jake answered curtly. "She wanted help in finding him."

"And she just naturally called on you?"

"Why not?"

"No reason," the sheriff said with a shrug. "I just didn't know your families were all that close. You'd think she'd call on some of Blackie's friends." He looked at Dusty. "Did you call Ed Taylor?"

"Yes. He hadn't seen Blackie."

"I see," the sheriff said thoughtfully and walked into the house.

"What was that all about?" Dusty demanded when the sheriff disappeared behind the screen door.

"Don't let Dan Reed disturb you," Jake growled. "He gets a kick out of being irritating sometimes. He can't even manage basic decency."

Dusty shivered in the brisk air, and Jake eased one arm around her shoulders to gather her into the shelter of his body. The men, waiting in the yard to tell the sheriff their story, looked discreetly toward the barn.

The sheriff returned shortly. He walked straight to Hooter and the sheepherder without a glance toward Jake and Dusty. "I guess I better get the facts here." He raised an eyebrow in the direction of the sheepherder, a small, leathery man who fidgeted uneasily under the scrutiny. "Hooter said on the phone that you found the body."

The sheepherder turned his stained hat round and round in his hands and kept his eyes carefully directed toward the ground.

"This here's Gomez," Hooter spoke up. "He found the body and brought it down on Blackie's horse."

"You speak English, Gomez?" the sheriff asked.

"*Sí*, Sheriff."

"Huh, we'll see," Reed said. "Who do you work for? Aren't you one of the herders on Morgan's place?"

"*Sí*, I work for Señor Morgan, it makes fifteen years now." Gomez straightened a bit and spoke proudly, "I work for Señor Morgan more longer than any sheepherder."

"You speak English pretty good, Gomez," said the sheriff.

"A little, Señor Sheriff." His eyes twinkled. "I speak pretty good. I speak for some people to the boss man."

Reed squinted at the old man. Then he nodded in understanding. "You mean you translate the Spanish for Morgan. You translate for the other herders."

"*Sí, señor*. I write English words. I write coffee, flour..." He demonstrated, scribbling with an imaginary pencil on his hand.

"Oh," Reed said, nodding. "You make out the grocery and supply lists for the herders."

"*Sí*, when herders in mountains or in desert."

"You pack those supplies up in the mountains for Morgan?" When Gomez nodded eagerly, the sheriff went on, "You must know the mountains pretty good."

"*Sí*, I know the mountains. Today I go for ride. *Nieve, no se*... Ah, snow." He smiled brightly with the accomplishment. "Snow in mountains. I go to see snow." His smile disappeared. "I find Señor Blackie."

"You knew Blackie, then?"

"*Ah, sí, señor. Claro que sí.* Señor Blackie ride mountains. He drink coffee *conmigo* many time. I say, 'Señor Blackie, where you cows?' He say, 'Gomez, where you sheep?'" Gomez laughed briefly. Then his face sobered, and he shook his head sadly. "He don't say nothing when I find him. Face—" his hand indicated the whole of his own weathered face "—all snow. Snow cover body." He gestured to include his chest and legs. "One hand and—*brazo, no se*—ah, arm, no covered by snow." He grasped his own arm to emphasize his meaning. "Hand stand up straight. *Como* say, 'Hello.'"

"What? What are you trying to say?" interjected Hooter, stepping forward. His moustache forged a grim line across the top of his mouth. "His hand—his hand looked like it was waving to you?"

Gomez nodded gravely.

"Lord, have mercy," Hooter said, turning his back.

Jake gathered Dusty closer against his chest. She buried her face in the rough material of his jacket, letting the brushed suede muffle her gasp of dismay. The sheriff looked over at them speculatively.

Returning his consideration to Gomez, the sheriff said, "You say he was lying on his back?" Gomez nodded again. "Didn't he have a horse with him? Where was the horse?"

"From this place to—" Gomez moved his head back and forth to see around Jake and Dusty "—to barn."

"His horse was standing that far from the body?"

"In trees."

Shifting out of Jake's grasp, Dusty looked from Gomez to the sheriff. She opened her mouth to speak, but the sheriff spoke first.

"You mean, the horse was sheltering in some trees? Smart horse. But the horse was with him this morning?"

Gomez nodded.

The sheriff turned to Hooter, "I'll want to see the horse."

"He's out in the barn, Dan," Hooter said. "I didn't let nobody fool with him. I figured you'd want to see how he was rigged."

Jake's deep voice rumbled from close behind Dusty. "What do you have on your mind, Reed? Do you think somebody might have murdered Blackie?"

Dusty gasped out loud, her gaze frozen on the sheriff. Reed seemed to take his time answering. Wind whistled around the corner of the house, stirring up heavy swirls of dirt between the knot of people in the sparse grass of the yard and the silent barn.

The sheriff rocked on the heels of his boots and stuck his thumbs in his belt before slowly raising his gaze. Then he tilted his head and looked at Jake with squinted eyes. "Why do you ask that? You know something I don't know, Valiteros?"

Jake flinched and his voice had a knife edge when he spoke. "Maybe you should tell us what you suspect. After all, Blackie's daughter has a right to know."

"Why, of course. Blackie's daughter." Reed narrowed his eyes even more.

"What happened to my father? Do you think somebody murdered him?" Dusty's jacket gaped open, but the brisk wind that slipped inside only matched the cold that gripped her heart.

The sheriff's gaze slid slowly to Dusty. "Doc said Blackie had a bad blow to the back of the head. He guessed it was hard enough to kill him. We're gonna have to get a postmortem done before we'll know for sure." His eyes flicked back to Jake. "I'd hate to say right now exactly what happened."

"But it probably was an accident, don't you think, Reed?" Jake put a reassuring hand on Dusty's shoulder. "He could have hit his head falling from his horse."

"Could have," the sheriff said stiffly. "I'll have to see where Gomez found him."

Hooter spoke up, "I can't imagine Blackie falling from his horse. Not Blackie, he knew more about horses than anybody." Dusty shivered and wrapped her coat closely around her middle.

"We'll see," Reed said. "Gomez, can you show me where you found the body?"

"*Como no,*" Gomez said. "*Sí*, Sheriff. I take you. Is far in mountains."

"Tomorrow morning then. We'll start from Morgan's place."

"I want to go with you, Sheriff," Dusty said.

"No need."

"There's every need. I have to see where Blackie was found." Dusty's eyes blazed at the sheriff and her fists clenched with determination.

"Why don't you start out from my place, Reed?" Jake interjected. "That way you'll pretty much go over the same ground Blackie did."

"I suppose you'll want to go, too," the sheriff said, crossing his arms and leaning back on his heels. "That right, Valiteros?"

"No reason not to. After all, Blackie worked for me."

"Yeah," Reed said, "he did. I was thinking of that myself." The sheriff looked significantly at Dusty and then back at Jake.

"Look here, Reed," Jake began, but the sheriff stalked off toward the barn. The rest followed in the sheriff's wake. Jake paused a moment, taking a deep breath, before trailing after them.

In the dark rich-smelling barn, the sheriff inspected the horse. Dusty stood at True Blue's head to reassure him. She talked quietly and kept her eyes on True's ears for signs of unexpected movement.

The sheriff's brusque examination didn't take long. He said nothing beyond several gruff grunts as he noted the gear attached to the saddle and ran his fingers over the leather. He finished as abruptly as he began and stalked toward the barn door.

"Are you through with this horse?" Dusty shouted, stroking True's long silver nose.

"Why?" Reed asked, stopping in the doorway.

"Because I want to unsaddle him and brush him down," Dusty said impatiently. "He's had a hard time of it the last twenty-four hours."

"Go ahead. Nobody's stopping you."

Jake silently shook his head and followed the sheriff back into the yard where the ambulance attendants were loading Blackie's body.

Through the wide barn door, Dusty could see what was taking place in the yard. She was glad for an excuse to stay in the barn. Someone had covered Blackie's body with a blanket, but that wouldn't have made it much easier for her. She turned her attention to True Blue and crooned softly to him. True had lived up to his name, loyally standing by Blackie all night. He was a good horse, well bred and well trained.

Once True Blue was tended to, she walked him through the back door of the barn and released him into the corral with the other horses. She thought he had earned a romp in today's sunshine. She paused to watch him trot off to the water trough for a drink.

The sun shone brightly, sparkling in the moisture on the grass. By the creek, the willow limbs glowed yellow with renewed life, and a mountain bluebird chased his lunch in the crisp air. Dusty looked up at the sky, at the bright bowl of clear blue. Last night's storm had vanished completely. Only the fresh snow on the mountains gave any evidence of its ever having been.

When she turned back into the barn, Jake was leaning against the frame of the open door at the other end of the wide work area. Bright sunlight was behind him; he was backlit, all his features obscured in the deep shadow of the barn's darkness. The lean male figure silhouetted by the sunlight reminded her of Blackie. More, it reminded her of all the cowboys she had known in her life, all the rough-working men who rode horses across sagebrush hills and prodded cattle and lived hard.

His hat was tilted low on his shadowed forehead, as if it had been tugged down securely. One booted foot was cocked over the other, his knee bent, at rest. Lean thighs were covered with worn denim that stretched easily over work-hardened muscle, seasoned by long hours in the saddle.

The man in the doorway, like Blackie and all the cowboys she had known, carried a naturalness about him, the naturalness of long acquaintance with ranch work. He was in his element here—as Blackie had been before him. From the top of his work-softened hat to the tip of his scuffed boots, he was a cowboy, born and bred. No one, especially not Dusty, had to see his face to know that.

Unconsciously, she walked toward him, drawn like steel to a magnet. He pushed away from the doorframe and met her in the middle of the barn. She paused in front of him and closed her eyes to let the scent of man and leather and crisp air wash over her. Reaching out to him, she spread her fingers on the soft chambray shirt beneath the shearling lining of his jacket. He made a sound of surprise, and she looked up into his eyes. They gleamed at her from under the brim of his hat.

She read questions and caution in his eyes, like the sly eyes of a cornered fox. The severe lines of his face were grim, stern. Dusty reached up to touch one sharp cheekbone, her fingertip brushing into the hollow of his cheek and coming to rest in the groove beside his slash of mouth.

He flinched in response to the coolness of her touch on his face, but she didn't stop the disturbing contact. Instead, she lifted her gaze once again to his, her eyes vulnerable with the green of aspen leaves, reminding him of their swift change of color at the auction when she'd learned about the loss of her ranch. That same intense pain was now reflected in the tender green of her eyes.

Her touch through the fabric of his shirt had made his heart pound, just her touch. He had known women who were more beautiful and more seductive, but never had a woman shaken him as easily as this woman. Then the sweet green of her eyes pulled at him, closing out everything but his need to hold her, to stroke away her pain. His hands closed on her hips, pulling her into his body until he could feel her softness against his hard thighs. When soft breasts pressed against his chest as she lifted her arms to his shoulders, hunger rose in him, choking off any words of comfort he might have given her.

She saw in his eyes the heat to cauterize her wound. Her hollow grief needed the heat, the fire that came so naturally from him. Her fingers touched the leanness of his cheeks, and she fitted his mouth to her own. His lips were firm and warm. When the tip of her tongue brushed them, his mouth opened immediately, and he wrapped her tightly in his arms.

So this is what it's like to kiss Jake Valiteros, she thought, as his mouth moved against hers. His urgent heat burned her, wrapped her in flames. For the long moments in Jake's arms, there was no father's death to face, no echoing loneliness in the house across the yard. They stood in the sweet pungency of the barn, holding fiercely to each other.

When he lifted his mouth from hers at last, he buried his face in her hair and neck, holding her close, postponing the moment when her body no longer touched his. He'd always felt disdain for all the poor suckers who let a woman wrap them into knots, including his cold, reserved father, who had mourned his wife's desertion. Since his own disastrous marriage, he had kept the safety of distance between himself, his life on the ranch and a woman, any woman. Yet this woman's touch had shaken him.

He pulled away to look into her face. Her eyes were closed, sun-tipped lashes making a fan against her cheek. Her eyebrows were brought together as if the pain of death had returned after the force of the kiss. He wanted more than anything to ease the pain, to smooth the worry from her brow. He wanted to trace the straight line of her nose with his finger, to touch each of the faint freckles with his tongue. It hurt, actually hurt, to move back from her, to put space between their bodies.

"Let me take you to get some lunch," he said, his voice husky.

"What?" she said, blinking at him in the barn's darkness.

"Lunch," he said after clearing his throat. "You haven't eaten today." He felt awkward talking about such a mundane subject when he was still quaking from the force of her kiss. "You can't eat here. I looked around in the kitchen, remember? I know how low the provisions are. I'll take you out to eat."

"No, Jake. If we went to a restaurant, I'd feel like I was on display. I'd feel like everybody in Big Piney was staring at me."

"We won't eat in Piney. I'll take you to a café over in Pinedale. It's not far. Nobody'll recognize you there."

"Sure," she said, actually grinning at him. The grin almost drove away the knot of anxiety in his stomach. "You know as well as I do that everybody in the valley would recognize both of us."

"We'll pretend we don't recognize them." He put his arm around her shoulders and steered her toward the sunlight. "Come on, Dusty. You have to eat."

"Are you making yourself my keeper?"

"Something like that."

Chapter Four

When Jake and Dusty returned from lunch, a strange truck sat outside the house, and Ruth came bustling out the front door onto the porch. She recognized Jake and stopped dead, waiting impatiently for Dusty to get out of his truck.

Dusty jumped out and rushed up the steps before Ruth had a chance to duck back in the house. She didn't want her aunt to shun Jake, not after his kindness. Lunch had been an easy escape. All the other customers in the little café seemed to be tourists. She had forgotten that Pinedale attracted so many strangers.

Ruth opened her arms to Dusty and hugged her. Ruth's big-boned frame enveloped Dusty's smaller one.

"Thanks for coming, Ruth."

"By the looks of that kitchen, it's a good thing I did," she said, casting a weathered eye on Dusty's pale face. "You're about ready to starve."

"That's what Jake said."

"Oh?" Ruth stiffened and pulled back to peer down the steps at Jake.

"Jake took me to Pinedale to eat some lunch," Dusty said quickly.

Jake said nothing. He stood at the bottom of the steps, feet slightly apart, meeting Ruth's gaze evenly.

"Hmm," said Ruth, refusing to give ground or speak to Jake.

"I'll see you in the morning, Dusty," Jake said in a low rumble. He relinquished his time with her reluctantly. Damn that interfering woman for showing up right now, aunt or no aunt.

"In the morning," Dusty agreed.

Ruth's left eyebrow arched threateningly. Jake touched his fingers to the brim of his hat and returned to his truck.

As the dust rolled up behind the fast-disappearing vehicle, Ruth asked curtly, "What happens in the morning?"

"The sheriff is riding up in the mountains to see where Blackie was found."

"Hmm." Dusty's worried frown stopped Ruth from further comment. Instead, she herded Dusty into the house.

Dusty let her. It felt good to have someone else manage things, all the plans and details that death brought. Ruth took care of the phone calls. She made arrangements for a memorial service the following Saturday. She said Saturday was a good day. Most of Blackie's friends could get away from their ranches then. They would want to pay their respects even though late spring meant a busy season on the ranches of the Green River Valley. Ruth bustled about the house, slanting a worried look now and again at Dusty's frozen posture on the worn sofa. Dusty's eyes stared straight ahead, focused on nothing.

When Ruth had the arrangements set and the refrigerator stocked, she pulled on her sweater and picked up her handbag.

"Are you going to be all right, hon?" she asked, placing a work-toughened hand on Dusty's shoulder.

Dusty tried to concentrate on what Ruth was saying. "Don't worry, Ruth. Thanks for everything."

"What's family for?" Ruth shrugged. She started out the door, then abruptly stopped. "I know I should keep my mouth shut, but I don't guess I intend to." Crossing her arms determinedly, she looked squarely at Dusty. "Some of the folks at church this morning couldn't wait to tell me about seeing you at the Waterhole last night. They were practically salivating about your dancing with Jake Valiteros."

"What?" Dusty looked up, her eyes wide in her pale face. "I just danced with him once."

"Well, all I can say is, it must have been some dance because they were all full of it. They couldn't wait to tell me." Her voice softened. "Now, honey, you just don't know what you could be getting yourself into. I don't think you ever knew Jake Valiteros very well, but he's picked up some bad habits the last few years. He's gotten himself into the taking habit. Land or women, it doesn't seem to matter. He takes whatever he can pry loose."

"I don't think I want to hear this." Dusty felt the ice creep back around her heart.

"You're not going to have to listen to any more. I've got nothing else to say. I just wanted to warn you, is all." With a wave of her hand, she walked out the door. "What you do with it is your lookout." She turned around on the porch and stepped back in, slower this time. "By the way, I plan to drive on out to T.J.'s cabin before I go home. I hate to think how he's going to take the news. Hard enough on the rest of us. Seems like the real cowboys are dying off one by one." She tugged her sweater close. "Anyway, I thought I'd spare you having to tell T.J."

"I appreciate that," Dusty said, her eyes filling suddenly at the memory of T.J. wearily plodding around the barn, his heavy bulk bent with grief.

When the sound of Ruth's truck had died away, Dusty wrapped her arms around herself to stave off the echoing silence. More than anything, she wanted this day to be over.

The ring of the phone shattered the brittle silence like glass splintering from a blow. Dusty clamped a hand over her mouth to force back a startled scream. Falling across the room, she grabbed at the phone with cold hands.

"Hello." Her voice was weak with strain.

"Dusty? Is that you, little one?" a male voice said in a cultivated bass drawl.

She gripped the receiver against her chest and shook away the absurdity of her disappointment. The caller wasn't Jake. Putting the receiver back to her ear, she tried to focus on the identity of her caller. Charlie.

"Are you there, Dusty?"

"Yes," she whispered, "I'm here."

The voice slipped into her ear like warmed syrup. He said he had just this minute returned from his first faculty reception at Texas Tech. And, he went on, he had to call to tell her what happened. He had mentioned, just mentioned mind you, her thesis to a small group of his fellow faculty members, and they had shown decided interest. He was sure he could wrangle a doctorate program for her.

Her master's thesis. As the voice slipped on, she pictured Jake in the café, leaning on the table and asking about her thesis. They'd traded stories about Wyoming pioneers, she and Jake, talking about cattle drives and blizzards and snowmelt-filled rivers. She knew he was trying to keep her mind off Blackie, but she'd enjoyed the stories. He'd said he liked to read what the old-timers wrote about settling the Green River Valley.

"Dusty? Did you hear what I said?" The syrupy voice hardened a bit.

"Blackie's dead," she said.

Silence, then the voice clicked impatiently, "Did you say your father's dead?"

"Yes," she whispered. "Blackie's dead."

"Good Lord, Dusty, you're all alone there. No ranch and now your father's gone, too. I'll come for you. I don't know when right now, but I'll—"

"No," she said, cold and final. "I'm staying here."

"Dusty, you don't—"

"I can't talk now, Charlie." She hung up the phone. She knew she could never make Charlie understand. All I have is this empty house, she thought, and the memories. I'll live here where I can see mountains outside every window. And where I can find out what happened to Blackie.

At ten o'clock the next morning, Dusty was standing by a lone fir tree trying to get the courage to join the others just above her. The sheriff, his deputy, the sheepherder, Jake and Hooter had halted on the scree slope above, examining one particular spot. Without the horses, which were left to munch on the grass beyond the fir tree, the five men looked out of place and tentative, as likely to slide downward as the tumbling pebbles around their boots.

It had taken most of the morning to ride up. Their way, a well-worn game trail, wound upward beside a twisting creek. They had disturbed a couple of mule deer does and a yearling at the foot of Bull Creek, where it spread out between clumps of reeds before it joined Big Piney Creek. This bigger creek flowed below her house, and ran between Jake's big log house and the two-story main house, where Hooter now lived and where the solemn procession had begun their trek. The does had run away, quickly climbing the ridge that divided the drainage from the next one. The riders had been slower, plodding their way upward, sometimes through open meadows still filled with snow, sometimes across an incline so steep, the horses seemed to cling like magnets to the side of the hill. When the creek seemed little more than a trickle, they had entered trees, weaving their way through them in wider places where the snow wasn't too deep. At last they'd climbed up out of the trees to a saucer-shaped hanging valley crowned by the sharp walls of a peak. The snow was just beginning to recede from the openness of the valley, leaving long brown ropes of dead grass to mark its edges.

Dusty could imagine what brought Blackie up this drainage: he'd want to know just how far he could get at this time of year. She reluctantly pulled herself up the slope within earshot of the men. Jake stood above the others. He impatiently slapped his riding gloves against his thigh as he watched the sheriff and his deputy outline where Blackie's body had been in the rocks. The deputy had a tape measure and was using it to block out a rough outline. The old sheepherder was watching the deputy carefully. He stepped forward to push one end of the measuring tape farther up the slope. Then he nodded his satisfaction.

"Gomez," said the sheriff, "you say the body was all covered with snow?"

"*Sí.*"

"That must mean Blackie was up here before the storm got going yesterday." The sheriff aimed his remark at his deputy.

"Must have been," said the deputy. "Snow sure has melted now. I always forget how fast snow melts in sunshine."

"Must not have covered much up here." Reed's boot kicked at the thin sheets of crackling ice on the rocks, all that remained of the late-spring storm. "I guess Blackie's head could have hit any of those rocks." The sheriff settled his hands in his back pockets and looked around.

"I don't see blood on any of them, Dan," the deputy said, imitating his boss by looking carefully at the rocky slope.

"No matter. The snow could have done away with any sign. Besides, he could have fallen up higher and crawled down here before he collapsed.... Or he could have just rolled down here until this rock stopped him." He put his foot on the large rock lodged next to where Gomez indicated the body had been found.

"What are you saying, Reed?" Jake asked, scowling from under the brim of his hat. "Do you think Blackie's death was an accident?"

The sheriff looked up to where Jake was standing above him on the slope. He squinted at Jake and twisted his mouth to spit into the dirt before he spoke. "You got any better ideas?" Jake shifted to balance his rangy body equally on both legs and returned the sheriff's squint with a steel-eyed stare.

Hooter spoke up, "I gotta say it. I don't see how Blackie could fall off a horse, specially his own horse. Why, Blackie packed in these mountains all his life. Nobody was better on a mountain trail than Blackie."

Dusty stepped up beside Hooter and looked uneasily at the spot where Blackie's body had lain.

"Stranger things have happened up here with bad weather threatening," said the sheriff, still squinting at Jake, whose nostrils flared in frustrated anger. "Besides," Reed drawled with cold speculation, "we all know Blackie's been doing a lot of strange things lately."

The deputy glanced from the sheriff to Jake. "The fact is, he just ain't been himself for some time now."

"A man can do all sorts of things when he loses what he's worked for all his life," Reed said. A muscle jumped in Jake's tightly clenched jaw, and he glanced uneasily at Dusty. The sheriff, following Jake's lead, shifted his attention to Dusty.

"I don't believe it," said Dusty, still staring at that awful spot on the ground. "Nothing could disturb Blackie's way with his horse. He rode by instinct. Besides, he'd never be on his horse on a loose slope like this. He'd be leading it."

Jake nodded, carefully observing Dusty's concentration on the slope. "That's right," he said, softening his voice. "He'd probably dismount down below where we did."

Reed shrugged. "Maybe. And maybe he got back on his horse up above there where it kinda levels off in those stumpy aspen. And maybe lightning or something spooked the horse while Blackie was off balance getting into the saddle and he fell."

"Blackie was never off balance getting into a saddle," Dusty said defiantly. The near break in her tension-stressed voice brought Jake quickly down the slope to stand protectively at her side.

The sheriff eyed the two of them, his mouth puckering in consideration. Then he turned his back dismissively and spoke to Gomez, who had retreated down the slope a few feet. "Where did you say you found Blackie's horse?"

Gomez nodded toward the thick stand of black timber below them. "Down there, Señor Sheriff."

"All the way down in those trees?"

"*Sí.*"

"Was the horse tied up?"

"No, *señor.*"

Hooter spoke up, "He would have been trained to stand with his reins hanging to the ground. Blackie trained his horse to ground-tie."

The sheriff gave Hooter an irritated look. "You don't say."

"Why would True be all the way down there?" Dusty said, automatically turning to Jake. "If Blackie was up here, you'd think True would stay here, too, wouldn't you?"

Jake felt her bewilderment as if the sharp-edged cold of the high mountain wind pierced his chest. Stuffing his riding gloves into his back pocket, he reached out to place a reassuring hand on the sleeve of her jacket. She was trembling. Was she in shock? Her face had the same pasty paleness that had alarmed him yesterday.

"Wouldn't he?" she asked again. "True wouldn't run off that far, would he? Something's not right about True's being found in those trees. Not if Blackie really did fall off and hit his head. True would stay with Blackie, I know he would."

Jake gripped her arm firmly. "Let's start back, Dusty. We've seen what we came to see." He had to get her moving. On her horse, she would feel more like herself.

"You do that," said the sheriff, nodding toward his deputy. "We'll stay up here a while longer. The rest of you go on."

"No," said Dusty, her hands clenching into fists inside her leather gloves. "I'm staying. I want to look around here. I have to know."

"No need," Reed said laconically. "The snow probably did away with anything we haven't already seen. We're not going to learn any more up here."

Jake said softly close to Dusty's ear, "He's right about that. There's nothing left to see up here." He pulled her gently in the direction of her waiting horse. "Come on. Go down with me now. If you want to, you can come back some other time." She resisted the pull of his hand on her arm. Her gaze had returned to the place on the ground where Blackie had lain. Jake said again, "Come on, Dusty."

She sighed and gave in, moving down the slope behind Hooter and the sheepherder. She would look around later. Without the sheriff.

Jake followed her, all the way down Bull Creek to the open country of his ranch. Despite her protests, he insisted on following her home, as well. He wanted to be sure the trembling stopped, that she rested.

Dusty stood silently staring out her living-room window. Jake was rumbling around in the kitchen; he sounded as awkward as a raiding raccoon. It was obvious that Jake

Valiteros spent little time in a kitchen. Listening to the clatter of dishes and the frustrated mumbling, she stared at Ol' Yeller, Jake's horse, tied to the fence beside the barn.

Horses and cowboys, she thought. On horseback, Jake was in his element. He and Yeller moved with grace and ease, the cowboy in the saddle and the yellow cow horse. Every movement was liquid, nothing wasted, everything smoothly rhythmic like ripples on water. But on the ground or, worse, in a house, he moved like a grounded duck. Across open ground, he waddled, shifting back and forth from leg to leg as if he expected the ground to lurch underneath him.

Oh, give him a real reason to cross an open space, like chasing down a calf, and his motion changed abruptly. His gait smoothed out the second he hit the ground, and he was as graceful as a dancer. Or as graceful as a good cow horse.

Out by the barn, Blackie's horse, True Blue, stuck his neck over the corral fence and regarded Ol' Yeller curiously. That's just like True, Dusty thought, he likes to know everything that goes on in his territory. He learned that from Blackie. When a good cowboy had a good horse, they started acting alike. Ol' Yeller, she noted wryly, was shifting back and forth, showing the same impatience in the yard that Jake showed in the kitchen.

Ruth said the real cowboys were dying off, like Blackie. She said Jake was greedy, land greedy, the worst kind. The sheriff believed Blackie was upset by the loss of the ranch, upset by the loss of what Jake had taken. He seemed to think Blackie had an accident up in the mountains because he wasn't himself. His implied accusations, she sensed, had come just short of making Jake retaliate. Why hadn't he? she wondered. Despite the awfulness of seeing the spot where Blackie's body had lain all night, she had felt the sizzle of Jake's restrained temper, the effort he had exerted to maintain control in the face of the sheriff's provocations.

Sighing, she leaned her forehead against the coolness of the windowpane. She wished she knew what to think. Especially about Jake.

The shrillness of the ringing phone made her jump. She turned to stare at it blankly, as if she wasn't sure what it was used for. On the third ring, Jake stepped through the connecting door from the kitchen to answer it. He looked uneasily at Dusty.

"Hello," he growled into the phone, then stiffened at the response on the other end of the line. He stuck the receiver in Dusty's direction. "Here," he said and stood there glowering at her as she put the receiver to her ear.

Charlie's voice, brittle and irritated, brought her immediately back to the present. Startled, she flashed a glance at Jake, remembering how she couldn't get him out of her head when Charlie had called last night.

"Hi, Charlie," she said, forcing her gaze away from the glowering cowboy in the kitchen doorway. "No, I'm fine," she protested in answer to Charlie's question. When Charlie asked, rather indignantly, who had answered the phone, she again glanced nervously at Jake before trying to answer.

"He's a neighbor," she said, and Jake quirked an eyebrow at her. "He's helping me," she added, turning her back on the knowing grin Jake gave her. She'd never be able to get Charlie off the phone as long as she was looking at Jake. She couldn't concentrate on the conversation.

She muffled her voice, "Don't worry about me, Charlie. I'm fine. I'll call you in a few days. I have too much to do right now to talk." Jake snorted behind her, but she heard him move away, back into the kitchen.

"Look here, Dusty. What's that man doing in your house?" The disgruntled demand in Charlie's voice was one Dusty knew very well. Until a few months ago, she had ignored it as unimportant. She had smiled at him or stormed at him and gone on to do whatever she'd wanted to do in the first place. But when Charlie got the job in Texas, she learned that the demand was serious and Charlie expected her to obey.

"I don't have to answer that, Charlie," she said grimly. "I appreciate your concern about me, but you and I don't have that kind of relationship anymore. We're just friends, that's all."

"We're much more than friends," Charlie objected. "I can help you get into the best doctorate—"

"Goodbye, Charlie," Dusty interrupted. "I can't talk to you right now."

The abrupt slamming of the receiver into its cradle startled even Dusty. She moved quietly into the doorway to the kitchen. Jake was putting a couple of plates on the kitchen table. He looked at her, his eyebrow cocked again.

"Can we eat now?" she asked, silently cursing her nervousness. "I think I'm finally hungry, and that roast looks pretty good."

Jake's expression didn't change. "Charlie?" he said.

Dusty sighed. "Actually, Dr. Charles Bradford Benson, history professor with a new position at Texas Tech," she said. "He called last night after Ruth left. I told him about Blackie. He just wanted to know how I'm doing, that's all."

His expression still didn't change.

"Look, I don't owe you any explanation." She jutted her chin at him, but he didn't even flinch. She dropped into a chair at the table and gave up. "Charlie and I broke up last semester when he got the job in Texas."

"And before last semester?"

She might object again, but it wouldn't do any good. He was stubborn. It was a trait she knew well.

"He and I lived together."

Jake halted in the act of sitting across from Dusty. "What...did...you...say?" He bit out each word separately.

"You heard me. We lived together, shared the same apartment." It was still painful to remember the sweet romantic dream that had been her love for Charlie. Only the sour taste of disillusionment remained.

"You lived with some man in Laramie?"

"You're shocked!" If she hadn't been so uncomfortable talking about Charlie with Jake, the expression on Jake's face would have been funny. "Aren't you being a little hypocritical? I've never heard that you live like a monk."

"Don't you know any better than to listen to gossip," he grumbled. He knew his neighbors linked his name with every female for miles around, but he didn't expect or need their goodwill. After his wife left, he built his big house, with its exposed log walls and oversize custom-made furniture. No woman had ever lived there. Despite the suspicions of his neighbors, no woman had even spent the night there.

"Surely you don't expect me to think you don't know any women," she said, gaping at him.

"No," he said shortly, "I know my share." Then he shrugged, "Your professor surprised me. I guess I have a hard time remembering you're a grown woman."

She glared indignantly. "I thought we cleared all that up at the branding."

He grinned at the memory of her brandishing those damn pinchers. "Okay, point made," he said, but the irritation that came with hearing about a man, any man, in Dusty's life grated on him. "So what's the story with Charlie? Is he allergic to marriage, or what?"

"Oh, he expected to marry me, all right."

The irritation opened like a raw wound. "So why didn't you marry him?"

"I thought about it. I just decided against it, is all." She stared back at the grumpy man, sternly regarding her from across the table. Such a contrast he made to handsome Charlie, the charming history professor. Two different worlds. She remembered Charlie's thick hair always looked rumpled, as if he had absentmindedly run his hand through it. Curls fell boyishly down on his forehead. In contrast, Jake's hair was flattened from hours under a hat; it was darkened by sweat and untouched by any attempt at grooming. Not one self-consciously vain bone is his body, she thought. "Charlie had a bad habit of accepting praise for my work. He couldn't understand why I was annoyed."

"He thought he deserved praise for your thesis?"

"Among other things." She nodded. Actually, she hadn't noticed Charlie's proprietary attitude until she finished the thesis. Most of the short papers she had done had been suggested by Charlie because of some research he was doing himself. But the thesis was her idea, born from the family stories she had heard from her mother. Then, one day in Charlie's office, the dean stopped by to praise the excellent work she had done. Before she could respond, she heard Charlie accept the praise as his own. He and the dean conversed about the thesis as if she weren't standing there at all. "I decided ol' Charlie wasn't good for my sense of humor."

"Maybe you just weren't ready for the sacrifices of marriage," Jake said belligerently.

"You're a strange person to be defending marriage," she snapped. "You weren't exactly a success at it yourself."

The air in the kitchen turned suddenly wintry. The silence cracked in her ears like breaking icicles. Jake's stare didn't waver, not even the flicker of an eyelash; the only indication of any reaction was the tic of a muscle in his tightly clenched jaw.

She directed her gaze at her plate, away from the laser intensity of his stare. "I heard you were married once," she mumbled. "Ruth mentioned it."

"I'll just bet she did." His voice was as hard as his eyes.

She looked up defiantly. "All I meant was, I'd think you wouldn't be the person to tell me about marriage."

"No," he said dryly, "I don't recommend marriage for anybody. Especially not for me. My ex-wife would vouch for that." He attacked the roast beef on his plate with the side of his fork, crushing it into two pieces. "She didn't like me any better than she liked being a ranch wife."

Watching him tear his roast, she speculated about that last incredible statement. What did this too-stern rancher ask of his wife that made her dislike him enough to run away? Unmoving, she watched his strong hand grip the fork, the fork and the roast overmatched against the steel force of his hand. How would that hand feel on a woman's skin? Icy shivers flashed across her scalp and down her back.

"Charlie expected me to marry him and go wherever he went," she said, forcing her attention back to her plate. "I couldn't leave Wyoming, and he couldn't understand why not." She looked up with a small smile. "Blackie understood. All I had to say is that Charlie went to Texas. Blackie just grinned. He knew I'd never leave my mountains. Not for any man."

Jake scowled at her smile. He resented Charlie the professor for existing, for having been a part of Dusty's life, but, at the same time, he resented the easy way she dismissed the man, returning to the mountains without a backward glance. The lines in his face became even more rigid in denial of his resentment.

Years ago, he had closed himself off from feelings that required jealousy. All of his life and his energy was ordered around work on the ranch. When he wasn't working, like as not, he relaxed in the big chair in front of his rock fireplace and looked out on the Wyoming Range through the massive windows in the front wall. When his body wanted what only a woman could give, he satisfied the urge with a trip to Jackson. He knew from bitter experience that living with a woman ruined his contentment and destroyed his peace of mind.

"He thought he could tell me what to do," she said. "Nobody makes my decisions for me."

"Am I supposed to take that as a warning?" he said evenly. "Be careful. I may see you as a challenge, and I won't be as easy to convince as your professor." His eyes turned to cold blue flame, flicking over her, from the golden highlights of her hair to the fullness of her lower lip. Unconsciously, the tip of her tongue slipped out of her slightly open mouth to moisten her bottom lip, and Jake smiled slowly, remembering how that moist lip felt under his.

"What's going to happen when I tell you what to do on the ranch?" His expression sobered. "I do expect you to work for me, Dusty. I'll need somebody to take Blackie's place."

"Yeah, I guess you will," she whispered, feeling the ache creep back around her heart. "I might as well accept your job. Working with horses is what I want to do now." She didn't say she wanted to work close to home so she could figure out what had happened to Blackie. "Are you sure you'll be able to trust me with your horses? After all, I'm just a woman."

One end of the straight line of his mouth quirked upward, and he leaned back in his chair, feeling suddenly relieved. "Don't get the wrong idea. I'll keep a close watch on your work. I expect the best from everybody who works for me."

She smiled. "Fair enough." She wished he didn't look so good stretching in his chair. She couldn't help but notice the way his shirt pulled across the lean muscles of his chest. This cowboy was used to having his own way. He would expect her to jump when he said jump, and she knew she would defy him out of pure stubbornness.

His narrow-eyed gaze took in the high cheekbones of her face. The day's sun had flushed them with a light sprinkling of freckles. Her eyes, fringed by long sun-kissed lashes, blazed like the sun behind the mountains. He knew he had to kiss her; more than life itself, he needed to kiss her. Slowly he unfolded from the chair, lazily coming to stand beside her.

"Come here," he growled, pulling her from her chair.

His demand stiffened her. Maybe she would have struggled against him, but his hard lips brushed ever so lightly across hers, a whisper of a kiss, almost a prayer. Fascinated, she stood absolutely still while he brushed her lips a second time, pausing at the corner of her mouth to flick the tip of his tongue in their seam, tasting and teasing as he traced the fullness of her bottom lip.

Then his mouth opened slightly and moved against hers, edging slowly into hers until his tongue slid against her own. Her hands grasped the strong shoulders, and she savored the salty taste of his mouth, the hardness of the body pressed against hers.

His hands measured her strong, straight back. He cupped the round firmness of her buttocks in the tough denim and pressed her against his own swelling firmness. He held her there, learning her body against his, and drank in the nectar of her mouth. He hadn't wanted to need a woman. But Dusty had taken away his choice. This woman, like no other he had ever known, fascinated him, tempted him, made him want to soothe and protect.

All the high emotion of the day surged through Dusty, heating her body and pressing her closer to the hard cowboy who held her. All of it came together in that one searing kiss, all the grief and all the need for comfort. She wrapped her arms around Jake's neck and pulled warmth from his mouth into hers. His arms tightened, his chest rose and fell against her breasts as his body cradled hers.

Slowly, Dusty pushed herself into consciousness, drugged by his kiss and the comfort of his strength. At last, she rested her heated forehead against the wall of his chest and silently cursed her own weakness. Hadn't her experience with Charlie taught her to hold on to her independence?

He stared down at her bowed head. "Fight it all you want to," he said in a rasp, roughened by uneven breathing, "but you can't win. I want you and you want me. That's the way it has to be."

"No."

"You can't escape seeing me, you know. You work for me now."

She looked up at him, her eyes widened with alarm. "Maybe it's not such a good idea to work for you."

"Too late to change your mind. I'm holding you to your word." He grasped her wrist firmly in his hard fingers. "I won't press you now. Take a few days. I won't expect you to start work until after the memorial service. And I'll stay away from you until then. But remember, I won't go away." He jerked his head in the direction of the window. "I belong in these mountains, just like you. You can't send me to Texas."

He left by the back door. She didn't move until he was gone. She didn't want to see him riding off on his big buckskin. She wanted no reminders of just how much he belonged here, of just how much he was a part of everything she loved.

Chapter Five

When the house settled into silence, Dusty moved to the back door and pushed the screen open, standing with one foot outside. A breeze blew up from the willows by the creek. Her eyes closed and she pulled in the smell of it, the sharp smell of sagebrush and the sharp edge of mountain wind.

A sudden brisk gust shivered up her arms and made her rub them to get back the warm feeling. What had invaded her safe space? She looked involuntarily toward the break in the willows. The old sheepherder, Gomez, had come from there, trailing her father's body behind him. She swallowed hard, trying to force down the panicky feeling. Something was disturbing the willows. They jerked arbitrarily, not from the rhythmic sway of wind.

She thought she could make out the top of a worn black hat, high-crowned and nodding with the rocking motion of a rider. Slowly, the hazy form of a man on horseback detached itself from the clinging willows. The horse slogged toward her, its head nodding with the same motion of its rider, the two beasts forged into one worn-out and dreary image.

As the bowed shape of man and horse moved closer, Dusty recognized the rider. It was T.J. She smiled at her foolish fear, and her shoulders slumped in relief. She had watched T.J. ride just that way countless times. Blackie was never able to urge T.J. into a faster gait, no matter how much he cursed. Cows could run and calves could bolt, but T.J. kept right on slogging down the trail.

Dusty walked out to the gate to meet him. Sitting grumpily in his saddle, he rode up to where she stood on the bottom rung of the big wooden gate. Then he sagged to one side to spit a stream of tobacco juice into the dirt. Long ago, Dusty's mother had told her, laughing as she said it, that T.J.'s name stood for Tobacco Juice, and T.J.'s gloomy expression hadn't changed one bit when he nodded his agreement. Dusty leaned over the top of the gate to stroke the nose of T.J.'s old mare.

He moved the wad of tobacco into the pouch of his cheek. "I come t' check on you. I tried t' stay away, but I wuz worried." His voice sounded moist, as if his throat were a clogged drainpipe.

"I'm doing okay." She shaded her eyes with her hand to get a better look at him in the bright sun. He hadn't shaved in a while and tobacco juice stained his chin. His jacket and jeans were slick with grime. "You don't look too good, T.J. Are you sick?"

"Naw," he said, looking off into the distant sagebrush. "It's jist hard, is all. Seein' this place without Blackie bein' here." He swiped at his eyes with the back of his dirty sleeve.

"We're going to miss him," she said softly. "I haven't gotten used to it yet."

"You be careful," he said, his voice taking on a hollow sound like wind across an empty barrel.

"What?" She squinted her eyes to see him better.

"Jist be careful, is all. They's some around here ya better off stayin' away from."

"What are you talking about?"

"You jist lissen to me." He nodded grimly. "You keep away from the thieves and murderers. They's out to git us all. Best you jist leave here. Go back to school where you belong."

"I can't do that, T.J. I belong here."

"You cain't protect yerself here. You don't know what's been goin' on." He gripped the saddle horn with his grimy, work-toughened hands. "I seen you this mornin'. I seen all of yuz ridin' up into the mountains with the sheriff."

"We wanted to see where Blackie's body was found," she said, watching him carefully.

"I knowed what you wuz up to, all right. I knowed you'd want to see where Blackie wuz found. But I seen you ridin' along with 'im." His eyes burned like red-hot coals. She drew back, gripping the top of the gate. "I seen you ridin' with Valiteros. He wuz ridin' right beside you. I seen you talk to 'im."

"He was trying to—"

"He killed Blackie. Killed 'im dead. Took his ranch and killed 'im," T.J. snarled. "And you ride along with 'im like you wuz goin' to a picnic." His voice rose to a roar. "You stay away from Valiteros." The old mare, screwing its ears around and whinnying uneasily, shifted beneath him.

"None of this wudda happened 'cept for his takin' Blackie's ranch." His voice dropped to a whimper. "Nothin's right no more. This whole valley's goin'. The ranches dryin' up. Blowin' away on the wind, jist like Blackie said they would." He snarled again, "There's nothin' here for you. You hear me. Nothin'." He pulled the old mare's head around and started back from where he came. He paused and jerked back toward Dusty. "Git out now. While you can. 'Fore Valiteros gits you, too."

Dusty watched him nodding back into the willows, fading away into the creek like in a dream. She shuddered, cold brushing up her arms like a dripping willow branch.

The long week dragged by, as slowly as T.J.'s nodding old mare. T.J. didn't come back. She thought about making a trip out to his cabin to satisfy her nagging worry about him, but she couldn't find the courage. Nor could she find the courage to go back up into the mountains where Blackie's body was found. She wasn't ready to face the reality of Blackie's death. If she didn't check on T.J. or go into the mountains, maybe she could believe her father wasn't really dead—for a little while longer.

Jake left her alone. She knew he was busy moving cattle. He and Hooter would be drifting the cows and their calves onto early-summer grass. This was the time of the year, after branding, to move the cows from their winter pasture. During the harsh winter, all the cattle had been kept in the hay meadows close to ranch headquarters, where they could be fed when the snow covered the grazing. The calving was done there, too. Now it was time to move them. The hay meadows would be irrigated for the summer crop, and the cattle moved in stages toward the high mountains for summer. In July, they would be drifted for the last time onto mountain pasture.

The calves they had branded on Saturday were still healing. They and their mamas would be the last ones moved to early-summer grass. That would probably be done next week, and Dusty expected to help. Drifting cows meant a long day on horseback, hard work but some of the best of ranch work.

It was during drifting she had gotten her name. She had been barely five years old, a miniature cowboy perched on the broad back of her horse. By the end of the day, her brother Mac said she was all one color—"dusty" from head to toe. When she took off her hat, he laughed because her head was still the same color as the rest of her.

Looking forward to the drifting was all Dusty had to get her through the week. She told herself she would start to face things then. She would be drifting cattle without Blackie, and Blackie's death would begin to be real.

The memorial service was at the end of the week. Jake was there. Dusty knew he would be. After the service, she saw him standing in the back corner of the church. She stood up front with Ruth and Ed while Blackie's friends came to offer their condolences. Some of the roughest-looking cowboys had tears in their eyes. Some of them even hugged her before they ambled off with that lurching gait reserved for solid ground.

She looked for T.J., but she didn't see him. She asked Ruth where he could be. Ruth looked surprised. She said T.J. never came around people much anymore, not that he ever had really. Oh, he might hang around outside, on the edges of a get-together, but he'd never come inside, especially not inside a church.

Several times, Dusty looked over some cowboy's shoulder and saw Jake watching her from the back of the sanctuary. He didn't approach her nor did he say a word to anyone. He just stood there, separate from everyone else, keeping watch. Hooter was at home with the collection of hands in the church as he clapped them on the back and shook their hands. But not Jake.

When Hooter came to hug Dusty clumsily, he whispered in her ear that he'd expect her for the drifting early Monday morning. He leaned back to smile at her and said, "I'm gonna like havin' Blackie's daughter workin' on the ranch."

Monday morning, she rode Early Snow into the pasture to meet the other hands. She was all alone, like Jake standing at the back of the church or sitting by himself at the Waterhole. She was no more comfortable with her own loneliness than she was with his. His loneliness had touched her, bringing out a protectiveness she hadn't known she possessed. She wanted to caress his forehead, massaging away worry lines, or, worse, to stand with an arm around him, daring their neighbors to say anything against him.

"Damn," she cursed to herself, "I must be soft in the head. That man owns my ranch and bosses me around and I get the urge to protect him. I even disgust myself."

By the middle of the day, Dusty wasn't sure she had ever seen any human weaknesses in Jake. His face stony, he bit out orders as if he begrudged anything that took a second away from his concentration on the cattle. The only time he uttered a word in her direction, he shouted at her to follow a straying calf or to keep a reluctant cow moving. All business.

Of course, everyone on the ranch had plenty to keep them busy. There were two hundred cows and their calves to move up the county road. These cattle had to be moved farther than any other part of the herd. They were the cows that had belonged to Blackie before Jake bought him out. Jake wanted these cows moved to grazing land near the rest of his herd. He planned to use most of the land he had bought from Blackie for growing winter hay. Blackie's land was easy to irrigate because of the creek flowing through it.

The easiest way to move the cattle for a great distance was to use a public roadway. Some roads had narrow drift fences along them to make moving cattle even easier. There were no drift fences for this move, though. All six of the hands working the herd had to stay alert for traffic on the road as well as for the stubborn temperament of the cows themselves. The cows bawled in protest at walking on the pavement. After all, enticing grass grew on both sides of the road. Apparently, they saw no reason to walk on anything that didn't grow grass.

Dusty drew drag duty. She and Ollie and Jeep brought up the rear, riding in the dust of the heaving bodies plodding along between the borrow ditches on either side of the road. No sign of any standing water anywhere, not even mud. The freak snowstorm that had hit the day Blackie died was no more.

Dusty pulled her kerchief up over her nose and her hat down low over her sunglasses. She had learned long ago to protect herself from the burning sun and driving dust. Moisture didn't last long in the dry air and the almost constant wind. She knew she could shrivel like the long-departed snow.

We need rain, she thought, as she trotted Snow up close to a stalled cow, urging it to move just to get out of her way. Then she snorted at her own foolishness. Rain would turn the shallow soil to a gooey mess. Cows and horses would bog down to their knees. Hands would be covered in the stuff. They would have to dismount to pull calves out of the mire, getting covered in mud and manure from boots to hats.

Oh, please keep us from that, she prayed.

From time to time, she looked warily at the western horizon. Gray clouds were gathering behind the red peaks of the Wyoming Range. Yes, the land needed the rain, but not now. She was prepared for the inevitable. A slicker was tied into a roll behind her saddle. No experienced hand was foolish enough to mount a horse in Wyoming without being prepared for any kind of weather. Experience also told her that rain, if it came, wouldn't be long in making itself unpleasant. Weather moved fast in Wyoming.

The only hope was that the clouds would dry up before they made it over the high peaks. Dusty saw Ollie keeping an eye on the clouds. Up ahead, Hooter's head turned in that direction when he had successfully maneuvered a recalcitrant cow around an oncoming truck.

Jake rescued a stranger's sedan, stuck behind two stalled cows. He rode in between the cows, shouting in the stunted sounds cowboys use to talk to cattle. The cows bawled back at him and moved off into the ditch. He stopped by the side of the road and checked the horizon. He pulled down his hat abruptly with one gloved hand and kicked his horse into motion.

In the early afternoon, they watched the rain move down the near side of the mountains. They felt the moisture in the wind that moved ahead of the rain. As if by an unseen signal, all the hands picked up the pace of the herd. They slapped their ropes against the chaps that covered their legs and shouted at the cattle. Horses moved into a trot, anxious to escape the cold rain. Even the cows seemed to know what was best for them. They, too, moved along, bawling to urge their calves closer to their sides.

They almost made it. Just as Jake moved aside the wide opening in the fence, the rain rushed over them. Dusty huddled into her slicker and crooned to the nervous cows, slowly pushing them through the bottleneck of the gate. By the time the last cow trailed through the gate, the ground had become a viscous mire, sucking at the feet of the horses. Ollie got the worst of it. He had to wrestle a calf that was trying to get itself trapped in the wire of the fence. He slipped in the slick mud, landing flat on his back with the calf on top of him. Calf one, Ollie zero.

Dusty slipped a rope around the neck of the calf and pulled it through the gate. Ollie stumbled to his feet and stood there looking forlorn.

"Get out of that mud," Jake shouted at him.

"Hey," shouted Hooter, "let him be, Jake. That boy needs a beauty treatment."

Jake didn't appear to catch the joke. The rest of them enjoyed Ollie's misery. Jeep paused in his laughing to bring Ollie his horse. Even Early Snow seemed amused as she and Dusty passed by, trotting onto the pavement in the wake of Jake and Hooter.

True to the fickle nature of mountain weather, the rain stopped in time for the ride home. Slickers came off and heads lifted. Nothing like a leisurely canter down a country road.

Dusty rode along, keeping Hooter between her and Jake's testy mood. Naturally, the traffic that had been such a problem when they were driving the cows disappeared completely. They were able to ride easily without having to wade through the mud of the borrow ditches. Even after a long day in the saddle, Dusty enjoyed the easy rhythm of Snow's even gait and the shiny brightness of the rain-washed air.

She was pondering the wild iris dotting a pasture just beyond the fence when something Hooter said to Jake caught her attention.

"Whatta you say I go back through the rest of the herd tomorrow and check the ear tags? I'd like to see which cows are missing."

Dusty looked at Hooter curiously. Did she hear him say there were some cows missing? He'd said it so matter-of-factly. Missing cows meant big trouble on a cattle ranch, especially at this time of year. She couldn't imagine Hooter's not being disturbed by it. Obviously, it was not new information.

Jake picked up on Dusty's sudden attention to Hooter. He had spent the day covertly watching her. He couldn't help but notice what a canny ranch hand she was. She would know the significance of missing cattle, and her very intelligent mind would start working on a link between the cattle and Blackie's death. He felt a solid coldness in the pit of his stomach at the idea she might get herself involved in something that could be terribly dangerous.

"I don't know," he said, trying to put Hooter off. "I'm not sure we got a good count last week. After all, ten missing cows is a good round number. Maybe the tally was off by ten."

"Couldn't be. I went back and checked the branding tally with the count I made last week. There's ten cows and their calves missing, all right. No doubt about it."

"Okay," Jake said quickly. Damn, Hooter, she's hanging on every word you say. "We can't get too excited about it until we know for sure. Go ahead and do a check on the ear tags."

"Jake, if there're some cows missing—" Dusty began.

"By the way, Dusty," Jake interrupted, "you can get started working with the horses tomorrow. After the workout we've given them today, they'll need a good going-over." He turned in his saddle to speak to Ollie and the two hands following behind. "You three get the irrigation going in the hay fields. That'll keep you busy the rest of the week, maybe next week, too."

"Yuck, farming," moaned Ollie.

Dusty grinned. Cowboys always complained about working in the hay fields. The work was necessary to feed the cattle during the winter, but it was dirty, sweaty work that couldn't be done on horseback. For a regular ranch hand, most of the summer was taken up with hay "farming." Only a few blessed days put them on horseback for a whole day of working cows.

Dusty knew Jake was changing the subject for her benefit. She saw Hooter glance her way when Jake cut her off so quickly. It wouldn't do any good to press the issue right now. But missing cows put a whole new light on Blackie's death.

The others cut across the pasture to follow the creek when they reached Dusty's house. Jake stayed behind. Ollie tried to look anywhere but at Dusty when Jake told them to go on without him. Hooter grinned at Jake's scowl and said, "Anything you say, boss."

Jake dismounted and trailed his horse behind Dusty as she led Snow into the barn. While she worked on her horse, he stood by silently, slapping the ends of his reins against his gloved hand.

Finally, he said quietly, "Don't jump to any conclusions about those missing cows Hooter was talking about. There's probably nothing to it. We don't get much rustling in the valley."

Dusty gave him a sidelong glance but didn't say anything. She kept right on with her unsaddling.

"Are you listening to me?" Jake asked testily.

"Yeah," she said, pausing in front of him on her way to put up the saddle. "I heard you."

"Then," he said to her back as she walked off, "you know there's no reason to go off half-cocked and looking for trouble."

She finished putting up the saddle before she responded. "Now, just what do you mean by that? It sounds like you're pretty sure that there's some trouble. Maybe you figure that there's some connection between the missing cows and Blackie's death."

"There you go jumping to conclusions, just like I thought you would. Everybody, including the sheriff, believes Blackie's death was an accident. It's damn easy to fall off a horse up there, especially if there was some ice around. And don't tell me Blackie was too good with horses for that to happen to him. It happens to the best riders, and you know it." He added softly, "Besides, everybody says Blackie wasn't acting like himself lately."

"Oh, you mean the theory that Blackie died because you drove him to it," she snapped.

He winced as if she had actually hit him. "Well, even I have to admit that losing a ranch isn't a happy experience."

"No, it's not," she said.

"You should know." He glowered at her, daring her to deny his logic.

"I do know." She went back into the stall and began brushing down Snow. "But I also know what Blackie said about it. He wasn't bitter, and he wasn't upset. He wanted to breed Appaloosas. He did a little of it, using Early Snow as the mare for True, but he sold off the colts. He always talked about buying more breeding stock. He and I were going to build something here." As she said the words, the truth of them sank in. No, Blackie wasn't upset about selling the ranch to Jake. Regardless of the speculations of his neighbors, Jake held no responsibility for Blackie's death.

After a pause, she smiled and continued, "When he went up into the mountains that afternoon, he was just glad to be able to get up there for the first time this year. There was no reason for his last ride to be any different from any other ride he made in those mountains."

He felt a sudden tightening in his throat. He couldn't say anything, but he was glad to know Dusty didn't blame him for what happened to Blackie. He had worried about it. He knew Ruth and Ed were probably filling her full of bad news about him. He felt ridiculous to be so relieved. Why could this woman unsettle him so easily?

"I want you to promise me you won't take off by yourself and go into the mountains." He sounded gruffer than he had intended to, but he had to get through to her. He already knew her well enough to worry about her stubborn independence and the trouble she could get herself into. "I know you're champing at the bit to get back up there and look around. When you get ready to go, I'll go with you."

She paused in her brushing and gave him a questioning look. How did he know she *hadn't* already been back in the mountains? Had he been watching her all last week? "I'm sure that's very considerate of you, but I can manage all right by myself."

"Considerate, be damned. And I don't want any of your nonsense about how you've been riding in those mountains all your life, either. That national forest land is big enough to hide all kinds of hell. Blackie died up there, and I want to make damned sure the same thing doesn't happen to you."

He cursed himself for putting it so bluntly. He might as well go all the way and get her really mad.

"Just do the work I hired you to do and don't go wandering into the forest unless I'm with you."

"Is that an order, boss man, sir?"

"Yes, that's an order." He turned on his boot heel and left the barn. Damn, he'd done that badly. Now he'd have to really watch her, or she'd be in those mountains the first chance she had.

Her first chance came two days later when Jake thought she was safely working with Ollie on an irrigation ditch. Jake rode by the hay field to be sure she had plenty to do. Since she and Ollie were getting shovels from the truck, Jake assumed there would be plenty of work to keep her out of trouble. He didn't stop. He was on his way to help Hooter finish up the check on the ear tags, and he didn't want to do any explaining.

Dusty saw him cross the field and noted his direction. She guessed where he was headed and guessed why he didn't want to say anything to her. She didn't consciously decide that the time had come to slip out from under Jake's watchful eye. It was just that, when she and Ollie drove over to her place to pick up Blackie's toolbox, she saw an opportunity and took it. Ollie agreed there wasn't much left to do in the hay field. He'd take the tools over to a cranky irrigation gate himself. No need for her to come along.

Later, as she made her way up into the trees, she told herself she wasn't riding by herself to spite Jake. No, she had Blackie's ashes with her, and she wanted to be alone when she scattered them. That was true enough. She knew she would cry. That's why she had been putting it off. She hadn't cried once since Blackie died, and she didn't want a witness when she did. At least, no witness but True Blue.

She wanted to ride the silver Appaloosa stallion when she scattered Blackie's ashes.

She and True made their way up the Big Piney Creek drainage. She would always think of all that drainage as family land, no matter who held the title. Just as she thought of the creek as hers even where it began high on public land. Up there in a grove of aspen was where she scattered the ashes. And where she cried.

Since she was so close, she decided to ride over the ridge that separated the Big Piney Creek drainage from Bull Creek, where Blackie's body had been found. She might as well look around on her own while she had the chance. She picked a game trail that went the long way around but kept her low enough for easy riding.

Here and there she noticed evidence of horse traffic on the wide trail. She was surprised that the droppings looked so recent. Each fall, hunters trailed horses everywhere in the mountains, but evidence of their horses would have been more decomposed. She couldn't think of anyone else who might find it necessary to trail through the trees as she was doing.

Above the lone fir tree where she had dismounted before, she noticed True had no trouble with his footing on the rocky trail. He went straight up with almost no effort. She stopped him to look down at the spot where the sheep-herder said he found Blackie's body. A cold shiver went down her spine as she thought of Blackie's body lying down there covered with snow. True seemed to be bothered by something, too. He shifted around underneath her and twisted his head back in the direction they had come.

"Not yet, ol' boy," she said to True. "I'm not ready to go back down yet. We have to look around here first."

She urged True into the stand of stunted aspen above the rocky slope. The trunks of the usually straight aspen were twisted with the effort of survival. The trees were widely spaced and not much taller than she was as she sat on True's back. The harsh wind discouraged much height. Underneath the trees, very little grew in the rocky soil.

A coil of rope at the base of one of the trees caught her attention and pulled her off True's back. It wasn't a very long piece of rope. It looked well used, scuffed and frayed in several places. It was the kind of rope a rancher used around the barn, a different kind from the one used to rope calves. A cowboy didn't carry rope as thick as this. One end of the rope had been cut—recently. The ends were a different color from the rest of the piece.

Then she saw it. She sucked in her breath with an audible sound. True whinnied uneasily behind her and stamped a forefoot.

It was Blackie's glove.

It had been partially covered by the rope, lying there in the rotting leaves of last fall. Her hand trembled as she picked it up. It was stained from rain and snow, but, otherwise, it looked as though he might have just taken it off.

She turned around to show True, extending it for him to see. "It's Blackie's glove, True." The big horse looked at the glove carefully, as if he knew what it was.

"What's it doing up here, do you think? Why would Blackie's glove be under this piece of rope? It's not Blackie's rope. He never carried rope like this. And why would he take off his glove up here and fall way down there?"

She put her head against the big horse's neck and hugged him. He felt warm and solid, comforting.

As she put the rope and glove in her saddlebag, she heard thunder, deep-voiced mountain thunder. She stilled for a second to judge the distance. True pricked up his ears, listening as carefully as she did. It was pretty far away, but it could be moving fast.

"We better get down out of these mountains, True. Thunder means lightning, and we both know how dangerous that is in the mountains."

Then her eyes widened. "You know what else, True? I didn't bring my slicker. If it rains, I'm going to get soaked." She shook her head at her stupidity. "I guess I'm in for it with the boss now. I didn't follow his orders about coming up alone, and I didn't come prepared for afternoon thundershowers. That'll probably convince him I really am a helpless female."

She didn't dare rush the trip down, even though the thunder was loudly rolling around the peaks above her head. The footing was much too treacherous for speed. Getting soaked was inevitable.

She made black timber before the rain reached her. But this time, the thick growth of Douglas fir over her head didn't keep out the icy rain. It quickly penetrated her shirt and the denim of her jeans. It collected in her hat brim and spilled over into her lap.

And it didn't stop. It went on and on, all the way down the creek. Lightning flashed and thunder rumbled all around. Light and sound and frigid wet enveloped her, closing off everything but the horse beneath her.

Chapter Six

When Jake discovered Dusty wasn't in any of the places she was supposed to be, he knew where to find her. The sureness with which he headed toward the mountains didn't lessen his feeling of panic. A thunderstorm, even though it was a frequent afternoon event in the mountains, was always dangerous. This storm rolled down the mountainsides quickly and fiercely, as stubborn as the temper of the dusty-haired woman, who had undoubtedly wandered into its path.

My God, she was irritating. He hadn't had an easy moment since the morning she'd shown up at the branding. Hell, he hadn't had an easy moment since the auction. He knew she was too headstrong to do what he had told her to do. No way. He had expected her to take off for the mountains by herself, but why did she have to pick a day when the weather was treacherous?

Grimly he had tracked down Ollie at ranch headquarters, unloading the tools from the back of the pickup.

Wasn't she at her place? Ollie had asked, wide-eyed at Jake's agitation. The curses Ollie received in reply were warning enough to send him out of Jake's range. He quickly volunteered to help his father complete the count of ear tags in spite of the approaching rain making it wet, miserable work. The coming thunderstorm couldn't be as bad as the storm Jake was kicking up.

Riding as fast as he dared, Jake made his way toward the game trail the sheepherder had shown them. Storm clouds deepened, turning black with fury. The booming thunder threatened menacingly. When he counted the seconds between the flash of lightning and the reverberating clap of thunder, the nearness of the storm made his backbone feel like ice. He prayed as never before. *Please let her be down from the open meadow where Blackie's body was found.... Please.*

The icy rain hit him like so many bullets. He pulled up into a thick stand of trees to put on his slicker. Time to slow down, no matter how anxious he was. Although the sudden heavy rain made it impossible to see more than fifty yards, he knew Bull Creek flowed into Big Piney Creek just ahead. The game trail began there.

When he and Ol' Yeller stepped into Big Piney Creek, lightning and thunder simultaneously ripped open the air around him. Yeller, his rider's urgency prompting him forward, threw himself toward the opposite creek bank with no hesitation. Horse and rider had started up the steep incline that led to the trail when Jake saw her. Or rather when he saw True Blue. His heart stopped with fear. Had she been thrown from True the way the sheriff guessed Blackie had been thrown?

True Blue halted his forward motion when he saw Jake and turned his big body enough for Jake to see the pathetic load he carried in his saddle. True seemed to be traveling on his own without any guidance from his rider. Dusty's limp form draped itself over the saddle and clung to the sturdy horse's neck.

Jake, heart knocking in his chest like a sledgehammer, jumped from Yeller's back and slipped and slid to where True waited patiently. His first touch told him her body had turned to ice. So cold. No body heat. Fearfully, he growled her name and grasped her upper arms to wrench her from the saddle. To his surprise, she jerked away from him, her eyes tightly shut.

"No," she said, her voice a low painful rasp. "No," she said again, trying to cling to True's neck.

"Stop it, Dusty," he said, battling her resistance. "You have to get out of the saddle."

He doubted she comprehended what he said, but he knew how urgent it was to get her down from her perch and into safer proximity with the ground. As if to confirm his fears, a brilliant shaft of lightning struck high on the timbered slope across the creek. It made an ominous searing sound as it disappeared among dark green treetops. He concentrated on getting Dusty to some kind of safety. The cold had weakened her enough to allow him to overpower her resistance and pull her into his arms. Even so, he was surprised at her strength. If she was still strong enough to resist him, she would make it.

Clutching her slim body to his chest, he crawled and scrambled up a slippery rise toward the only possible protection he could see. The base of a rocky overhang offered shelter from the lightning even if it wouldn't keep out the cold and wet. He deposited her in the depression where the ground met the rock wall and covered her, head and all, as best he could with his slicker.

"Where's your damn rain gear?" he growled, tucking the tail of the slicker around her feet. "Stupid. Next time you listen to me."

It was just as well she couldn't hear him. She'd probably start fighting him again. Stubborn female. He had to get to the horses. He couldn't leave them standing out in the open. He left her slumped against the rock wall for a moment and went to tend to the horses. He tied them up, close together, in the trees. Neither horse protested.

"Damn sight smarter than she is," he said to True. "You know enough to come in out of the rain, don't you, ol' boy."

Pulling his collar up around his ears, he ran back to Dusty. He crawled under the long yellow slicker and pulled her against himself, nestling her inside his jacket, but her cold, wet shirt chilled him, and he felt the deep shudders that shook her. Fumbling between their huddled bodies, he ripped buttons out of buttonholes in her clinging shirt and peeled it off her unresisting arms.

"Wh-what?" she muttered weakly. "What are you d-doing?"

"Shut up," he mumbled against her ear as he unknotted his kerchief and blotted the beaded moisture on her upper back. "Damn, this thing has to go," he growled, yanking her wet camisole loose from the waist of her jeans and tugging it upward. A whispered "no" pressed coldly against the bare skin of his neck when he roughly pushed up her arms along with the soaked garment. "Shut up, I said." He ripped open his own shirt, briefly exposing his dry bare chest to the cold that seemed to rise out of the ground beneath their bodies, and clutched her shivering upper body against his, wrapping the open front of his shirt and denim jacket around her slender shoulders.

The skin of her upper body had almost a metallic coldness when he pressed it within the curve of his body. At first, that sensation of deep cold was all he felt, but, as her shivering grew calmer, he felt the prickling of her skin, pebbling into goose bumps. Then he closed his eyes and groaned aloud. Against the sensitive skin beneath his own nipples, he felt the cold puckering of hers boring into him with the white-hot heat of dry ice. Instinctively, his arms tightened around her, desperately drawing her into his body, until the soft mounds of her breasts flattened against him.

"God Almighty," he groaned into the wet strands of hair at her ear.

She responded by burrowing into him, her cold lips piercing his collarbone and her deep breath rasping through his chest hair. Gradually, her shuddering breath evened out, and he could feel some warmth return to her core. If the lightning would just let up, he could get them both safely back to the ranch.

He didn't know how long they stayed there like that, huddled together under his rain slicker. It seemed like forever. She was like a little animal snuggling into his chest, but his cursed body recognized the woman despite all the resolutions he had repeated to himself during the last few days. When he left her after the trip into the mountains with the sheriff, he told himself she was much too vulnerable emotionally for a tussle in his bed, which was what he had in mind every time he saw her.

All the long week before Blackie's funeral, he knew where she was and what she was doing at any given time. Usually, he checked on her himself, keeping himself shrouded in distance, but sometimes he quizzed Hooter or Ollie to see what they knew. Although both of them seemed to get an enormous kick out of his interest, he didn't let their snickers stop him. His obsession wouldn't let him go.

From his vantage point at the back of the church during the memorial service, she still seemed shaky, so he waited. By the day of the drifting, her cockiness was back in full force, and that attitude of hers irritated the hell out of him. He was even more irritated at his own contrariness. He didn't want her to be vulnerable, but when she wasn't, he got mad.

A glance at her riding in the dust of a drifting herd was enough to speed up his pulse rate. Watching her lift a shovel from the back of a pickup stopped him in his tracks, even across the width of a hay field. Now he lay within the narrow margins of a rain slicker with every delicious inch of her body pressed against his. How could he expect his body not to react?

Damn, he cursed himself. *Damn, damn, damn.* Gritting his teeth at the tense fullness in his groin, he tightened his arms around her and rested his cheek against her tawny hair. Even wet from head to toe, she felt good—too good.

He felt her stir, legs moving on his and bare breasts brushing his chest. She looked at him cautiously, her face so close to his that their noses were almost touching. She had to feel the changes in his body. The cold clamminess of her skin had decreased and its departure signaled her loss of numbness and a growing awareness of him and her situation in his arms.

"Jake," she said tentatively, "you came after me."

"Yeah," he said through gritted teeth.

"Can't we go down now? I mean, the lightning seems to have moved on."

He grumbled, "Just hold still a minute." He loosened his hold on her and struggled under the precarious shelter of the slicker to take off his denim jacket. Although he forced himself to look away from her bareness, he knew she shielded her breasts with her forearms. That small gesture of protection aggravated him into roughness when he pulled his jacket around her shoulders. "You stay put. I'll go get my horse."

"No, I'm coming, too."

"No?" He shook his head in disbelief, his nose brushing her hair in the close confines of the slicker. "You are the most contrary woman I've ever come across." He grabbed her arms to keep her from jumping up. "You didn't have the good sense to bring rain gear up here. This time you do what I say. Stay put."

"What do you think you're going to do? Carry me back on your horse like a wayward child?"

"That's exactly what I'm going to do."

"No. I came up here on my horse, and I'm going down the same way."

"Listen to me, Dusty," he said stiffly, his hands on the jacket that covered her bare upper body unconsciously tightening. "You're not making sense. You're wet and you're cold. Your teeth are even starting to chatter again. You got yourself into this condition, but there's no way in the world I'm going to let you make it worse. If I have to tie you up and carry you back like a sack of feed, so be it."

She could feel the strength in his hands and knew the futility of fighting him. If he said he would tie her up, he'd do it.

"Well, what's it going to be? Are you going peacefully, or do I have to use my rope?"

Her shoulders slumped in defeat. She felt so cold. "What about True? I don't want to leave him up here again."

"I'll send Hooter to get him just as soon as we hit the ranch." She looked at him doubtfully. "I promise. We won't let it be any harder on him than it has to be."

She didn't offer any further protest as he went to get Yeller. When he led his horse back to where she huddled under the slicker, she obediently slid into his saddle. He put on the slicker and swung up behind her, enclosing her in the roomy yellow coat. He groaned with the delicious misery of her shapely bottom fitting into his crotch.

"What's the matter?"

"Don't ask," he rumbled into her ear. "Just, for God's sake, don't move any more than you have to."

"Oh," she said, unconsciously clenching the muscles of her buttocks.

His arm tightened around her middle. "God, Dusty, don't do that."

"Sorry." If she hadn't been so cold, she would have laughed at the absurdity of their situation.

When they pulled up to ranch headquarters Hooter came running out of the barn.

"I was beginning to think I was going to have to go after the both of you," he shouted with obvious relief.

"You weren't far wrong," Jake answered. "You're going to have to rescue True Blue. He's tied in some trees where Bull Creek runs into Big Piney. Bring him back here and stable him in the barn."

"No, Jake, I'll take care of him at home," Dusty objected.

Jake's voice cut sharply at her ear. "Shut up, Dusty. You've caused me enough trouble for one day. I don't have any patience left for more."

The abrupt tightening of Jake's arm stopped her from trying to jump off the big stallion. When Hooter chuckled knowingly, Dusty ground her teeth in frustrated anger, her head full of purple curses.

"Jake," she said, carefully staring straight ahead, "Mac's horse has to have a workout before it gets too late. I have to go home."

"Mac's horse?" Jake paused behind her in the saddle, arresting his attempted dismount. "You mean the sorrel gelding you have at your place?"

She nodded. "Sunny Boy...he's a competition roping horse." No more explanation was necessary to make Jake understand.

"Don't worry, Dusty." Hooter chuckled in his high cackle. "I'll send Ollie over to your place to exercise Mac's horse. That boy'll quiver all over like a cow dog about to get his dinner."

"That should take care of Mac's horse," Jake said wearily as he swung himself to the ground, ignoring the slump of Dusty's shoulders. "Take Yeller into the barn before you leave for True Blue," Jake said to Hooter. He pulled Dusty down from Yeller's back, keeping one muscled arm around her to prevent her from getting any silly ideas. Hooter led off the horse as Jake half carried and half dragged Dusty into the waiting pickup.

"What do you think you're doing?" she protested making one last attempt at seizing some control.

"I said, shut up, Dusty." He sounded bone-tired.

They made the trip from the barn across the creek and up the hill to Jake's house in silence. Dusty resigned herself to the inevitability of going along with Jake. She had never been in his house before, and her curiosity about that showplace of a log house soothed some of her objections. The morning of the ride with the sheriff, the group had gathered at Jake's barn, and she had stared up at the big house's vaulted roof and tall windows that faced the mountains. She had itched to see it from the inside, to look out those tall windows at her mountains. But, entering the house being dragged behind a disgruntled Jake didn't add to her appreciation of the experience. Nor did she appreciate being hauled into a large bathroom, just beyond the entry, and dumped there.

"Get out of those wet clothes," Jake growled. "And I mean every stitch." He reached into a large cabinet and threw two enormous towels at her. Then, instead of leaving as she expected, he reached inside a shower stall and turned on hot water. "Take a hot shower and wrap yourself up in those towels. Get started or I'll do it myself." He stepped toward her threateningly.

"I want to go home." She couldn't believe she'd said that. She sounded like a lost little girl. Trying to undo the damage to her image, she gave her fiercest glare.

"Don't push me, Dusty." He moved toward the door. "Take off every stitch you have on and put it all outside this door." He paused to glare at her with his piercing eyes. "Do it, Dusty, or like I said, I'll do it for you." With that, he slammed the door behind him, leaving a sodden Dusty shivering in the middle of the bathroom rug.

When Dusty emerged from the bathroom, Jake was at the opposite end of the long living area, his back to her, feeding a fire in the huge fireplace. Clutching the towel around her shower-warmed body, she padded barefoot and silent into the room. She didn't get very far before the view of the mountains through the tall windows stopped her dead.

"My God," she gasped involuntarily.

At the sound, Jake jerked around to see her standing in a pool of apricot light, transfixed by the mountain sunset. The white towel that draped her body was golden in the light, and her exposed skin glowed a golden rose. Her tawny hair was damp, framing her with a glistening halo. He had never seen anything so beautiful.

Again he felt that aggravating quickening in his groin. "God Almighty," he groaned aloud. Last week he had reined himself in like a rambunctious stallion, but right now, when she stood still and bare as Venus, in the golden shimmer of mountain sunset, in the middle of his living room, he admitted to himself he had lost control, given up all restraint.

"Come over by the fire," he said.

The huskiness of his low voice drew her attention from the magnificence of the sunset. He was crouched in front of the huge fireplace, looking at her with a curiously subdued expression on his face. After the fierce stubbornness he used to get her down from the mountains, she didn't know what to expect. She came out of the bathroom prepared to fight him, but in the mellow light, with the warm glow of the fire behind him, he appeared softened, as invitingly comfortable as the room around her.

Her gaze took in the earth tones of the overstuffed furniture, arranged more for looking at the mountains or enjoying the fire than for social gatherings. The room was spacious but amazingly private, stamped with the individual taste of one man, suited for what pleased him. There wasn't one pretentious piece of furniture in the room, not even one hand-tooled leather chair. The chairs looked plump and purposeful: that one for reading magazines, another for watching television, a sofa for stretching out on.

The carpet, deep enough to make her bare toes burrow into it, was scattered with exquisite Navajo rugs that added their own natural colors to the mix. A bronze sculpture of a horse and rider stood on the massive coffee table in front of the windows. Paintings of western scenes covered the walls and surrounded the fireplace.

She looked at the man who had assembled this room and felt a shiver of recognition. All her growing-up years she had known he existed, but she'd paid him no more mind than a hundred other neighbors. He had been just a name she knew, a man who rode a beautiful horse at the Fourth of July rodeo. Nothing more than that. When she stumbled into the auction, he took on new significance. At first he was the center of her anger over losing her ranch, but he also made her feel nervous, as if she were teetering on the edge of a dangerous precipice. Her nerve endings sizzled at the sight of him. She resented the awkward weakness he made her feel.

But here in his house, in the room he had decorated to suit him, she suddenly knew him. And she was terrified by what she knew. Looking at him was almost like gazing in a mirror and seeing a lost part of herself staring back. How could she protect herself from so powerful a force? How could she keep herself separate from a man who appealed to her in so many ways?

He had been right. He said she would not find it so easy to send him to Texas. She had come home, to the mountains, to be ambushed.

"Dusty, your hair is wet and you're barefoot," he said with impatience. "Come over here where it's warm."

"Where are my clothes?" She realized she stood there in nothing more than a towel; she had nothing to protect herself from what she knew about this man.

"Your clothes are in the washing machine. I got you some of mine to wear temporarily." He indicated neatly stacked clothes on the hearth. She could see what looked like a white pajama shirt with a pair of boot socks on top of it. "They're over here by the fire where you should be."

"Your clothes?" He was wearing a clean, dry shirt that was hanging open, and clean jeans, softened by much wear, but she saw only his bare chest. His lean, muscular chest with the sprinkling of curling hair and the flat masculine nipples. She forced her gaze back to the stacked clothes. "Those things look like pajamas."

He chuckled, a low rumbling sound, intimate in the dusky light. "They probably look that way because that's what they are. I couldn't think of anything else that might come close to fitting you. The bottoms have a drawstring that you can pull tight. My jeans would just fall off." One corner of his mouth quirked upward. "Of course, I wouldn't mind that at all. Maybe I should get you some."

"No," she said quickly, raising one hand to stop him from getting up. "It's just that I'm going to look funny riding home in your pajamas."

He rose to his feet in one fluid movement, crossing to her in long strides. She recognized the easy way he crossed the room, remembering cowboys move gracefully across ground only when they have purpose. She stopped herself from backing up at his approach.

His hands on her bare shoulders were warm. He caressed her with fingers roughened by work and weather. His touch kindled a liquid warmth deep inside of her. When she looked up into the hard male face so close to her own, she saw what could have been a pleading look in the steel of his eyes.

"You're not going anywhere, Dusty," he said gently. "You're staying here tonight."

When she started to protest, he put his finger against her lips to silence them. His gaze followed his finger as he lightly rubbed her full bottom lip. "Hush," he whispered. "I know what you're going to say. You're going to remind me about your independence and how you don't need to stay here. I know all that." He lifted his gaze to her eyes again. This time she was sure she saw pleading. Amazement left her speechless.

"Stay here for me." He stroked the lustrous wildness of her drying hair. "You scared me very badly this afternoon. I couldn't find you fast enough. Every bolt of lightning burned though me like a branding iron until I got you on the ground next to me and under some protection." She heard the roughness that lingered in his voice. "I'm not ready to let go of you yet. Let me be sure you're safe before you take off again."

"I don't understand, Jake. You expect me to stay here all night? In your pajamas?"

"Hey, don't worry." He grinned. "I don't think I've ever had them on. So far as I know, they're brand-new." His eyes twinkled at her. "I don't sleep in pajamas."

"It's not the pajamas I'm worried about, and you know it."

"Yeah, you want to know if I expect you to sleep in my bed." He grinned again, but his eyes were serious. "How else am I going to be sure you're all right?"

"Jake," she warned, but the objection dissolved as she pictured Jake without his pajamas. Then she spoiled it all by sneezing.

He steered her toward the fireplace. "I think we better have this conversation later. Right now you need to get into some clothes. I'll go find us something to eat while you dress."

The soup he brought was warm and filling, driving the chill away. As she stared into the fire, her thoughts were on the man sitting quietly in the chair behind her. She wore his flannel pajamas that crinkled with newness and hung so loosely that she was even more aware of her bareness.

Jake hadn't bothered to button his shirt. She knew if she turned her head in his direction, she would see all that tempting maleness. Actually, she didn't have to turn; her treacherous imagination pictured his chest in the curling flames of the fire. He was work-hardened, bone and muscle clearly defined. His chest hair, only slightly darker than the sun-streaked hair on his head, spread across the muscle and reached upward to the base of his throat. The flame image of Jake warmed her face and chest while the reality of the man burned into her from where he sat.

Jake startled her when he moved, reaching around her to pick up the hairbrush he'd placed on the hearth with the clothes. His hand moved slowly, grasping the brush and bringing it behind her to stroke her hair. With his other hand, he kept her from turning to him, holding her shoulder as gently as he stroked her hair. The brush caught long strands of her hair and swept them back from her face until they fell like spun silk against her neck. Each stroke began with a caress of her scalp before measuring out the long tresses. Again and again he caressed her hair with the brush, massaging her scalp until it tingled with awareness of the strong hand that wielded the brush.

At last, his hands pushed aside the curtain of hair, and he buried his face in the exposed curve of her neck. His arms came around her, holding her in place, and she felt the sweet teasing kisses on the vulnerable skin of her neck. With a sigh, she let herself crumple in his arms, giving up the last of her resistance.

"Thank God," he breathed against her skin. His waiting was over.

Shaking like an aspen branch in a summer breeze, he lowered himself beside her. They stretched out together on the large Navajo rug before the fireplace. Fitting herself against his length, she wrapped her arms around his chest under his open shirt and pressed her cheek into the hollow below his collarbone. He held her with the same care he'd given to her under the slicker, but his arms jerked reflexively when he felt her lips feather across his skin.

His tenderness gave way to hunger, a hunger he had kept under control too long. He rolled her over onto her back and blindly sought her mouth with his own. His lips rubbed bruisingly over hers. He tasted her with his tongue, every part of her mouth he could reach, licking and sucking, memorizing the honey taste of her. She responded with equal hunger, sucking and pulling on his tongue and moving her hands along the long sinewy muscles of his back under his loose shirt.

He impatiently pushed aside the pajama shirt to kiss her bare collarbone, measuring its length with his mouth, memorizing through touch her straight, sure shoulders. The large buttons of the shirt slipped free and the loose garment settled on the rug, making a soft flannel shield against the rough wool. She lay back on the brushed softness, her head cushioned by her own hair, and gazed bemusedly at the concentration on the craggy face as he untied the drawstring of the pajama bottoms. His hand spread warmly on her hip and pushed at the soft garment. She lifted her hips and felt the heat from his eyes replace the covering of the pajamas.

He slid his gaze over her velvet skin, touching her everywhere with his eyes. Her body was golden in the firelight, perfect breasts, slender waist, tawny triangle of hair between her legs. He impatiently shrugged out of his clothes, tossing shirt and jeans to join discarded pajama bottoms.

She reached out fingertips to test the textures of his chest and abdomen and hip. The brush of her touch on his skin electrified him, making him tremble and weakening the arm that supported him above her. He looked down into her eyes, a translucent green in the light of the fire, and saw mountains and sky and sunshine.

He moved over her, joining his body to hers, and heard the deep voice of mountain thunder booming in his ears. As her body closed around his, he felt as if she pulled his very soul out of him. He made love to the mountains he saw in the green of her eyes, to the horsewoman he felt in her bones, to the open sagebrush he tasted on her skin.

Outside, the fickle weather of the mountains left the sky with new-washed stars, their bright sparkle unhindered by even a hint of cloud. The almost-full moon smiled brilliantly on the night-shrouded landscape. Everything, barn and fences and willows and open grass, took on the metallic glint of polished silver. The tall windows in the dark log house glowed with the golden reflection of flames.

And, inside, the fire in the large stone fireplace cast its spell on the two bodies that moved urgently together. The golden glow bathed bare skin, moving its light and shadow in unison with the movement of limbs and torsos.

Later, an eternity later it seemed to Jake, he lay upstairs in his giant bed, holding Dusty tightly to his side. Tracks of tears still marked her cheeks. After he had made love to her a second time, this time in his bed, she had told him about scattering Blackie's ashes and she had wept. Now, exhausted, she slept with her head nestled in the curve of his shoulder, and her even breathing brushed softly through his chest hair.

The trust evident in her sleeping form filled him with gratitude and a certain uneasiness. Looking at the childlike innocence of her face, he shuddered, cold brushing across his skin with the sough of her breath on his chest. Unbidden came the image of True Blue in the cold rain, and the icy-fingered terror that clutched him before True turned to show Dusty clinging to his back. The image touched something long frozen in the past, the cold memory of his sister's empty saddle and his long minutes of agony, a child's horror-filled agony, trying to push his way through the agitated cattle until he saw the crumpled form so still on the ground.

He touched the light sprinkling of freckles on Dusty's high cheekbone. "Penny," he groaned, his voice as rough as the skin of his fingertips, "little freckle-nosed Penny."

Chapter Seven

Long habit woke Dusty early the next morning, despite the strenuous activity of the day before and the deep weariness she felt in her limbs. She pushed herself off the empty bed, strewn with rumpled bedding, and stumbled to open the bedroom door. Voices drifted up from downstairs, Jake's deep rumble and a high cackle that could belong only to Hooter. She closed the door quickly. Until she found something to wear, she couldn't possibly leave the privacy of the bedroom.

She looked around for something to dress in. In a big easy chair in front of the windows that faced the mountains, she saw her own clothes, stacked as neatly as the pajamas had been last night. She pulled on jeans, shirt and socks and then looked out at the soft morning light on the mountains.

Last night, she thought as she hugged her arms around herself, she had felt fused with Jake, too much a part of him to separate where he began and she ended. Now she had to find some way to put the boundaries back again. Without them, Jake would take over as naturally as rain on the mountains. She knew with a weary grimness that Jake would never understand her need to forge a life for herself, an independent life in the shadow of the mountains.

Downstairs she found her way to the kitchen by following the smell of fresh coffee. Jake was perched on a stool at a counter, coffee cup in both hands, staring across the space of the dining room. She supposed he was looking at the morning mountains as she had done. But the preoccupied expression on his face told her he wasn't seeing much. He was too deep in thought.

"Morning," she said hesitantly.

He looked around as if he were surprised by her presence. Then he slowly grinned, his eyes watching her with a concentration he hadn't used on the mountains.

"How about a cup of coffee while I fix you breakfast?"

"Okay." She climbed up on the stool beside him and accepted the cup he handed her. He deftly set about providing the two of them with a gigantic breakfast of eggs, hash browns and toast.

When he placed an overloaded plate in front of her, she laughed in spite of her nervousness. "You're feeding me again. I'm really impressed with your talent at kitchen duty."

"I've had plenty of practice cooking breakfast. Ranch work takes lots of energy."

They ate in uneasy silence, neither one of them having the courage to look at the other. When he pushed aside his empty plate, Dusty took that as her cue.

"I guess it's getting late. I need to get to work." She turned around on her stool. "I don't want the boss to complain about my being lazy."

Jake stopped her from leaving with a firm hand on her arm. "You're not working today, Dusty."

She looked up with surprise at the steely determination in his eyes. "Are you firing me?"

"Of course not," he said, running an impatient hand through his hair. He sighed with exasperation. "I want you to rest. Yesterday you got cold and wet and—" He broke off, cursing his own inability to explain. She had scared him so badly yesterday that he needed to coddle her a bit today.

"I don't need to rest," she objected. "I don't melt when I get wet, and I don't need anyone to take care of me."

"You certainly couldn't prove that by me," he said, raising his voice at her belligerence. "From the way you looked when I dragged you off that mountain yesterday, I'd say you need a keeper."

"Are you volunteering for the job?"

"Yes, I am."

"Just you try it, Jake Valiteros."

She stood defiantly in the middle of his kitchen, her arms crossed on her chest, glaring at him. He shook his head at his own clumsiness. All he had wanted to do was keep her close to him, and he'd made a mess of it.

"Would it help if I said please?"

She couldn't help herself; she grinned at the picture he made. Even with his weather-beaten face, he looked as uncertain as a little boy. This hardened ranch boss was full of surprises. Starting last night with his gentleness as a lover. She would never have expected that.

"Oh, I guess if you insist, I could find plenty to do around my place."

"No," he said, startled. "I want you to stay here."

"Here? In your house?"

"Yes." He ran his hands up her arms and brought her close. "In my house."

"Why?" she said, eyeing him suspiciously.

"You could spend the day moving your things in here." There. He'd said it. What he'd been thinking about all morning and half the night.

Her eyes widened as if he'd slapped her. "What did you say?"

He might as well go all the way now. "You could take my truck over to your place and pack up your things. Whatever you think you'd need to be comfortable living here."

"Are you asking me to live with you?"

He shrugged. "Why not?" Then his eyes gentled like a horse's in new grass. "You know we started something last night, Dusty. Something that feels like it has a life of its own. We're not going to be able to stop it, and I doubt if we're going to control it, either." He paused, his eyes clouding over. "Besides, I want you close enough to be sure you're not doing something stupid." His voice dropped to a barely audible whisper. "And dangerous," he added.

"No." She closed her eyes and reached down into herself for the will to resist him. When she looked up again, her eyes glinted like green glass. "I won't live in your house, Jake Valiteros, and I won't let you tell me what to do."

In spite of everything he had said to himself, her rejection hit him like a blow to the gut. He turned away from her and gripped the edge of the counter with both hands. "I'll wait," he said, staring through the large window at the morning mountains. "You can't change what's already happened, Dusty. You stayed with me last night, you slept in my arms." He turned to her, his eyes gleaming in his stone face. "If you won't live here, I'll show up at your house. You'll get used to me." He opened his fists, working his fingers. "I'm not a patient man, Dusty, but I'll outlast you."

As Dusty swung onto True Blue's back, she remembered the load she carried in her saddlebags. How could she have forgotten about the rope and Blackie's glove? She sat back in the saddle, collecting herself for a minute. Naturally, she knew the answer to her question. Jake. She smiled ruefully at herself. Certainly Jake would turn up at her place later today. Hadn't he promised her that he would? She would tell him then. She had no reason to hurry. After all, the cut rope and the glove had been lying on the mountainside almost two weeks before she found them and put them in her saddlebags.

As she sat forward in her saddle to urge True toward home, she heard the slow plod of an approaching horse accompanied by Ollie's uncertain tenor voice. To her amusement, he was singing a Garth Brooks song, "Much Too Young to Feel This Damn Old." She wondered how many cowboys felt that way in the morning. The song stopped immediately when he rounded the corner of the barn and saw her. Just yesterday they had laughed together while they shoveled the muck that clogged an irrigation ditch. Today he reined in his horse and looked embarrassed, his eyes trying to find somewhere to light.

"Morning, Dusty," he said. "How are you feeling this morning?" Then an incredible blush washed over him, climbing out of his collar and creeping up to his hat brim.

Dusty felt heat flush over her face, as well. The quiet rang in her ears, and she shifted uneasily in her saddle. "I'm fine," she mumbled finally. True Blue shook his head in an impatient horse snort.

"I guess you didn't see your hat," Ollie said, turning his horse into the barn. "I'll get it for you." He returned on foot with a battered facsimile of a hat in his hand.

"Oh, my!" she said, reaching down to take the battered thing from him. The flat crown on her already well-worn hat was tilted to one side, and the uneven brim curled under where it should curve up.

"Yeah, it's in pretty bad shape. I guess True must have stepped on it." True looked around at the mention of his name and gave Ollie the evil eye for telling on him.

"Anyway," Ollie continued, stepping back from True's retaliation, "Dad found it on the ground."

Dusty bit her lip in consternation at the idea of Hooter and Ollie discussing last night's activities. She knew it was obvious to Ollie, and probably everyone else on the ranch, where she had spent the night. In fact, she was sure she had seen Gaylene, Ollie's mother, hovering behind the curtains in the big ranch house. Damn. Dusty smoothed the hat in her hands, turning it round and round trying to restore some semblance of its original shape.

"Hey, I enjoyed working Mac's horse last night. I bet he was a great roping horse," Ollie said.

"Yes, he was," she said, biting her lip to keep from adding, when Mac was alive. The past tense slapped at her, reminding her of the empty house that had been so full of life. She could feel the mist gathering in her eyes. "What are you doing today?" she asked, forcing herself to smile at Ollie.

His guilty look said as clearly as a shout that he knew Dusty wouldn't be working today. "Aw, we're shifting a few cows from one field to another."

"Oh, I see," she said. That meant cowboy work for Ollie, not the hay farming he hated. No wonder he had been singing. "Well, I'll let you get to it." She didn't miss the relieved look on his face when she headed True Blue down the road to her place. The front curtains dropped back into place as she passed the house.

Within the familiar warmth of her own barn, she unsaddled True and put away the tack, taking the time to oil the saddle and bridle. She didn't fool herself, though. She knew she was just putting off dealing with the contents of her saddlebags, but, regardless of all the busy work she made for herself, the coiled rope and the glove circled around and around in her head. They made no sense. There didn't seem to be any reason for them to be up there. Not in the stunted little aspens.

When she couldn't postpone it any longer, she took the saddlebags from the stall partition where she had draped them and gingerly opened up the full side. She reached into the darkness of the bag and pulled out the leather glove. Blackie's glove. A couple of weeks ago, she had stood in the

IT'S FUN! IT'S FREE!
AND IT COULD MAKE YOU A
MILLIONAIRE

If you've ever played scratch-off lottery tickets, you should be familiar with how our games work. On each of the first four tickets (numbered 1 to 4 in the upper right) there are Pink Strips to scratch off.

Using a coin, do just that—carefully scratch the PINK strips to reveal how much each ticket could be worth if it is a winning ticket. Tickets could be worth from $100.00 to $1,000,000.00 in lifetime money ($33,333.33 each year for 30 years).

Note, also, that each of your 4 tickets has a unique sweepstakes Lucky Number . . . and that's 4 chances for a **BIG WIN**!

FREE BOOKS!

At the same time you play your tickets to qualify for big prizes, you are invited to play ticket #5 to get brand-new Silhouette Special Edition® novels. These books have a cover price of $3.50 each, but they are yours to keep absolutely free.

There's no catch. You're under no obligation to buy anything. We charge nothing—ZERO—for your first shipment. And you don't have to make any minimum number of purchases—not even one!

The fact is thousands of readers enjoy receiving books by mail from the Silhouette Reader Service™. They like the convenience of home delivery . . . they like getting the best new novels months before they're available in bookstores . . . and they love our discount prices!

We hope that after receiving your free books you'll want to remain a subscriber. But the choice is yours—to continue or cancel, anytime at all! So why not take us up on our invitation, with no risk of any kind. You'll be glad you did!

PLUS A FREE GIFT!

One more thing, when you accept the free books on ticket #5, you are also entitled to play ticket #6, which is GOOD FOR A GREAT GIFT! Like the books, this gift is totally free and yours to keep as thanks for giving our Reader Service a try!

So scratch off the PINK STRIPS on all your BIG WIN tickets and send for everything today! You've got nothing to lose and everything to gain!

© 1991 HARLEQUIN ENTERPRISES LIMITED

Here are your BIG WIN Game Tickets potentially worth from $100.00 to $1,000,000.00 each. Scratch off the PINK STRIP on each of your Sweepstakes tickets to see what you could win and mail your entry right away. (SEE BACK OF BOOK FOR DETAILS!)

This could be your lucky day—GOOD LUCK!

TICKET 1

THE BIG WIN

Scratch PINK STRIP to reveal potential value of cash prize if the sweepstakes number on this ticket is a winning number. Return all game tickets intact.

LUCKY NUMBER

4G 850387

TICKET 2

THE BIG WIN

Scratch PINK STRIP to reveal potential value of cash prize if the sweepstakes number on this ticket is a winning number. Return all game tickets intact.

LUCKY NUMBER

2Q 741705

TICKET 3

THE BIG WIN

Scratch PINK STRIP to reveal potential value of cash prize if the sweepstakes number on this ticket is a winning number. Return all game tickets intact.

LUCKY NUMBER

9P 865761

TICKET 4

THE BIG WIN

Scratch PINK STRIP to reveal potential value of cash prize if the sweepstakes number on this ticket is a winning number. Return all game tickets intact.

LUCKY NUMBER

7J 725711

TICKET 5

FREE BOOKS

Scratch PINK STRIP to reveal number of books you will receive. These books, part of a sampling program to introduce romance readers to the benefits of the Reader Service, are free.

AUTHORIZATION CODE

130107-742

TICKET 6

FREE GIFT

All gifts are free. No purchase required. Scratch PINK STRIP to reveal free gift, our thanks to readers for trying our books.

AUTHORIZATION CODE

130107-742

YES! Enter my Lucky Numbers in The Million Dollar Sweepstakes (III) and when winners are selected, tell me if I've won any prize. If the PINK STRIP is scratched off on ticket #5, I will also receive four FREE Silhouette Special Edition® novels along with the FREE GIFT on ticket #6, as explained on the back and on the opposite page. 235 CIS AQYC (U-SIL-SE-10/94)

NAME _____

ADDRESS _____ APT. _____

CITY _____ STATE _____ ZIP CODE _____

Book offer limited to one per household and not valid to current Silhouette Special Edition® subscribers. All orders subject to approval.

© 1991 HARLEQUIN ENTERPRISES LIMITED.   PRINTED IN U.S.A.

THE SILHOUETTE READER SERVICE™: HERE'S HOW IT WORKS

Accepting free books places you under no obligation to buy anything. You may keep the books and gift and return the shipping statement marked "cancel". If you do not cancel, about a month later we will send you 6 additional novels, and bill you just $2.89 each plus 25¢ delivery and applicable sales tax, if any.* That's the complete price, and—compared to cover prices of $3.50 each—quite a bargain! You may cancel at any time, but if you choose to continue, every month we'll send you 6 more books, which you may either purchase at the discount price. . .or return at our expense and cancel your subscription.

* Terms and prices subject to change without notice. Sales tax applicable in N.Y.

mudroom and looked at Mac's glove. At the thought, tears prickled behind her eyes. A cowboy's glove held a special life of its own.

Within her cupped palm, the leather of the glove felt warm, probably a result of sun on the saddlebag, but the warmth gave the curled fingers of the worn glove a feeling of recent use. A tear splashed onto the supple leather. Then more tears, dropping one by one into the worn palm, made dark splotches on the light tan leather, splotches as dark as the weathered places at the base of the thumb and the crooks of the fingers. The tears pooled in the cup of the glove until the palm, from thumb to little finger, looked uniformly used, as if Blackie, himself, had spent the day working sweat into it. Stuffing the glove back into the saddlebag, she swiped at the tears on her cheeks with her shirtsleeve, cursing herself for crying again.

Unaccountable tears. She never cried. Blackie used to say he didn't raise a crybaby—if she couldn't solve her problems, tears wouldn't do any good. She had wanted to scatter his ashes by herself, in the mountains, alone, because she knew no amount of toughness would keep the tears back when she did that. Those tears didn't surprise her. She just let them be. After all, no one was there to see. But last night, in Jake's bed, she had cried again.

He had made love to her twice, both times slowly, so slowly that time seemed to stand still. No time, no moon-escaping storm clouds, no night-softened house—only the two of them and the glow of the fire and, later, the soft caress of crisp sheets. The second time had been on Jake's bed with the diffused light of the moon shining through high clouds. Jake had touched her as if he couldn't believe the first time had really happened and repeated it to make sure, not speaking a word until he spilled himself into her and collapsed limply in the cradle of her body. Then he rasped her name, over and over, as if he spilled himself again in the repeating of her name, giving the sound of it the rawness of new discovery. And, like the sound of her name, she felt new, changed somehow. And, more than anything else, at peace. The storm and Jake's loving had cleansed her, purged the hollow grief of death, and had reached back even farther to rub away the anger, her deep abiding anger—at Charlie's insensitive male arrogance, at the loss of her ranch, at the unexpected and cruelly abrupt death of her father.

That's when the tears came. They poured from her. She lay there in Jake's enormous bed with her hands grasping his lean, sinewy back and wept into his shoulder. He rolled off her and pulled her into the lee of his arm, stroking her hair and her shoulders and crooning to her in a soft voice. He guessed she had scattered Blackie's ashes on her trip into the mountains, and he asked her to tell him about it. She did, letting Jake's soft kisses and her memory of shady aspen beside a trickle of creek soothe her. She also let Jake think the scattering of Blackie's ashes was the sole reason for the tears.

She knew that wasn't true, and that disturbed her. She knew that Jake's lovemaking was as responsible for the tears as was the solemn communion with the spirit of her father. Something inside herself had shattered, some defense she had thought necessary to her survival, some carefully constructed fortress where she had felt safe. In Jake's arms, she hadn't wanted to hide. She had let him open her up like a flower, opening petal by petal in the sun. Then she had cried.

"What have I done?" she said now in the quiet of the barn. Then she proved once again she was Blackie's daughter by turning on her heel and marching up to the house. Whatever the consequences of her night in Jake's bed, she couldn't avoid them by pretending it didn't happen. She would face the problems as they arose.

* * *

After Dusty left his house, running away to the safety of her own, Jake encountered one frustrating situation after another. Hooter's count had confirmed the missing cows, and a check of his computer files revealed that the missing cows, fifteen in all plus their calves, were all prime stock, representing the best the herd had to offer. In recent years, he had greatly reduced the number of cattle he grazed on the land, keeping careful records on each individual cow to maximize the productivity of the herd, while minimizing the negative impact of a large herd on the sensitive ecostructure of the mountains. Sitting at his desk in the study and staring at the computer screen, he thought it almost seemed as if whoever stole the stock had carefully selected them, taking several here and several there of the best-producing cows he owned. A few of them were even from the stock that had belonged to Blackie.

Constructing a new file of the missing cows, he tried to find some pattern, some commonness that would help explain their disappearance, but the only thing the cows had in common was their quality: excellent calf weight, excellent health records for cows and calves, prime ages for production—no green heifers or old cows at the end of their producing years.

In frustration he sat back in the deep cushions of his desk chair, worriedly rubbing his jaw and letting his tired eyes rest on the book-lined shelves that circled the room. The books reminded him of Dusty, and for a few minutes, he let himself forget about the problem of the missing cattle. As his eyes strayed over volume after volume of western history, he pictured Dusty talking about her thesis in that café in Pinedale, the day her father was brought down from the mountains. He recalled the sparkle in those green eyes when she talked about the personal histories of the people she'd interviewed. The somberness of the day hadn't been able to extinguish her love for Wyoming history. Even in his study, where she had never been, his wayward mind conjured pictures of her stretched out naked in the glow of the fire, tawny hair, apricot skin, rounded breasts, firm thighs—and, between the thighs, the slick wetness of heaven. He cursed himself and angrily switched off the computer. He slammed out of the study, stomping away from all those books that represented one more way Dusty had insinuated herself into his private world.

Then again, he thought as he peered into the gray ashes in the cold fireplace, maybe he could use his history collection to lure her to his house. If she knew about the treasure trove he had in the study, perhaps she wouldn't be able to resist living in his house.

"She's turned me into a damned fool," he snorted grimly as he stomped through the empty room toward the massive front door. "Why should I want a woman to live in my house?" he stormed at himself, banging shut the door of his pickup with a hollow clank. "I've gotten along just fine without a woman around to stir things up." He gunned the pickup down the hill and across the creek, cursing himself the whole way and, at the same time, knowing that the only thing he wanted to do with his day was to drive over to Dusty's house and take her to bed again. "Damn fool," he repeated as he screeched to a halt in front of the empty barn.

He sat staring dumbly through the windshield. A moment later, the ranch pickup with Hooter driving came careering around the barn—with more bad news. A stack of last year's hay was smoldering in the middle of one of his best hay fields. Of course, lightning could have ignited the hay, lightning helped along by spontaneous combustion in the heart of the stack. Hooter didn't think so; he was sure the bales had been shifted to allow air and fire into the stack.

Whatever caused the fire, putting it out was a nightmare, destroying the whole stack and trampling the new hay crop with equipment and shredded bales of sodden, partially burned hay. But through it all, Jake worried that Dusty would see the black smoke from the burning bales and come to investigate. He kept one eye cocked in the direction of her house in case he should see her riding toward the soot-streaked men battling the hay, miserable with the stench of fire.

Jake was right to be apprehensive. Dusty should have seen the black smoke, since she worked outside most of the day. Probably her dogged determination to force her mind away from Jake Valiteros and the night in his arms kept her from looking toward the smoldering field tucked away behind rolling hills on the far side of the creek.

Instead, she found the wooden practice steer Mac had used when he took up team roping. It was sitting in the back of Blackie's pickup, which was parked neatly in the shed attached to the far side of the barn. She guessed Blackie must have planned to do some roping himself with his new-found spare time. Team roping would have been the perfect hobby for Blackie. In the teams, one roper, the header, threw a rope loop around a steer's head or horns and the other roper, the heeler, slipped a loop around the steer's feet. Team roping was a beautiful event that ended in a per-fect tableau, two horses, poised, facing each other in the middle of an arena, with a steer stretched motionless be-tween them. It was cowboy skills turned into art.

Dusty pulled the wooden frame with steer horns on one end out of the truck, musing about all the rope loops that had flipped down over those horns, ropes thrown by Mac or Blackie. Then, quickly making up her mind, she pushed the practice frame back onto the truck bed and jumped into the cab. Why not, she thought? She'd take the frame out into the pasture and spend the afternoon exercising Mac's horse.

When she came back to the barn for Sunny Boy, she made a detour by the house to pick up Mac's best rope that was coiled on a peg in his room. She took the horse and the rope into the pasture where it flattened out by the creek. There she spent hours playing at being a roper. Most of the time she had to suffer Sunny's impatience because the years without a rope in her hands had left her clumsy.

Sunny was only a little rusty, and his performance improved with more ease than Dusty's. Late in the afternoon, much to her satisfaction, Dusty snagged the horns with a loop, and Sunny continued smartly straight ahead, neatly turning the wooden steer as if to present the heels to the other roper. Then, at Dusty's signal, he wheeled sharply to face the horns, keeping the rope taut. Dusty cheered jubilantly and reached forward to pat Sunny's neck.

With the smile still on her face, she froze in place. Unbidden came the urge to tell Jake, to share with him the perfection of Sunny's performance. She could have understood if she had felt the need to tell Blackie or Mac. But why Jake?

"No," she groaned aloud. "How could I be so stupid?"

She sat back in her saddle and shook the loop free of the horns, coiling it slowly and carefully. The sun was sitting low in the sky, just above the gray top of Lander Peak. Jake would show up soon. He'd expect to pick up where they left off last night.

"Come on, Sunny," she said. "Time to quit for the day." Time to quit fooling myself, she thought. After Mac died, she had drifted into a relationship with Charlie, succumbing to the illusion that falling in love with the charming professor might block out her grief for Mac. Not again, she thought. She couldn't let the same thing happen with Jake—just because of the devastation of Blackie's death.

After leaving Sunny in the corral with True Blue, she slammed back into the house and into Mac's room with the rope. Hanging it back in its place, she said aloud, "Well, Jake Valiteros, you're in for a surprise. One night doesn't give you permission to take over my life."

She picked up the picture sitting on the small table Mac had used as a desk. It was a newspaper shot of Mac standing by Sunny Boy and holding on his hip the saddle he had won in a roping competition in Pinedale.

"What do you think I should do, Mac?" she asked her brother's image. "Is it safe to work for Valiteros, do you think?" No, she thought, definitely not safe, but helpful for finding out about Blackie. "As long as I can keep some distance between the boss and me."

Out in the sodden, blackened field, the damned day dragged on—relentlessly—for the fire fighters. Finally, when the sun loomed over the western mountains, Jake climbed into his pickup and headed back to his house. He wanted to wash off the stink of the hay before he saw Dusty.

After he had bathed and after he had fought with himself in front of his shaving mirror, he gunned his pickup down the hill again, leaving in his dust Hooter and the ranch hands, unloading the rakes and shovels and buckets at the barn. They stopped to watch his pickup disappear down the road, staring after him with knowing grins. Gaylene stepped out on the front porch as he passed the house, openly watching him drive away.

"I'm a damn fool," he said in the cab of his truck, but he was preoccupied with worry. Would Dusty find out about the fire in the haystack? Would she start poking around the ranch looking for rustlers and getting herself into more trouble? Aw, hell! Would she be glad to see him tonight?

By the time he hit the top step on Dusty's front porch, he had worried his hat down low on his forehead and the stern lines around his mouth had deepened. For some reason, perhaps a vague sense of movement in the periphery of his vision, he glanced out the end of the porch toward the creek in time to see someone on horseback amble across a hill on the far bank and out of sight. Something about that hunched figure and the shambling gait of the horse pulled him to the end of the porch. He stared out at the empty sagebrush on the hillside, searching for some remnant of the figure, some explanation for his unease. Shaking himself out of further foolishness, he turned his attention to the stillness of the house. The front door stood open behind the screen but there was no light inside, no sign of movement or life. He entered quickly, banging the screen door and calling Dusty's name. No response. In the hallway he could see the door to Blackie's room standing open. Inside the room he found Dusty, sitting cross-legged on the floor in front of Blackie's dresser with her back to the door.

"Dusty?" he said anxiously to the back of her bent head. "What is it? What's wrong?"

She swiveled in his direction, her raised hands spilling snapshots and her eyes brimming with tears. He squatted beside her, balancing on the toes of his boots and gathering the snapshots that had dropped from her hands.

"I know," he said. "I found these the day the sheepherder brought Blackie down from the mountains."

She took the snapshots from Jake, carefully avoiding contact with Jake's flesh as she did. He flinched at her avoidance.

"I've never seen them before," she said. "All those years since Mother died, and Blackie never showed them to me. We had school pictures and a few newspaper shots, but I don't even remember a camera in the house."

The picture on top showed a laughing woman on horseback holding a squirming little girl in front of her. The child, obviously Dusty, was trying vainly to take the reins in her own hands. Her mother laughed at her young daughter's single-minded determination. In spite of his increasing anxiety, Jake couldn't help smiling at the resemblance between the child Dusty and the woman she had become. She'd wanted to ride her own horses even then, he mused.

"I thought there would be time," she said, staring at the pictures in her hands. "I thought there would be time to understand why Blackie sold out, time for him to teach me how to survive without the ranch."

She choked, her head bending lower over her crossed legs and her hands losing the snapshots again. Jake stopped himself from reaching out to pull her in his arms, unwilling to face her rejection of what he offered. She lifted her head to stare at the clutter of snapshots on the faded rug.

"There's so much I don't know," she whispered. "I learned all about the history of my family, but I never learned about the feelings. How he must have loved her," she said, her voice choked. "I don't even know the story of how they got together, how they came to be married. Now I'll never know."

Jake couldn't speak. The sight of her anguish struck him dumb. He wanted to wrap her in his arms and carry her away to the safety of his big house and never let her out again where she could be hurt. His whole body stiffened as he fought the urge.

"Look at this," she said, lifting a modestly bound document from the cradle of her crossed legs. "It's my thesis. It was in the drawer with the pictures. I sent Blackie a copy because I was so proud of it." She opened it, folding back the stiff brown cover. "See, the corners of the pages are bent. He must have read it so many times that he bent the page edges." She closed it quickly, clutching it to her. "How could he read what I wrote and not understand how I felt about the ranch? I lived all my life in this house.... Didn't he understand how I felt?"

Jake silently cursed the obstinate silence between parents and children. He and his father had lived for years in the same house, neither of them speaking to the other. All the softness and understanding in his own family, what there had been of it, disappeared with the death of his little sister. He couldn't explain away Dusty's pain, but he needed to keep her safe. He had failed his little sister; he couldn't survive if something happened to Dusty.

She placed the thesis back in her lap, smoothing her hands across the cover as if it had been mistreated. She sighed. "I guess all this is just history, dry stories about a lot of dead people."

"I want to read it, Dusty."

She looked up at him, startled. "Why?"

He shrugged, refusing to face the implications of his determination to protect Dusty and everything important to her. "I read everything I find about the history of the West."

Reluctantly, a frown knitting her forehead, she handed him the thesis. She regarded his averted eyes under the brim of his hat, those narrow coyote eyes that had the power to paralyze his prey. She was thankful they were not turned on her, but she couldn't suppress the shiver of vulnerability she felt knowing that those eyes would read what she had written.

He stood up, his knees creaking in protest, and looked at the title on the cover: "Pioneer Wyoming Ranch Families" by Dusty Macleod. One end of his straight mouth twitched upward.

"What's so funny?" she said, wanting to grab her thesis back from him and the grin on his face.

"Dusty Macleod, it says. You didn't use your real name."

She smiled at that, leaning over to pick up the pictures. "No, Dusty is my name now. I never have used Vera May."

"Not even before you were called Dusty?" he asked.

"No," she said, looking at the snapshot of her and her mother sitting on the same horse, "I've been told they called me Sissy. Mother was Vera."

"Oh," he said, covering his discomfort by taking off his hat and turning away. Penny had been Sissy to him from the time she began toddling after him everywhere he went. His mother had sternly rebuked him for the fond nickname, but he persisted, out of stubbornness and small-boy defiance. He had known, even then, the sting of his mother's rejection.

"I need a drink," he said, stalking out of the small room.

Dusty watched him suspiciously, pulling herself to her feet. "All I have is Blackie's whiskey," she said, returning the pictures to the dresser drawer and shutting it firmly. By the time she paused in the doorway to the living room, Jake was returning from his truck, minus her thesis but carrying an expensive bottle of bourbon in one hand and a small box of cigars in the other. He walked right by her with his cowboy's lurch, obviously heading for the kitchen. She followed reluctantly, observing how easily he found Blackie's shot glass.

"I brought my own," he said unnecessarily as he leaned against the counter and sipped, eyeing her above the rim of the glass. "I like to drink good bourbon, and the stuff you keep is an insult to good taste."

"Don't get too comfortable," she said sharply. "You're not staying."

"We've already been through this." His narrowed eyes burned at the glass in his hand.

"You can't move in here with your bourbon and your cigars—" she looked around him at the small box he'd placed against the back wall of the cabinet "—and take over my life."

"We want each other."

She flinched, unable to deny the truth of what he said. Last night's intimacy filled up the space between them. She forced herself to remember how, with Charlie, she had come to herself too late, after she had been neatly tucked into Charlie's life with nothing left to call her own.

"Bad timing," was all she said.

He slammed the shot glass loudly down on the countertop, gritting his teeth against the anger surging inside him. He turned abruptly, his strong hands reaching across the empty space to grasp her arms. His fingers closed around the slenderness of her upper arms, as he struggled to even out his breathing. She slumped between his hands, her head bowed. How could he convince her when she looked so defeated, so little like herself?

"Tell me you don't want me to kiss you or hold you," he defied that bowed head.

"I want you to leave," she said, her voice a raspy whisper.

His grip went slack, and his hands dropped from her arms. He felt numbness at his fingertips rising up his arms and creeping into the hollowness around his heart. When had he become so lonely?

"I'll wait," he croaked, huskiness swamping his throat.

At the front door, he stopped, halted by the fear of what Dusty might do in the morning—without him to stop her. He turned to see her still standing just inside the kitchen, her back to him and her head lowered. "I'll expect to see you at the barn tomorrow," he said. "Early."

She didn't move. "I'll be there."

She listened to him drive away before she dared raise her head to see the closed box of cigars and the open bottle of bourbon.

Chapter Eight

The next morning, Dusty put the rope and the glove in her pickup, and drove to ranch headquarters. When she reached Jake's barn, he was waiting by his truck, impatiently slapping his work gloves against his thigh.

"You're late," he growled as he opened her truck door.

She shrugged, gathering the rope and glove from the front seat before sliding out from under the steering wheel.

"Get started training those two three-year-olds," he barked, his grim face turned toward the corrals. "I need good cutting horses and those two have strong hindquarters." He wasn't even looking at her, just snapping out orders. "Those two need to come along before you start the breeding."

"With all your plans for your horses, you could use a separate horse barn," she said, cocking her head at him.

"Yeah, I know," he said slowly, his eyes glittering at her from narrow slits. "I plan to start on that this August—"

He paused briefly "—now that you're here to work the horses."

"Jake, I'm not—"

He cut her off. "Get started on the horses. I can't stand around waiting for you any longer."

"Wait a minute," she said, reaching out to stop him, placing her hand on his forearm, which was exposed below a rolled-back sleeve. Touching him was like touching a hot stove. She jerked her hand back instantly. He stopped just as quickly, looking down at his arm, where her hand had been, as if he didn't understand what had happened. He turned, lurching around, oddly off balance.

She swallowed and thrust the rope at him. "I found this in a stand of aspens about fifty yards above the place where Blackie's body was found."

He stuffed his gloves in his back pocket and took the rope from her.

"Look at the cut end," she said. "It's not the same color as the rest of the rope. It's a fresh cut, and the rope's too big. It's not the kind that's used for animals, and it's not the kind of rope Blackie had with him."

His forehead puckered in a thunderous scowl.

"That's not all. Look at this." She thrust the worn leather glove at him. "That's Blackie's. I found it under the rope."

"Blackie's work glove? Under the rope?" The hushed words barely moved his mouth.

"Does any of this make sense to you?" she said.

"No." He turned the glove slowly in his hands. He looked from the glove to the rope. "Would an outfitter use rope like this to tie a load on a packhorse?"

"I probably wouldn't, but I guess you could."

"You don't suppose Blackie's body—" He stopped mid-sentence, looking up quickly at Dusty.

She shuddered, a chill shooting down her backbone. "That's what I've been thinking. I can't get the picture out of my head—Blackie's body tied to his saddle with this rope.''

"Don't jump to conclusions," he said, his eyes flint-hard. "If someone killed Blackie, there's no reason to believe he'd take the body all the way up there to dump it. There are plenty of places to hide a body around here without making that long ride.''

"He might if he wanted the body to be found, but not right away. That meadow up there grazes sheep every summer. The body was sure to be discovered then. It was just a coincidence that Gomez made such an early trip there and found Blackie so soon after he died." She took the rope and glove from him.

"That still doesn't explain why anyone would kill Blackie in the first place.''

"Jake, you're missing cattle.''

"Okay," he said, his jaw stiff, "we'll take this stuff to the sheriff. But I want you to promise me you'll let Dan Reed do his job, that you won't get in his way by trying to investigate on your own.''

She glared at him, and, cursing her stubbornness, he grabbed the rope, shaking it at her. "Dusty, if rustlers killed Blackie, they're dangerous, deadly dangerous. You're going to have to promise me that you'll leave this to Reed or, so help me, I will tie you up wherever I can keep you safe.''

"Are you going to let Reed investigate your cattle losses?'' she challenged him.

He sighed, rubbing the tired lines in his forehead. "If you leave Blackie's death to Reed, I'll let him find out what happened to the cattle. Is it a deal?''

"Hey, Jake," Hooter shouted, lurching up from the direction of the main house. "Ain't you ready yet? We need to get out there and look at those—''

"Dammit, Hooter," Jake barked at him, "I know what we have to do. Get in the truck.''

"Okay, Jake," Hooter said, halted by the anger in Jake's voice. "I guess I'll just get in the truck."

"Be here when I get back," he said to Dusty. "We'll go to town then."

When Jake returned two hours later to pick up Dusty for their trip to town, he didn't mention what exactly he and Hooter had checked out. Hooter barely said anything to her before he disappeared into the main house, and Jake remained grimly silent all the way into Big Piney.

Jake knew she watched him, suspicions running riot in her overactive brain, but he couldn't tell her Hooter had found a cut place in the north fence. Someone had cut the wire at the post and carefully repaired the opening, restapling the wire. The post had been pulled only slightly out of alignment. Anybody riding fence would have to look closely to see what had happened. There was no telling how long ago the damage had been done.

The sheriff extended no welcome to Dusty and Jake. He leaned back in his chair and watched them come into his office with what passed for a patient expression on his face. Dusty tossed the rope and glove on his cluttered desk and explained how she found them. She made a point of carefully describing their location in respect to the body.

Sheriff Reed scratched his chin and moved the tobacco around in his cheek. He speculated that the glove could have belonged to anybody. After all, a lot of people, sheepherders included, wore gloves like that. And the rope, why, the rope could have been left by hunters. He wasn't impressed.

Dusty bristled at his skepticism. "Tell him about the missing cattle," Dusty urged Jake.

The sheriff cocked his head at Jake. "What's the matter, Valiteros? You got some rustling on your place, do you?"

"As a matter of fact, I do have cattle missing," Jake said grudgingly. "I have at least ten missing cows and their calves."

"At least?" said the sheriff. "You mean you're not sure how many are gone?"

Jake glanced at Dusty. He didn't want to say that he and Hooter had the count up to fifteen and that they suspected more had been taken through the damaged fence. "We're sure about ten."

"And their calves?" Jake nodded, and Reed went on, "Well, I tell you, Valiteros, I don't hardly know where to start looking for somebody who'd take your cows. I mean the Waterhole over there'll be full of likely suspects tonight. Just full of folks who might be real happy to see you lose money." He gave Jake a baleful look. "You want I should go over there tonight and start asking about your cows?"

"If you believe the Waterhole is a reasonable place to start," Jake answered him, "yes, I do."

"Sheriff," Dusty said, covering her anger with careful control, "it seems a reasonable assumption that my father's death is connected with Jake's missing cattle. After all, Blackie was hired to work those cattle. He might not take it kindly if somebody tried to steal them." She smiled coldly. "How many dead bodies do you need before you find the time to investigate?" The smile vanished. "Maybe I should talk to the local newspaper instead of you. Those folks really jump at a juicy controversy."

The sheriff chuckled wryly. "Okay, I'll look into it, but I can't promise you anything."

"Give it your very serious attention, Reed," Jake said, quickly steering Dusty toward the door and closing it behind her without waiting for a reply from the sheriff. He wanted to get Dusty out of there before she dropped that fake coldness and started a fistfight.

Once they were back in the open air, he put his hat back on and breathed deeply, watching her. She had rejected him, practically kicked him out of her house. Why was he trying to protect her from rustlers and Dan Reed and her own bad temper? Why was he standing on a Big Piney sidewalk wanting nothing more than to hold her safely in his arms? "Well, that's done," he said, instead, and climbed into his truck.

"That jerk," Dusty said, slamming the passenger door. "A lot of help he's going to be."

Jake started the truck. "Before you arrange an interview with the newspaper, I think I better mention Reed has a pretty good record for doing his job. He may not have the world's best personality, but he'll do what he says."

"You can't really believe he's going to do any investigating?" she scoffed.

"As a matter of fact, I do."

"I don't believe this," she said. "You're saying he did that sneering routine because he likes to play the big, bad sheriff?" Jake shrugged, backing the truck into the street. "How am I supposed to trust somebody like him to take Blackie's death seriously?"

"I know. I heard him." Pulling into the empty street, he gripped the steering wheel to keep himself from touching her. "But no matter what he says, he'll do his job. He may not do it as fast as you'd like him to, but he'll do it." He hoped, in spite of the gnawing anxiety in his gut, that what he said about Dan Reed was, at least, close to the truth.

June moved in wet, unusually wet. For an area that averaged less than ten inches of moisture a year, frequent soaking rains constituted good weather. The hay fields loved it. The ranch hands didn't. They slogged through fields and pushed at muddy cattle. Dusty decided nothing was more miserable than a muddy cow—unless it was a muddy calf. Muddy or not, the hard work kept her mind occupied and left her exhausted enough to fall asleep most nights—despite her constant awareness of Jake's hard, watchful eyes. Wearily, she realized that Jake never let her out of his sight.

And even her stubborn independence hadn't been enough to make her object.

By the middle of the month, it was time to put the bulls in with the cows to begin next year's calf crop. Ollie joked that the bulls would slip right off when they tried to mount a cow's muddy flanks. Hooter reminded him the calves didn't have any trouble finding their dinner, and he doubted the bulls would have any trouble finding what they were looking for, either.

Sheriff Reed came around to check out Blackie's rope, the one that came back on Blackie's horse. He said as little as possible to Dusty. She watched him fiddle around in the barn, looking over Blackie's tack. He made no notes, and he asked no questions.

A couple of times, he rode out from ranch headquarters with Hooter. Each time, Jake busied himself with the haying equipment in the barn while she worked a horse in one of the corrals. She knew his sudden interest in mechanics was supposed to be a message: he was letting the sheriff investigate the rustling, and she should let the sheriff investigate Blackie's death.

Days and weeks of hard, satisfying work ground by, and Jake never let up his surveillance of everything she did. At the beginning of every workday, he growled at everyone, especially her. But, contrarily, he jumped on anyone else who said a cross word to her. Poor Hooter had his toes stomped for complaining to her about the amount of alfalfa cubes she fed the horses. When Hooter had ambled off mumbling to himself, she did her own yelling at Jake, but he flashed his glittering eyes at her, silently stifling her protest.

It wasn't all silence and bad temper, though. Each day, as the work went into full swing, he mellowed until sometimes she was able to coax a smile from him, occasionally a laugh. She loved those laughs; they were rare jewels indeed. They came rumbling out of him as if they grated over the cracked surface of rock, as if he had never laughed before in his life.

Then, on the first of July, she pulled up to the barn earlier than usual to get horses ready for the hands. They were scheduled to rotate a few hundred head off one pasture and onto another. The cattle wouldn't be moved far, but there would be a full day of working cattle on horseback.

She smiled remembering the last time they rotated cattle. She had come early that day, saddling and rigging a horse for Carl. She had added a special touch, a braid in the horse's tail, just six inches, but she had used hot-pink ribbon in the braid. As usual, Carl came out of the bunkhouse, bleary-eyed and stumbling, grateful to Dusty for getting his horse ready. He nodded at her as he rode out of the barn, and she nodded back, straight-faced and sober. Jake came in, griping that she wasn't saddled already. He griped and growled at her all the way out of the barn. She earned several puzzled looks from Ollie because she didn't snap back at Jake. Instead, she maintained an uncharacteristic expression of serenity. By the time they reached the cattle, Jake had quieted down enough to smile when Dusty and Ollie started trading cowboy jokes.

They were ready to split up to chase down cows when Carl came roaring up in a cloud of dust. He was sputtering at Dusty. He said Jeep had been calling him Sue and laughing at him since they left the barn, and he said he was feeling sorry for the ol' codger until he twisted in his saddle and saw what Dusty had done. "Just you wait, Dusty Macleod," he shouted at her. "I'll catch you when you're too sleepy to defend yourself and make you look like a durn fool, too."

"What're you jawing about, Carl?" Jake frowned at him.

"Don't you try to defend her, neither. She done went too far this time." Carl glared at Jake, and Jake opened his mouth to give Carl a piece of his mind when Ollie, who had pulled his horse around to Carl's back side, started laughing.

"It wudden enough to use ribbon on my horse, but she had to use pink!" Carl's face flushed the same color as the ribbon, and he turned his horse so Jake could see the humiliation.

That's when Jake's face broke open in a laugh. Dusty joined in, enjoying the rusty sound Jake made as much as the pink on Carl's face.

But this morning, when she climbed out of her truck, the barn was empty. Then Ollie came wandering in, saying that he and Jeep would be moving the cattle by themselves. Jake and Hooter and Carl had gone off in the ranch truck to do another job. According to Ollie, her job for the day was to work horses in the corrals at headquarters.

"What's Jake doing that couldn't wait?" she asked Ollie, who suddenly became busy rigging his horse. "Ollie," she said a little louder, "what's the big, important job that wasn't on the schedule for today?"

There was a full minute of silence. Ollie's horse looked back at him in puzzlement as the cinch was readjusted for the third time.

"Ollie?" Dusty prompted, gloved hands on her hips.

His face was flushed when he looked back at her. "Well, uh, Dad said they'd probably be gone all day, and he told Jeep to be sure and get those cattle moved. That pasture they're on right now needs a rest."

"Yeah, I know," Dusty said grumpily, resigned to Ollie's lack of information. "Time to move the cattle to grass that could use some pruning." She resumed the rigging of one of the three-year-olds she had been training. "I guess I'll just give you a hand with the cattle. You'll need the help."

Ollie stumbled against his horse, his foot slipping out of his stirrup. "Oh, I don't know, Dusty. Jake will blow a fuse if you're not working here when he gets back."

"Yeah, well, I'm training this horse to work cattle." She patted the strong horse, a handsome brown horse with one white sock. "I'll give him some good field training."

Jeep and Ollie rode out quickly, trying to leave her behind, but she caught up with them before they reached the cattle. Grudgingly, they accepted her help, the three of them scattering out over the pasture to push cattle toward the west fence.

The day on horseback working cattle was perfect, well, almost perfect. All day, Dusty fought the nagging feeling that something was missing—or someone. She was disgusted at herself. Hadn't she been chafing with resentment because Jake wouldn't let her work outside headquarters unless he was along to keep an eye on her? She should have been glad for one day without those narrow eyes on everything she did. And here she was missing him.

Then, sometime after the middle of the afternoon, she was trying to get the brown horse to practice a little cutting when she heard a low-pitched growl behind her.

"What're you doing? You're supposed to be working green horses today."

Confoundedly, she had to fight a glad spurt of laughter at the sound of that voice, disgruntled tone and all. She turned her horse abruptly toward him, struggling to rearrange her face into an expression more consistent with his irritation. "I *am* working a green horse today," she said. "Can't you see?"

"Yeah, I can see," he barked. "You're out here having fun with that horse instead of taking care of your job back at headquarters."

"Oh, come off it, Jake. You're mad because I took off without you playing watchdog. Look," she said, extending both arms, "I'm all in one piece. Nothing terrible happened to me."

Taking in the picture she made, sun on her cheeks beneath her hat brim and shoulders straight and sure under the bold stripes of her Western shirt, he shifted uneasily in his saddle. The heat of anger transformed itself into a hot ache in the area of his groin. It was a transformation he had become well acquainted with over the past few weeks. The shock of it hit him every morning, the first time he saw her each day. No matter how much he cursed himself for it, he found that every damn day he fell into enjoying her company, her laughter and her skill, especially with the horses. Every damn day the ache got worse.

Across the pasture, riding up from a steep coulee, Ollie urged a couple of stragglers on their way. When he caught sight of Jake and Dusty, he slowed to a stop. "Damn," he muttered, "the boss'll have my hide for bringing Dusty out here." Then he heard Dusty laugh and saw Jake relax in the saddle. Ollie shook his head at the pair of them. "She's doing it again. No need to worry about the boss's temper now." He pushed at the two cows, speeding them up.

With Jake's help, it wasn't long before they were closing the gate on the new pasture for the last time.

"Look at that grass," Dusty said from across the fence.

"Yeah," Ollie shouted back at her as he rode away, "those cows just found heaven."

Jake pulled up beside her, gazing with satisfaction at his cattle spreading out to make good use of the food supply. She studied his quiet posture, aware that his restless eyes were busy checking out the pasture and the animals. He examined every detail, looking for disease or injury or lack of vegetation or just plain trouble. His vigilance never rested. He watched over the land and the cattle the same way he watched over her. He's a good rancher, she thought, and the thought reminded her of Blackie and the rankling mystery of his death. She reined her horse, heading back to the barn with a burst of irritation. Startled, Jake watched her ride away, his scowl gathering, before he followed.

After she finished her chores at headquarters, Dusty walked out of the barn to find Jake and Hooter leaning against the ranch pickup. Jake slumped tiredly, his hand covering his eyes. Hooter saw her coming and, raising his voice, said, "You know, Jake, we're going to be ready to cut some hay along about next week."

Jake looked up. "What?"

Hooter nodded in Dusty's direction. "I said we can cut some hay next week." Jake shot a look at Dusty as she walked up, frowning at Hooter. "At least two of those fields down at this end of the creek should be ready. Of course, that big one on the other side hasn't recovered from—"

"Okay, I heard you," Jake said, irritated, glancing uneasily at Dusty. Dammit, Hooter, watch your loose tongue, he thought. All I need is for you to mention the fire. "Go into town and hire a couple of high school kids to help Carl with the cutting."

"Why couldn't I help?" Dusty asked. "Carl and I could handle two fields by ourselves."

"No," Jake said quickly, stopping Hooter from responding. "You've got enough work to do with the horses."

"Jake," she said wryly, "I can't get into any trouble if I'm busy with a hay field."

"I said no, Dusty," Jake said sharply. "We'll hire some kids to take up the slack."

Hooter scooted off toward his house, and Jake unloaded the back of the pickup, hauling wire and tools, fence repair equipment, into the barn. So, she mused, they had been repairing fences today. Jake said nothing, concentrating sourly on the unloading.

"Where were you repairing fences?" she asked.

Jake paused, a spool of wire balanced on the open tailgate, and glared at her. "What is it with you today?" he growled. "Can't you do your job and leave the rest of the ranch alone?"

"No," she said, glaring back at him, furious at one more secret she wasn't trusted with. "You want me to be a nice little prisoner, who doesn't object when you keep me blindfolded and hog-tied. No more, Jake. I'm through with your secrets and your evasions. You can take the busy work you think up to keep me occupied and shove it. I'm going to find out what happened to my father." She stuffed her gloves into her back pocket and strode off toward her pickup. "I quit, boss man," she shouted over her shoulder.

She heard him yelling at her to "Come back here" as she backed out, but she spun away from the barn, hoping he'd choke on the dust.

When she pulled up in front of her house, the sun was hanging low over the mountains, sending shafts of light like golden arrows into the sagebrush-softened rise across the creek. There, silhouetted on the brow of the hill, stood a bent figure on horseback, blackened against the beams of the setting sun. Was it T.J.? She shivered in the darkened cab of her pickup. Behind her she heard the unmistakable roar of Jake's ranch truck approaching on the double-track road, and she glanced over her shoulder in unaccountable relief. When she looked back across the creek, the image of the old man on the old mare had disappeared. Had Jake's arrival driven it away? Giving herself a small shake, she got out of the truck and went into the house.

She waited in Blackie's chair as Jake stomped up the steps, across the porch and into the house. She braced herself before she looked up to see him halt just inside the front door. The angry greeting churning in her head slowed and stopped dead when she saw him. He wore no hat. The lines in his face had deepened into canyons of weariness, and his eyes were bleak. Incredibly, his shoulders, his lean, capable shoulders, drooped as he shifted his weight to one leg and stuffed his hands awkwardly into his pockets.

All of Dusty's resolve melted. For weeks she had felt the force of those keen eyes constantly following her. Now their light was gone, worn away, and she read an almost desperate pleading there.

She knew why, suddenly, she had spent the last month doing only what Jake asked her to do—because the night she had spent in his arms, over a month ago, had taught her about his fear, his gnawing, anguished fear that something would happen to her. She had felt it in the trembling of his arms and in the rasp of his breath and the blazing heat of his body. And hurting him, causing his anguish, was like stabbing herself with a dull blade, a slow, ragged pain. For weeks, she had avoided that pain at all costs—because she loved him.

"Oh, Jake," she said on a sigh, going to him and wrapping her arms around his shoulders. His arms clutched her close, holding her so tight she could barely breathe. She thought he whispered "Please" into the hair near her ear.

Later, in the dim light of the lamp on her bedside table, she leaned against the headboard of the rumpled bed. Jake had collapsed, exhausted, into a pillow, snoring lightly, his cigar and whiskey forgotten on the bedside table. She reached across his broad shoulders to turn out the lamp. He snorted at the warm brush of her breasts on the bare skin of his back, before resuming the even rhythm of sleep-deep breathing. She looked down at him in the darkness, at the sheen of man-sweat that covered his shoulders in the silver light sifting through the curtains. He needed rest, she realized. Over the last month, he had gradually looked more and more worn, eroded, as if the constant worry etched his face and sapped his strength.

She leaned over and softly kissed his rugged cheek, shadowed by moonlight. She smiled when he, in his sleep, breathed in deeply, one deep breath, soughing in and out, like a contented sigh. Making love had washed the fear out of him. She had felt his body relax, stretching in pleasure. The trembling had eased and died away.

But the fear would return.

She admitted to herself that she loved him, but he was smothering the life out of her. He was taking away her choices, her ability to act on her own. She knew what she had to do; she had to block him out of her life. She couldn't work on his ranch or sleep with him or let him touch her.

He would fight her, and, after tonight, he would know where she was most vulnerable. All he had to do was touch her or hold her, and she forgot everything except loving him and needing him.

Somehow, she had to find the strength to refuse his touch, if she expected to have a life she could call her own. And if she expected to solve the mystery of Blackie's death.

She put off confronting Jake and quitting her job at the ranch until after the celebration for the Fourth of July. In Big Piney, the Fourth meant Chuckwagon Days. There was a parade and a free barbecue and an afternoon rodeo, all time-honored traditions that dated back to long before Dusty was born. She usually missed the parade, but she wouldn't think of missing the barbecue and rodeo. People came from all over western Wyoming to join the fun.

At the show barn on the fairgrounds where the barbecue was being served, she talked the grumbling server into giving her two helpings, enough to take some of the succulent meat out to the rodeo arena to Jake. She flushed when she saw that Ruth was the next server, who plopped potato salad on the two plates. Before handing back the second plate, Ruth paused, looked down at it and raised her eyebrow at Dusty. Then she moved on to the next hungry person.

Inside the gate to the rodeo grounds, it didn't take her long to spot Jake. He had parked on the edge of the grounds to give him plenty of room to tend to his horse. Other horse trailers were parked nearby. Workers and rodeo contestants were busy with their horses, grooming and saddling, while they greeted one another.

Dusty saw Jake crane his neck to observe the traffic around the show barn, and, seconds later, she saw him stiffen into stillness, when his impatient gaze picked her out of the crowd. While she made her way to where he waited for her, she noticed no one stopped to talk to him. Several men nodded as they walked by, but no one greeted him with the same enthusiasm they gave to the others. She carefully said nothing when she handed Jake a plate of food and crawled up on the open tailgate. Ol' Yeller's reins were draped loosely on the side of the truck at her elbow.

"Hello, ol' boy," she said softly to the big animal. Yeller's ears perked up at the sound of her voice. He had already learned to anticipate her touch, her experienced fingers working small circles on his strong neck. Jake had told her she was spoiling a good horse, but he'd grinned when he said it.

He wasn't grinning now. "It's about time you got here," he growled as he leaned against the truck and started in on the food. He didn't like the angry, restless look she had, staring up at the mountains as if she were trying to force them to reveal their secrets about Blackie's death. He wished he could lock her up and throw away the key. Dammit, why did looking after a woman have to be so damned much trouble?

"Hey, Jake," Ollie shouted, running up to them from the direction of the arena. "Hello, Dusty," he said, nodding self-consciously at her.

In spite of her sour mood, Dusty couldn't keep a smile out of her voice. "Hello yourself." Ollie had reason to be nervous and excited. All through June, he had been working out in the roping arena at ranch headquarters, getting ready for this rodeo. Jake and Ol' Yeller had worked with him several times a week, giving him tips and checking his progress.

"I was just wondering, Jake, if I could use your saddle in the roping. I mean, if you're not going to enter anything except the team stuff," Ollie apologized. Late last week, Ollie had finally talked Jake into entering the team roping. Jake had caved in to Ollie's constant badgering but had resolutely refused to concede anything else. "What do you think? Would it be okay with you? I mean, I get a much better dismount with your saddle, and I'm gonna need all the edge I can get. These guys have been working at this a lot longer than I have.''

Jake pulled a can of beer from the cooler in the bed of the truck and popped it open. ''If you've got my saddle on your horse, what do you think I'm going to use in the teams?''

''My rig?'' Ollie asked hopefully. ''You can manage with it much better than I can. Besides, you've got Yeller.''

Jake shook the beer can in Ollie's direction. ''Yeah,'' he said, ''I've got Yeller. And don't go getting any ideas about borrowing my horse.''

''No, I won't.'' Ollie laughed, hopping with excitement. ''I guess I can stick with my horse. Of course,'' he said, slanting his eyes in Dusty's direction, ''I probably should've tried to borrow Mac's sorrel from Dusty.''

Dusty laughed out loud; she couldn't help it. ''Too late, cowboy,'' she said.

He grinned at her and then looked uneasily at Jake. ''Uh, Jake, you know you gotta get over to the pay window pretty soon to pay your fee for the teams.'' He started backing up in the direction of the arena. ''Don't forget. And thanks a lot for the loan of the rig. I'll just go get my rig out of Dad's pickup and bring it over.''

Jake sighed, pushing away from the truck. ''Well, I guess I better unsaddle Yeller.''

Dusty watched him, marveling at his lack of concern about lending his roping saddle, although she knew the saddle had been made especially for him. Cowboys, she thought, they are the most generous human beings on the face of the earth. Rodeo cowboys think nothing of lending whatever they have to someone who needs it. They might be competing against one another, but that doesn't stop them. You need a rig, just ask to borrow somebody else's. No problem.

''You look awful pleased about something,'' Jake commented. She didn't know he had given her the slightest glance.

"Oh, I was just thinking what a foolish lot rodeo cowboys are." She grinned. "They throw good money away on a chance to break their bones and roll around in the dirt with filthy calves. They ride around in small arenas trying to persuade angry bulls to go into tiny chutes instead of stomping on the cowboy on the ground. And, to top it all off, they lend their saddles and anything else they have to the first person who asks." She shook her head in mock consternation.

Jake grinned back at her, looping his lean arm on the neck of his horse. "So cowboys are foolish, huh?" He considered the question for a moment. "Yep, I guess you're right. But to my way of thinking, it takes a fool to live in this valley and make a go of it." He tapped her nose with a long finger. "I guess that makes you one of us."

"I hope so, but I haven't made a go of it yet."

His expression hardened. Stubborn female. She was determined to find some way of making it on her own. "Maybe you better remember that when cowboys help one another out, it's more than a tradition. It's a way of life. Nobody makes it alone out here."

"I don't mind being helped," she said, jumping off the tailgate. "I just like deciding when and where." She stuck her hands into her hip pockets and turned in the direction of the arena.

"Go over to Hooter's truck," he barked at her. "He said you could watch the rodeo from there."

Bristling at his tone, she looked at him. "I don't take orders on my day off." She pushed her hat back on her head and ambled out of his range.

Touchy, he thought, watching her retreating back. He worried the reins in his hand. Somehow, he had to figure out how to reach her.

Chapter Nine

Dusty avoided Hooter's truck by ambling around the opposite end of the arena fence. She silently accused herself of being self-destructive because Hooter's pickup was perfectly placed for the best view. Like so many of the locals, Hooter had parked in a choice location the night before. Locals backed their trucks up to the arena fence and seated family and friends in the empty truck beds, usually in lawn chairs with a beer-filled ice chest handy. A cold beer was a relief in the heat of the day with dust flying everywhere.

Out in the arena, a truck put water on the dirt to settle the dust. The rodeo announcer spewed out a line of gab on the public address system. He called out to some of the riders circling the arena. The riders loosened up for the competition or simply enjoyed the experience of riding inside a real rodeo arena, especially the kids. The announcer told the competitors, "Get ready. Pay up now or we gonna turn you out. If you were there right now, you'd be late." He called to one young rider, "Ride that white thang over here where

I can see ya. There's nothin' on earth prettier than kids and horses.'' Dusty smiled to herself at the familiarity of it all.

Soon enough the opening ceremonies were over and the barrel racing had begun. Dusty found herself pulled toward the fence. She fell once again under the spell of watching beautiful horses and good riders. The announcer declared, ''Now here's a handy girl on a handy-lookin' horse.'' Real Western flattery for the barrel rider, a high school student from Pinedale. ''Come a ridin', girl!'' And so she did, hat pulled low on her forehead and her splashy shirt matched with the leggings above her horse's hooves. The young rider hunched forward in concentration as she and her horse circled the barrels in the cloverleaf pattern, the horse matching his gait to the intricacy of the turns without touching the barrels. Then the burst for the finish line, the rider flicking reins back and forth on the horse's withers and the horse stretched out for maximum speed. Good-looking ride, Dusty silently cheered. Nothing prettier than a good barrel racer.

Following on the heels of the barrel racing came the first group of calf ropers. Ollie did all right, but his horse lacked the finesse of Ol' Yeller, and he had a little trouble getting his calf on the ground so he could tie off three legs. The announcer said, ''Let's give this rookie a hand for a good try.'' Later, when Ollie teamed up with Jake, Ol' Yeller looked great. Ollie managed to get his rope around the steer's horns before Yeller put Jake in just the right position to slip a rope under the steer's back feet to heel it. If Ollie and his horse had been as quick and sure as Jake and Yeller, they would have had the best time. Dusty heard someone down the fence say, ''Look at that horse. Ain't he havin' a great time?'' In fact, Yeller seemed to be disappointed that his time in the spotlight was over so soon. Jake's stone face showed no emotion at all. At least, that's the way he must have appeared to everyone but Dusty, but she could see the satisfaction in the easy set of his shoulders.

Dusty pushed away from the fence and made her way toward the roping chutes. She wanted to congratulate Ollie on surviving his first go as a roper. As she stumbled into the weeds beneath the metal framing of the bleachers, a burly hand closed around her forearm. She screamed in reaction to the sudden halt of her forward motion, and another hand pressed over her mouth. She looked up into T.J.'s red-rimmed eyes. At the same time her brain registered the relief of recognizing him, she gasped at his slovenly appearance. His face was puffy and covered with bristly whiskers. From the sticky smell of him, he hadn't bathed or changed clothes in quite a while. Concern replaced the jolt of alarm she felt when he grabbed her.

She looked around quickly to be sure her scream hadn't caused unnecessary attention. Fortunately, the people in the bleachers were yelling at the bull riders. Probably no one even heard her scream. She put a consoling hand on T.J.'s where he still clutched her arm.

"What's wrong?" she asked him. "Are you sick, T.J.?" She felt guilty for not checking on him. Blackie wouldn't have been so neglectful.

"Naw, I ain't sick." He looked down at the slender fingers patting his rough hand. When he raised his eyes again, they were filled with moisture. "Don't you worry none about the likes of me. I'm jist a ol' cowhand that's used to bein' alone. Why, I wudden know whut to do wit' comp'ny. Never liked it much nohow." He said the last with a touch of urgency, clutching her arm tighter as he said it.

"I'll always worry about you, T.J.," Dusty said, gently pulling her arm out of his grasp. "Blackie would be ashamed of me if I didn't."

"Blackie wuz th' bes' friend I ever had," he said broodingly. "He wuz like fam'ly. My brother wudden no closer to me'n Blackie." He wiped his dirty shirtsleeve across his eyes and, then, his nose. "I loved Blackie." His eyes clouded with moisture again.

"I know you did. I miss him, too."

"Sometimes I forgit and git on my horse to go over and give him a visit," he said eagerly. "One day I got all the way to Piney Crick." He shook his head at the ground. "I din know whut to do then. I wuz right there by Piney Crick where I growed up and I wuz jist lost."

Dusty felt her throat close up because she knew how he felt. She still expected Blackie to ride up every evening.

"I guess Blackie wuz th' bes' cowhand there ever wuz. In these parts, anyway." He stared at a spot between him and the cars that were sitting in their viewing places on the hill above the arena. "He din like cows much, but he wuz good to 'em. He liked horses, though. That's the truth." He wiped his eyes again. Dusty thought he wasn't going to say anything more when he began again. "My pa talked 'bout when Blackie's pa come into this country. He was a tie-hack. Did you know that?" His red eyes focused on Dusty. "Your grandpa was a tie-hack. He cut cross ties for the railroads."

"Yes, I know that, T.J.," Dusty said. "I've heard the stories. He came to the mountains to cut trees for crossties and stayed to marry my grandmother. He took over her ranch."

"Tha's right," he said, giving out a watery chuckle. "Blackie used to tease your ma 'bout that. I heard 'im."

"Yeah, I heard him, too." Dusty laughed. "Blackie told Mother he learned to marry well from his father."

"He meant 'cause she wuz from one of th' first fam'lies in th' valley. Like his ma." He breathed hard, letting air out in a bubbly sigh. "I come from one of them first fam'lies, too. My grandpa pioneered this valley. He staked 'is claim an' proved up jist like your grandma's fam'ly and your ma's."

"I know that, too. Remember? You came to my house last summer, and I interviewed you for the paper I was writing. We talked a long time about your family. You told me about your grandfather being a blacksmith before he took up ranching.'' Actually, Blackie had told her about the blacksmithing. Blackie said that T.J.'s grandfather never could quite get the blacksmithing right. He had more than one mad rancher threatening him over a bad horseshoeing job. He wasn't much better at ranching. The family constantly struggled to put food in their mouths.

"Do you remember talking to me about your family, T.J.?''

"You wuz writin' somethin'.'' He brightened. "It wuz a report, somethin' for school, you said. You talked to all the pioneer fam'lies. Did you ever finish that? I sure would like to see it.''

"Yes, I finished it. There's a copy of it in the Big Piney library.'' She remembered suddenly that Jake still had Blackie's copy of her thesis. "All you have to do is ask the people in the library to let you read it.''

"Right here in Big Piney? I'd like to read that.'' He regarded Dusty seriously. "I figured you'd be to th' rodeo. I come to see if I could find you.''

"Why didn't you just come to the house?''

"Naw, I wudden do that.'' His face twitched itself into a fierce scowl, furrowing like a black cloud pitching down a streambed. "I been watchin'. Tha's why I had to see you. I seen that thievin' snake come to your house. I know all 'bout it. I seen 'im go in your house and he don't come out. Th' nex' mornin' he leaves and he's wearin' a big grin.'' He grabbed her upper arms in his broad hands. "I tole you 'bout 'im. I warned you. You jist a little girl. Blackie's little girl. You don't know 'bout men like 'im.''

"No, T.J., you're wrong about Jake.'' She put her hands on his arms, hoping to calm him, but she could see he didn't hear what she said.

"He's tryin' to take it all. You, pretty little thing, you don't know nothin' 'bout 'im.'' One big hand touched her face. "That snake sees how pretty you are, so he wants you, too. But he's jist mean clear through. He's not gonna be sati'fied till he runs us all out.''

"Listen to me, T.J. Jake's a good rancher. He—''

He shook her to stop what she was about to say. His eyes were wild, haunted. "He's not like us. Don't you un'erstand? His pa come here when I wuz jist a young'un. I 'member 'im. He bought up stuff. He pushed people around. He pushed 'em off their land, so's he could have some.''

Something clicked in Dusty's head. She hadn't been able to understand the attitude of her neighbors toward Jake. Nothing he had done seemed to warrant the cool way they treated him. Not when she knew them to be warm, generous people. But if Jake's father had made enemies all those years ago, probably before Jake was born, that helped to explain their attitude. History lived in this valley. People didn't forget.

T.J. shook her again, bringing her back to what he was saying. "Don't you see? The ol' man's cub is jist like 'im. If somebody don't stop 'im, he's gonna run us all outta this valley. He ain't gonna stop 'til he does. He's got no right. This valley belongs to us. We gotta stop 'im.'' He swallowed hard and narrowed his eyes. "You gotta git outta here. Don't you see? You cain't stay. You gotta leave so that snake don't hurt ya. Tha's whut I come to tell ya. Git out. Go back to that school in Laramie.''

He stopped suddenly and looked over his shoulder. That's when Dusty saw Jake coming toward them. T.J. backed up and made a hissing sound through bared teeth like a cornered dog.

Jake's gait slowed, approaching carefully. "Hi there, T.J.,'' he offered tentatively. "I haven't seen you around in a while.''

"You do whut I said,'' T.J. snarled at Dusty. "I'll be watchin'. Don't you forgit.'' Then he circled around Jake and loped off. Dusty couldn't remember ever seeing T.J.

move fast before. His speed startled her almost as much as the wildness of his behavior. But he was still T.J. She had known him all her life.

"What did he want?" Jake asked, watching T.J. push his way through the crowd.

"I'm not sure," she said, staring bemusedly at Jake.

"Maybe you better stay away from him for a while, Dusty. He's acting crazier all the time."

"That might be a good idea." She shook off a shiver that ran up her back.

"Dusty," Jake said, one hand holding her chin to make her look at him, "was that old man threatening you?"

"Threatening me? No, not T.J. He would never hurt me."

The look Jake gave her said he wasn't convinced. "If you say so," he said. "Anyway, come help me load up Yeller. I'm ready to head back to the ranch."

Dusty looked around at the slowly emptying grounds, trying to spot T.J., but he was nowhere to be seen. He had disappeared. Trucks and cars were lined up at the gate, waiting their turn to leave. T.J.'s battered old truck wasn't one of them. Beyond the fence that marked the boundaries of the grounds stretched rolling hills of sagebrush. In the far distance, a band of antelope sped over a hill. They could simply be practicing, giving this year's babies a chance to learn the unique antelope skill of running. Or they could be running in alarm from some human intrusion on their territory.

Dusty felt an icy uneasiness slither down her back. She sympathized with the skittish antelope that ran away from the fearful unknown. Maybe T.J. reacted to the same alarm. Maybe his strange behavior came from an alarm at Blackie's death, something he couldn't explain or accept. If she could find out what happened to Blackie, perhaps she could help both T.J. and herself.

When Dusty approached the ranch pickup, Jake was deep in conversation with another rancher. She recognized Jim

Christenson in spite of the paunch he had added to his middle since she saw him last. That Jim had stopped to talk with Jake surprised her until she realized it wasn't a pleasant conversation. Jake's eyebrows knitted together in controlled fury. Jim's hand made stabbing gestures as he talked. She heard him say something about keeping cattle on the flats too long. She heard "public land" and what sounded like "any fool knows cattle'll turn that sage country into desert" and something about using "forest leases."

When the other rancher seemed to be running out of steam, she moved closer. Jake said, "I'll tell you what I'll do. Come August, I'll invite you to look over my sagebrush leases. If that land isn't in better shape than you've ever seen it, then I'll take you up on your offer to run my ranch for me." Jake poked the man deliberately in the chest. "But until then, keep your nose out of my business."

The other man said sharply, "Until August, Valiteros." He retreated a few feet before adding, "Somebody's got to look out for the land around here. If we don't, the damn environmentalists'll see we don't have any land." He wagged his head warningly and shuffled off.

Jake went back to unsaddling his horse. His jerky movements revealed the extent of his anger.

"What was that all about?" Dusty stroked Ol' Yeller's forehead consolingly.

"Nothing," Jake barked. He stopped and took a long breath. "That meddlesome fool wanted to complain about my cows being on the flats," he said finally, directing his remarks to the saddle instead of Dusty. "He thinks they should be up in the forest by this time of year."

"Doesn't he know how you've been rotating cows from section to section? I've seen grass in places that never have grass this time of year."

He looked at her suspiciously. "You been snooping around on my property?"

She sighed in exasperation. He wasn't concerned about her snooping. He was concerned about her looking for rustlers. "Did you ask any of these ranchers if they were missing cattle?"

"Nope, I didn't want to give them a chance to gloat. Hooter's been asking around." He settled the saddle in the back of his pickup.

"What's the matter with you?" she demanded, her voice edgy with impatience. "You won't talk to any of your neighbors about the rustling, and you won't explain to Jim Christenson about how you're moving cattle to improve the grass on the range." She grabbed his arm to get his attention. "Do you like being the only rancher in the valley that nobody will speak to?"

He cut his gaze to her hand on his arm, and she loosened her grip immediately, sticking her thumbs in her back pockets and staring at the toes of her boots.

"I'm a rancher," he snarled, "not a damned politician."

She looked up quickly. "If you ask me, it wouldn't hurt you to be a little more open about what you're doing on your ranch."

"Nobody asked you," he said coldly, slamming the tailgate shut.

"Too late, Valiteros. I'm counting myself in," she said, turning on her heel and striding away from his rigid expression.

"What does that mean?" he barked. "Dusty, where the hell do you think you're going?"

She stopped and turned toward him. "It's been a long time since I had a talk with Jim Christenson. I'll just see if I can find him back at the show barn." She whirled away, her shoulders squared with determination, and stomped toward the gate that marked the exit to the rodeo grounds.

"Dammit, Dusty, you stay out of this," he called after her, unconcerned that cowboys stopped working with their horses to watch. "Did you hear me? Come back here."

She didn't slacken her pace. "See you later, Valiteros," she shouted. "Take care of that big yellow horse. I have a job to do."

Jake slammed his hat into the dirt at his feet. "Damn. Damn. *Damn.*" There was nothing he could do. She knew he had to tend to Yeller and couldn't come after her. Damn female. He had spent the past six weeks trying to keep her from getting herself killed by rustlers and now she was messing around in the bad blood between him and his neighbors. Infuriating female. She was too damned much trouble.

The sun was setting in a red fury by the time Jake stormed into her house, demanding to know just what she had said to Jim Christenson.

"Jim seemed interested in learning more about what you're doing with your cattle," she said. "I suggested he come over and have a look. He said he just might do that." She cocked her head. "I think he would like to try the same approach on his land."

"I don't want nosy neighbors poking around on my land." He glowered at her.

"You owe it to the land to spread your methods around," she retorted.

"I'm not running a damned ranching school."

She moved quickly, toward the front door, propelled by her fury, but Jake moved faster. One strong hand whipped out to grasp her wrist. She tried to twist away, but he overpowered her. Letting out a long, exasperated breath, Jake yanked her into his lap as he sat on the sagging sofa. With Jake's arms holding her in place, she slumped resignedly. Jake should have noticed the determined set of her jaw before he relaxed his hold. Because as soon as he loosened his arms, she was up and out of his lap, her hands on her hips and her eyes spitting green fire.

"Don't you ever try to manhandle me again," she said in a low deadly voice.

Jake was too startled to stop her as she swept toward the front door.

"Hold on there," he shouted. "Where the hell do you think you're going now?"

"Out," she shouted back.

He reached her in two long strides, grabbing her arm and pulling her around to face him. The blazing fury of her expression stopped him in his tracks, and he dropped her arm.

"I said, don't manhandle me." Each word was like a slap.

He raised both hands as if she held a gun on him. "All right. Just stop long enough to talk to me."

"That's rich," she said. "I'm supposed to talk, but you keep everything to yourself. You won't talk to your neighbors, and you won't talk to me." She slumped into the soft cushions of Blackie's chair, pulling her legs up, and resting her forehead on her knees.

Jake switched on the table lamp next to her because he could barely see her in the gloomy dimness of the room. The light spilled into her hair, picking up the golden strands. His hands itched to stroke that tawny mane, loosening it from the clasp that caught it at the nape. Earlier today, at the rodeo, she had her hair in a braid. He liked it that way. There were so many colors in her hair, and the braid seemed to weave them together like textured silk. He stuck his hands in the pockets of his jeans to keep from touching her. She wouldn't appreciate being touched right now. She was spitting like a wet bobcat.

He knew there was more than irritation about Jim Christenson behind her anger. He wanted to assure her that, if rustlers were responsible for Blackie's death, they'd show up soon enough. Brand inspectors were pretty sharp these days. It got harder and harder to steal cattle. That's what he told himself. Sit tight. Nobody can get away with stealing cattle in this valley. His confidence in the system kept him from going off half-cocked, but he knew nothing would calm Dusty down. After all, he had lost only cattle. No matter how dear the money they represented, his loss didn't come close to losing a father.

He sat on the edge of the sofa, his leg close to Dusty's chair, and propped his elbows on his knees. He braced himself for an inevitable fight.

"Okay," he said quietly. "Let's have it. What's got you so steamed? I know it's not just Christenson."

She lifted her head, fixing him with hot eyes. Her knuckles were white where she clasped them around her knees.

"Tell me what you've been keeping from me for weeks now. I'm not stupid. I can see the signs of something going on." Her cold voice, a sharp contrast to the fire in her eyes, cut at him, slicing little chunks out of his resolve. "First there were the trips you and Hooter made out into the flats. You came back with tired horses. And don't tell me you were working cows. I know better. You didn't ride Ol' Yeller. When you work cattle, you always ride Yeller." Her hot gaze didn't waver. "Then all the hands, except me, became real active, riding out to check cattle. One, then another, was gone for long hours. Regularly. Don't tell me they were moving cattle around. That was your excuse then. But I don't buy it. I rode with you when you moved cattle. When I asked Hooter, he mumbled something about fencing and walked off before I could ask anything else." She got up out of her chair and paced in the small living room, going in and out of the lamplight. "Then last night, I caught Ollie riding out at dusk. The surprised look on his face when he saw I was still in the barn was almost comical. I guess I was supposed to have gone home already." She stopped in front of Jake. "He had a rifle in his rig. He looked so rattled when he saw me that I didn't even bother asking what he was doing. He volunteered that he thought he'd do a little rabbit hunting. His rifle was powerful enough to kill elk. It would completely destroy a rabbit, with nothing left but the tail."

Jake lifted his eyes from staring at the hands that hung helpless between his knees. He looked bleak again, his eyes pale, all color washed out of them.

"Sit down," he said, "and I'll tell you."

"No," she responded in automatic defense. "Don't try to soften me up or protect me or whatever. Just tell me. Right now. All of it."

"There isn't much," he said, slumping back into the worn cushions of the sofa. "Hooter found a break or two in the fence."

"A break or two? Exactly how many breaks did Hooter find?"

"Five. At different times."

"Five? Hooter found five separate breaks in the fence?" Jake nodded reluctantly, and she went on, "When did he find the first one?"

Jake shrugged. "A few weeks ago."

"And when did he find the last one?"

"Last week."

"Now we get to the interesting part." She pierced him with a look as if she had him under interrogation lights. "What was so special about that last break? Why did you start night patrols? And armed ones, at that."

He shifted uncomfortably. "There wasn't much special about it. Just that it was left open. Like somebody was in a hurry or deliberately letting cattle loose. The first few had been repaired."

"Repaired," she repeated incredulously. "You mean, whoever cut the fence stayed around long enough to repair it?"

"The first few times. But not the last ones. Those were left hanging loose, and cattle strayed through. The last time, they were grazing along the creek and had already done some damage to the bank."

Dusty knew Jake treated creek banks with extra care, even if it meant having to carry water to the animals. Unprotected banks eroded under the onslaught of trampling cattle.

"Tell me about the cattle. How many more have you lost?"

"Not many. In fact, that's what is so strange. Somebody has gone to a lot of trouble, and I don't think I've lost more than twenty cows, all told."

"Twenty cows and their twenty calves?" Jake nodded slowly. "Forty head is enough," she whispered. "You'll have a tough time making up that much money."

His expression told her how worried he was. She sat back down in Blackie's chair. Jake immediately reached out to take her hand.

"Dusty, I was waiting for the sheriff to find out something before I told you. We had a bargain."

"No, Jake." She yanked her hand out of his. "Our bargain is not the reason for the big secret. You were protecting me. That's why you ordered everybody to keep their mouths shut."

"Of course, I was protecting you," he said, slamming his hands against his knees. "What would you expect me to do? The last time you got a wild hair, you got yourself caught in a mountain storm and damn near scared me to death."

"I'm not a child, Jake, and I've got a right to know. It was my father who was killed. Don't try to tell me that your missing cattle have nothing to do with Blackie's death."

"The cattle just may have nothing at all to do with Blackie." At her indignant look, he said, "You don't know that cattle thieves murdered Blackie. It seems to me if somebody killed Blackie, they wouldn't hang around to be found out. I'd think a murderer would hightail it out of the country as fast as he could go."

"Not if they had a ready supply of somebody else's cattle."

"That's another thing. Why are my cattle the only ones being stolen? Why not somebody else's? Hooter says nobody he asked is missing any cows. They all think I'm paranoid. A few wanted to fight with him. They thought he was accusing them of being cattle thieves."

"Jake, if you're the only rancher missing cattle, that must mean the rustlers have better access to your herd. They're probably hiding out someplace close by. They could ship out the stolen cattle and then come back to snag some more, a few at a time."

He could see her mind working, exactly what he'd been trying to avoid. Next thing he knew, she would be playing detective, riding off by herself to look for a rustler's hideout like some hero in a cowboy movie.

"No, Dusty. Just calm down. If they're staying anywhere near here, the sheriff will find out about it. They're not going to stay around where somebody might accuse them of murder."

"They wouldn't be scared about that. The sheriff said Blackie's death was an accident. It was even in the newspaper."

"Dusty, you will not go looking for any cattle thieves. Not if I have to tie you up and lock the door."

"What makes you think I'm going to let you get close enough to tie me up?"

Jake gripped both her arms to hold her in the chair. She was pale with fury, each freckle across her nose standing out starkly against her white skin, a furious hellcat with the freckles of a little girl.

"No matter what you say, Dusty, I won't let you go looking for trouble. You will stay put and stay safe."

"I don't need permission from you. I'll do what I think necessary. And I'm the one to decide what that is, Jake Valiteros, not you."

"No, Dusty, you're not thinking straight."

"I'm not thinking like you want me to, you mean. What I do is not your concern. I don't belong to you."

"That's where you're wrong," Jake growled. His hands gripped her arms tight enough to leave bruises. She was no more aware of the pain than he was of inflicting it. "You do belong to me. I've staked a claim on you. You're mine and I'll do whatever I have to do to protect what's mine."

"No! I won't be your property. I don't need your protection, and I don't want it."

When he was hit with the urge to shake her, when he tightened his hands even more to do just that, he suddenly became aware of the strength in his hands and the feminine slenderness of her arms. Horrified at himself, he released her immediately. With the sudden withdrawal of his hands, she slumped in the chair before drawing herself up in proud defiance. Her hands rubbed at the places on her arms where he had held her.

"God, Dusty, did I hurt you?" he said, his voice choked.

"Yes, you hurt me, but I'll survive. Now get out, Jake. This is my house and my life. Get out."

Jake ran his hand tiredly through his hair and stood up. He had handled this badly. Nothing and no one had ever been this important to him, and no one had ever made him feel so helpless.

"I'll go, Dusty, but promise me you won't take off into the mountains by yourself. Promise me you'll get someone to go with you."

She looked up at him. This was harder than she expected. "What I do is my business. I'm not promising you anything."

"Dusty, listen to reason...."

"Get out," she yelled. "Leave."

He stood for a moment longer looking at the fragile little spitfire who had crawled inside his soul and clutched his heart in a death grip. He knew that in spite of all his precautions, she would be up in the mountains the first chance she got, and he wouldn't be able to stop her.

She was as stubborn as he was.

So he left. He couldn't think of anything else to do.

All night long, Jake paced through the empty rooms of his house. He worried the problem of Dusty up and down the stairs and back and forth across his living room. He leaned against his stone fireplace and stared into its sooty black coldness. In the last month, he had lost valuable livestock, livestock he couldn't afford to lose. His whole ranch could very well be in jeopardy and the only thing that really got to him was Dusty. Nothing seemed important except her.

And he couldn't think of a single way to keep her safe.

Before dawn, he saddled Yeller and rode out. Maybe if he did some investigating on his own, he thought—at least it was better than going crazy in that great empty house. He rode toward Bull Creek, toward the place where Blackie's body was found. He rode slowly, observing his cattle along the way, checking the fences and scanning the edges of the forest for anything unusual, but he saw nothing more than the pearly gray light of morning as it washed over livestock and grass and forest.

Up on the fatal mountainside, he encountered sheep, hundreds of them, and as the sun climbed above the eastern horizon, he was hunkered down by a campfire having coffee with Gomez. He always thought sheepherders made the best coffee.

Gomez told him no other sheepherder would come up there this summer, not since the body had been found. He shivered when he said it. Jake asked him if he had seen anybody, anybody who didn't belong in the mountains.

Gomez shook his head sadly. "No, *señor*. Nobody up in these mountains. Just sheep."

Jake was climbing back on his horse when Gomez said, "That one they call T.J., he come up here. This summer not so much. Only once."

Jake pulled his foot out of the stirrup and turned back to the old man. "Tell me about seeing T.J."

Fighting a sense of urgency, Jake made his way down the mountain toward Dusty's place. He told himself that T.J.'s behavior constituted no reason for anxiety, but it worried at him, nonetheless, especially after what happened at the rodeo yesterday.

He heaved a sigh of relief when he saw that Dusty was apparently at home, entertaining a guest, not roaming the mountains and getting herself into trouble. But his relief was short-lived because the strange car, a yuppie-model sedan, parked at her front steps, had Texas plates.

Chapter Ten

Sitting at the kitchen table across from Charlie, Dusty suppressed a yawn and got up to pour another cup of coffee for the two of them. He had driven up just as she reached the barn this morning. She had been late getting up, probably because she had spent an agonizing night after the scene with Jake. Then, before she could saddle True, Charlie drove up. He stepped out of his car looking crisp and virile, as usual. He never missed a beat, that Charlie, she thought, irritated. His dark curly hair fell boyishly down on his forehead, and his oxford cloth shirt was a dazzling pink with sleeves carefully rolled back to reveal tanned forearms. His jeans were freshly ironed, and his Italian loafers shone with fresh polish. She wondered, grouchily, how it was possible to keep a fresh shine on a pair of loafers.

He was telling her about the conference he was attending in Laramie. Something about taking the opportunity, since he had to be in the state, to drive over to western Wyoming and see her. Just as she started in on another yawn, Charlie leaned across the table and slickly drew her hand into his, giving her the full benefit of his heavily lashed brown eyes.

"Dusty," he said, making her name sound seductive. "Dusty," he repeated, "I was so sorry to hear about Blackie. You came all the way out here to take care of him, and now he's dead." That woke her up with a start. Take care of Blackie? What was he talking about? "But, since his death, there's no reason for you to stay here now, Dusty." Charlie deliberately misunderstood her reason for returning to the mountains. "I can help you. The dean of my new history department read your thesis, and he thought it was wonderful. He suggested that I could do some work with it and develop it into a book." So that was it. Ol' Charlie wanted to publish the thesis, her thesis, under his name, and he wanted her to help him do it. "We could have such fun working on it. You remember all the good times we had when you helped me with research."

There he sat, oozing charm with those big brown eyes and the curly brown hair falling casually on his forehead, and, with a start of recognition, Dusty saw something else in his handsome face. Fear. Not like Jake, who was afraid something would happen to her. Oh, no, not like Jake. Charlie was afraid for himself and to hell with anyone else. Ol' Charlie was afraid he couldn't make it in the new history department all on his own. Charlie, the big authority on the history of Western settlement, was a fraud. He needed the daughter of an authentic pioneer family to make it all real. He had used her at the University of Wyoming, and he wanted to go on using her at Texas Tech.

Sitting there, listening to his cultured drawl as he went on and on about all the things he could do for her in the department at Texas Tech, she heard his mother's voice on the telephone, calling from her palatial home in Dallas in that same cultured drawl. She called him Charles, or Charles Bradford. Never Charlie. No, he wasn't Charlie. Even his name was part of the performance, part of his attempt to fit into Western culture, to be one of the boys.

A rattling at the back door broke through her absorption with her new and clarified image of Charlie. She refocused her bemused gaze just in time to see Jake open the door and stroll into the mudroom. The pain, the ragged burning she had fought all night shot through her with new force. He tossed his hat and gloves on the shelf, before turning his narrowed eyes on her. His eyes flashed a moment of uncertainty before they hardened into determination, and she gasped, a sharp intake of breath, at the sight of him, hat-flattened hair, sweat-stained shirt, boots and jeans coated with dust. His presence crashed head-on with her clearer understanding of Charlie. Her head swam with the realization. Ruth had said the real cowboys were all dying off, but she was wrong. Jake was the real thing, as authentic as Blackie or her grandfather or any of the other legendary cowboys who had ridden the range. Jake was as authentic as Charlie was fake. And, oh, how this cowboy gripped her heart.

"Hi, honey," Jake said, sauntering over to the cupboard by the sink. "Thought I'd come back for another cup of coffee." He barely paused in the act of taking out a cup to say, "Got a visitor?"

"You know very well I do." Dusty reined in a contrary bark of laughter.

Across the table, Charlie's chair legs hit the floor with a thud. Jake leaned against the cabinet and considered the startled expression on the other man's face. Dammit, this guy had the dark-haired good looks of a television perfume ad.

"Honey," Jake said to Dusty, the straight line of his lips curled only slightly at each end, "I don't think you told me our guest's name."

Charlie stood abruptly, his chair banging into the wall. "Who the hell are you?"

"Oh, excuse me, both of you," Dusty said, employing as much wry emphasis as possible. "Jake, may I present Dr. Charles Bradford Benson." She indicated Charlie. "Charlie, Jake Valiteros of the Diamond V Cattle Company, Big Piney, Wyoming." She smiled with satisfaction at Jake. Take a look, Charlie, her smile said. Here's a version of the male animal you've never seen before.

"Dusty," Charlie demanded, "is this the rancher who bought your father's property?"

"The one and only."

"I'm the one," Jake said, taking a cigar out of the box on the counter. "The one and only."

Dusty's eyes widened at the cigar. Jake had smoked a cigar, or part of one, in bed the other night after they had just... She forced her eyes shut, stopping herself from picturing what the cigar suggested. That is, she tried to stop herself, but the image of a buck-naked Jake, propped up in bed and smoking one of those damned cigars brought an unbidden flush to her face. When she opened her eyes again, damn Jake, she knew he'd seen the red creep up her neck, and she watched as his tight smile widened into a grin.

"I thought you told me," Charlie said to Dusty, "that your father retained this house and the land it sits on. Was that information wrong? Does this cowboy own your house as well as the rest of your land?" Charlie made "cowboy" sound like a dirty word.

"Nope," answered Jake, deftly assuming responsibility. "This house belongs to Dusty, free and clear. As do the barn and corrals and fifty acres between here and the creek." He added, "Fifty acres of the sweetest pasture you ever saw."

He didn't need to say that he knew Charlie wouldn't know good pasture even if he stepped in a fresh cow-pie in the middle of it. He was sure Dusty got the message. He wanted to add that the house belonged to Dusty—and Dusty belonged to him.

"If this house is Dusty's," Charlie asked stiffly, "what are you doing here?"

"Why, I'm getting myself a cup of coffee and—" Jake looked meaningfully at Dusty "—smoking one of my cigars. A morning break, you might say."

"Dusty, does this mean what I think it does? Are you having an affair with this cowboy?" Charlie demanded imperiously, his drawl slipping somewhat in the process. "Answer me, Dusty."

Jake straightened from his slouch against the counter. "Now look here, buddy," he said around the cigar clamped between his teeth.

"That's enough, Jake," Dusty said, stopping him. "You've had your fun." Jake's lean body didn't lose any of its rigidity, but at least he unclenched his fists. "Charlie, as for you, you no longer have a right to ask me that question." Jake winced at the reference to a relationship between Dusty—his Dusty—and this city slicker. "I did not," Dusty continued, "ask you to come here." Jake relaxed slightly at that. "I owe you no explanations."

"How can you say that?" Charlie asked, amazed. "After all we've meant to each other?"

Jake's fists clenched and unclenched. He wanted badly to punch this guy's face in. When Jake perched his cigar on the edge of the sink, Dusty panicked. She stepped quickly in front of Jake, and faced him with a determined look that said she expected him to let her handle this. His eyes narrowed, staring back at her for a tense moment before he relented and reclaimed his cigar. She didn't let the relief settle in before she whirled on Charlie.

"You wasted your time driving all the way out here, Charlie. I'm not interested in any doctorate program at Texas Tech, or anything else except ranching."

"But, Dusty, you can't ranch anymore. This cowboy standing here with his damned cigar stole your ranch."

"No, Charlie," Dusty said, using her most even tone. "Jake did not steal my ranch. He bought it from Blackie, fair and square."

"That's not the impression I got last spring. Back then you were practically foaming at the mouth."

"I'm still not happy to lose the ranch, but that's not Jake's fault. In fact, he can do things with the land that I would never be able to accomplish on my own." She flashed Jake a surprised smile, suddenly aware that an admission of limitations didn't hurt, didn't even scare her. Jake's eyes softened with pleasure, but he refused to let himself smile. He was smart enough not to show any triumph. She went on, still looking at Jake, "And I have some plans of my own for what's left of my property. I've had time to think and to adjust to what's possible."

"So once you thought about it, you decided that Jake was one hell of a guy and jumped into bed with him. Is that what happened?"

Jake said in a deadly cold voice, "Back off, Professor. You've got no claim on Dusty. Whatever is going on between Dusty and me is none of your business."

A scowl settled on Charlie's handsome face as he confronted Jake. "As a matter of fact, I've got first claim on Dusty, and that makes whatever happens to her my business."

"Shut up, both of you," shouted Dusty, barking like a drill sergeant. "I think it's time the three of us sat down in the living room and tried polite conversation." She smiled sweetly at their incredulous expressions. Taking advantage of their surprise, she indicated the door to the dimly lit room. "After you, gentlemen." She hoped getting out of the tight confines of the kitchen would defuse the tense atmosphere.

To Dusty's amusement, Jake took Blackie's chair. He wasn't above using his greater familiarity with the territory to make a power statement. Charlie sat awkwardly on the far end of the sofa, as far away from the "cowboy" as he could get.

"Now, Charlie," Dusty said, standing carefully out of range of both of them, "I've already told you I'm not interested in an academic career." She glanced uncertainly at Jake, whose cigar glowed red fire at the tip.

Charlie shifted a bit, casting a wary eye at Jake. "I'd prefer talking to you in private, Dusty. I've been worried about you. I could tell when I talked to you on the phone that you're not thinking straight."

"I'm rather busy at the moment, Charlie. I'm sorry you've been worried, but there's really nothing for you to be concerned about. I'm doing just fine. I like working on a ranch." Jake noisily chomped his cigar and smothered his triumph again.

"You can't mean that you want to be a ranch hand. I can't believe you prefer mucking out stables to directing the work of history students. Your mind is too fine to waste, Dusty. You should be in a university doing the work you were meant to do."

Jake sat up, cigar smoke curling around his head, and looked from Charlie to Dusty. How could anyone think Dusty belonged someplace besides here in the high country?

Dusty sighed. "Charlie, you didn't listen to me." As usual, she thought. Besides, buster, if my thesis gets developed into a book, I'll do it myself, here, on the ranch. "University life was exciting, but that part of my life is over. It was time for me to come back home, back to the ranch."

"But you don't have a ranch anymore, Dusty," Charlie reasoned stubbornly.

"Now there's where you're wrong," Jake interjected, taking the cigar from his mouth. He wanted to say Dusty had a ranch as long as he had one, but one look at Dusty told him she would stuff that back down his throat. "Dusty's home isn't a ranch. It's these mountains. Look

outside there and you'll see where she belongs. Dusty can't
be cooped up or fenced in, not by anything." He said each
of the last words slowly, looking directly at Dusty. Then he
smiled at her, his eyes soft again. "She has to be free to ride
her horse on the open mountainside, with nothing between
her and the sky but sunshine."

She smiled back, her smile dazzling. Oh, God, please let
him mean that. Then his smile widened, taking in his eyes,
and the recognition that passed between them shimmered in
the dim light, as brilliant and magical as a mountain sunset.

"He's right, Charlie," she said huskily, unwilling and
unable to break the shining bond between Jake's eyes and
hers. "The university was a foreign land to me, interesting
for a while, but my heart is here. I belong in the mountains
where I grew up."

Unaware of the magic that passed between Jake and
Dusty, Charlie stared stubbornly at the floor. "Look, I've
driven long miles to get here. I'm not going to leave until
I've made my case." He looked up, startled to see Dusty
place her hand in Jake's. "Listen to me, Dusty," he insisted. "The conference in Laramie has another week before I return to Texas. I think you should drive back to
Laramie with me. You could visit friends and attend my
seminar. The conference would show you what you're
missing up here in the backcountry."

"No, Charlie, I'm not going to Laramie with you," she
said tolerantly, grasping Jake's hand. "Not now and not
ever. I'm not missing anything here. In fact, this is probably the only place in the world where I'm not missing anything." She smiled softly at Jake, the bright mountain
sunshine dappling the space between them and their joined
hands. She turned back to Charlie. "Charlie, I don't have
anything else to say to you. I've said it all over and over.
You're going to have to accept that I've made my deci-

sion." She squared her shoulders. "I think it's time you leave."

Jake stood up as if to enforce her statement, and Charlie pulled himself to his feet to face Jake across the battered coffee table. "Don't get the idea you've won," he said to Jake. "Dusty and I were together for three years, and I'm not ready to let her go. She'll get tired of playing with the cowboys sooner or later and come back to me. I know her, you don't."

When she felt Jake flinch beside her, she squeezed his hand to reassure him. He visibly brought himself into control, but he chafed under the restraint, his straight mouth twitching with impatience. His obvious effort at self-control touched her like a warm finger tracing around her heart. She ached to hold him, to caress that hard cowboy's body.

"Come outside with me, Dusty," Charlie said. "You can't refuse to say goodbye, can you?"

"Okay, Charlie." She sighed. "I'll see you to your car." In the doorway, she smiled at Jake and promised she wouldn't take long saying goodbye to Charlie. "Trust me," she said to Jake.

Jake stood in the middle of the cramped room and watched her go outside with Charlie, handsome Charlie who thought he had first claim on Dusty. The walls of the dingy room closed in. Tossing the cigar in an ashtray, he paced across the worn carpet like a caged animal. He paced and watched the two people out by the shiny sedan. The sun was like a spotlight on them, two handsome actors playing out a script he couldn't hear. The pretty professor talked and talked. Jake watched Dusty's face for any sign she might change her mind. She looked firmly resolved, not even a flicker of an eyelash. When the professor took her hand in his, Jake had to hold himself back from exploding through the window. Everything in him wanted to crash through glass and space to get to Dusty. He grasped the window frame, forcing himself to hold tight and wait.

It seemed forever before Dusty took a step backward and slipped her hand out of Charlie's. She clasped her hands behind her and said goodbye. Jake saw the word on her lips, and he wanted to kiss those lips more than he had ever wanted anything in his life. He felt like shouting with relief when Charlie got in his car and closed the door. Dusty stepped up on the porch and watched Charlie drive out of the yard. Jake couldn't wait any longer. He opened the front door and not so gently hauled Dusty into the house. She came willingly, wearing the same smile she had given him when he said she belonged in the mountains. As his arms enclosed her, she reached up to pull his firm mouth down to hers. Her cowboy, she thought in a sudden flood of possession.

The kiss was hungry. His hard mouth opened on the softness of hers, plundering with his tongue the treasure that was the inside of her bottom lip, the edge of her teeth, the pillow of her tongue. The sensations quaked through her, making her hands tremble on his shoulders. When he dragged his mouth from hers, he held her nestled in the hollow of his shoulder. His knees felt weak, and he wasn't sure if he could remain standing without her to lean on. Her ragged breath sang in his ear like the finest music.

"We have to talk," she said when her breathing had evened out. "We still have problems to resolve." She pulled back to look at him. "I don't want you to get the idea I'm going to give you control over what I do."

He chuckled. "Now where would I get a silly idea like that?"

"I'm sure, Jake Valiteros, you need little enough encouragement to get that idea."

"Okay," he agreed, caressing her cheek with his rough fingertips. "We'll talk. But first let me love you. I missed you last night. So much." His hand cupped her jaw as he looked deep into the rich green of her eyes. "Give me that much. Please."

"But, Jake," she teased, "you've already smoked your cigar."

He whooped with laughter as he scooped her up in his arms and headed toward the bedroom. "Let's just say, woman, that we got things a little out of order. This time, it's the cigar first and then the loving." He lowered her to her feet beside the bed and started to pull her shirt out of her jeans.

"What if Charlie comes back?" she asked, rapidly unbuttoning his shirt.

"Right now, I don't care who or what comes through that door. All I want is to lay you out on that bed like a feast from heaven." He shrugged out of his shirt and batted her hands away from his chest. "Not now. I need to see skin. Your skin." He yanked at her open shirt.

"Are you sure skin is all you want to see?"

His long fingers cupped a breast, and his eyes devoured the pearling nipple. His voice was husky. "Well, maybe there are a few other things I want to see."

Then her own urgency took over. She wanted to touch him, all the parts of him, all of his mountain cowboy body.

"Don't move," she said, jerking at her jeans.

"What are you doing?" he asked roughly.

"Shh," she warned, clambering onto the bed. She knelt on the bed's edge, her bare legs folded under her, and looked at him. Midday sunlight poured into the room through the unshuttered windows behind her. It shone on his bare chest, highlighting muscle and bone and hair.

"Now take off the rest of your clothes," she whispered.

Staggered by the hunger in her eyes, he dropped into the chair behind him and tugged clumsily at his boots. His fingers wouldn't cooperate. The strain stretched the muscles in his arms and back into ridges. She licked her lips in delicious anticipation and let her eyes enjoy the show. He kicked his boots aside and stood to strip off his jeans. Jeans and briefs came off together, rough denim sliding over lean thighs. When he looked up from disentangling himself from the jeans, there was no mistaking the direction of her gaze. He felt an embarrassing redness creep into his cheeks.

"Come here," she said in a feathery whisper. "Let me touch."

Jake stood before her, his legs slightly apart, exposed in the sunlight. Her fingers tested the tension in his chest and in his taut stomach. She examined him as if the eyes that followed the fingers were blind and only touch would satisfy her curiosity. He clenched his teeth and tried to even out his breathing. He amazed himself that he was able to stand. A few minutes ago, he was so lost in the taste of her kiss that his knees had almost buckled with weakness. Now he stood and let her touch him with fingers that nearly drove him insane. He felt a fierce pride at his own strength. With one hand, she reached behind him to grasp his tense buttocks, holding the firm muscle where it hollowed. With her other hand, she cupped and stroked, loving his moan and the sudden grip of his hands on her shoulders. Both her hands encircled the velvet length of him. She bent her head to touch the underside of the rounded tip with her lips first and then with her tongue.

"Sweet heaven," he gasped. He moved his hands on her shoulders and held his breath. The palms of his hands rasped against the soft skin of her shoulder blades.

At last she straightened and smiled impishly into the rigid tension of his face. Her expression was the last straw. Promising himself he would take care of her later, he rolled her back on the unmade bed, impatiently parting her thighs and sinking himself into her. Silken relief surrounded him and drove his body into pulsing thrusts. She gloried in the power of his thrusts and raised her hips to meet him, drawing her legs along the pumping muscles of his buttocks. She felt his body curl tightly, his muscles clenching as he groaned his release. She wrapped her arms and legs around him and held his spent body to her. The moist warmth of him between her thighs made her tremble. His body stirred in response, rubbing against her in a tantalizing rhythm. All her senses flooded with Jake, swirling her to the center of an explosion that left her floating in sunshine, her spirit mating with the cowboy in her arms. As the wonder of it spread into every extremity of her body, she groaned his name over and over. For that moment, only Jake was real to her.

He listened to her rasp out his name as her body arched in satisfaction, and the hardness in his wind-creased face softened. She knew who gave her such pleasure. His name seemed to come out of her soul. Before Dusty, he had never believed it possible for one human being to feel so close to another. No woman had ever touched him with such deep warmth, certainly not his mother and certainly not his wife. A strange moisture, suspiciously like tears, gathered in his eyes.

The sunlight was dazzling in the gentle silence. He propped himself against the headboard and cradled her to his side. They lay utterly still except for their stroking hands. He brushed his fingertips over the curve of her hip, and she caressed the hair-roughened contours of his chest. Long seconds passed without disturbing their languor.

At length, he sighed and tipped up her face for a brief kiss. "I think you made me forget I'm a working cowboy." He checked the clock on the bedside table. "I should've been helping Hooter cut out those bulls a couple of hours ago." He paused. "What are you doing this afternoon?"

Her eyes darkened, and the hand on his chest stilled.

"Dusty, I'm worried about you," he said raspily. His arms tightened around her stiffening body. "God, you're enough to drive me out my mind. I wish I could stay here and hold you in this bed. At least, I'd know you were safe, not looking around for cattle thieves who just might resent your interest."

"I have to look, Jake," she said quietly. "You know that."

"Yeah. You told me."

"Jake, no more of your coddling." She pushed away from him, her mouth flattened and her eyes glinting with dark pools of green. "You told Charlie that I have to be free, and you were right. I have to find my own way without any of your restrictions."

He held her face between his hands. "I'm not trying to stop you, Dusty, but, dammit, I have every right to be worried. You might be in God knows what danger. That's hard for me to take. Dusty—" he sucked in his breath and let it out with a ragged sigh "—I had a little sister, six years younger." Dusty looked at his hard face, startled by the deep huskiness in his voice. "She was a perky little thing, freckles on her nose—" he tapped Dusty's nose lightly "—and big blue eyes. Her first word was horse. Every time I walked out the door, she followed, pestering me to take her to the horses. And every time, our mother would come screaming out of the house to drag her back in." His mouth was a grim line, bracketed by the harsh grooves of his cheeks. "My little sister died when she was five years old."

She watched the thin line of his mouth twitch with suppressed emotion. "What happened?" Her hand soothed the tense muscles of his arm.

"She fell off her horse in the middle of a cattle drive." At the horror of what he'd said, Dusty's hand clenched his arm, unconsciously pressing sharp nails into him until he covered her hand with the abrasiveness of his. "My mother had fought with my father about Penny's going on the drive with us. She had long since given up trying to keep me off the ranch, if she had ever cared, but she hung on to Penny. She fought Dad every step of the way when he taught Penny to ride, especially when Penny rode her horse out of sight of the house." His eyes closed tight. "I need a drink."

Grabbing his jeans off the floor, he headed toward the kitchen and his liquor stash. Dusty stared numbly at the empty space he left in the bed and pulled the sheet up to her chin. Jake had suffered the same kind of loss she had. Instead of losing a brother as she had lost Mac, he was the brother who had lost a little sister, a sister who had followed him around as she had followed Mac.

He came back in the bedroom, sitting down on the edge of the bed, his bare back to her, and drank the burning liquor.

"After the accident," he rumbled into the drained glass, "my mother packed up all her clothes and a lot of the furniture and moved to Salt Lake City. She never came back, and Dad never even mentioned her name. I didn't see her again until I went to Salt Lake by myself after I was almost grown. She looked at me as if I were a ghost. I guess, in her mind, I was as dead as Penny."

Slamming his empty glass on the bedside table, he turned to face her, resting one jean-clad knee against her hip. "I'll never forget what she said to me. She called the mountains hard and cold. She said they killed everything human." He absently stroked the line of her leg under the sheet. "She looked at me with the coldest eyes I have ever seen, and she said only the hard and the ugly could live in these mountains. Then she closed the door in my face."

Dusty gasped and reached for him, pulling the coolness of his bare chest against her warm breasts. He shuddered at the warmth of the kisses she rained in the crook of his neck and up the plane of his cheeks and across his closed eyes. When he began to speak again, his voice was muffled in her hair as he held her close.

"I tried for years to forget seeing my mother. I told myself she was wrong. Then I married, and the woman I married, a girl really, left me, ran back to the city. She said that the city was a place made for people. She ran away from the empty space of the mountains and the cold silence of long winters. Then I remembered what my mother had said, and I decided she had been right." Dusty groaned in protest, but Jake's strong arms held her tight, silencing her. Against her cheek she felt the steady beat of his heart. "I knew I belonged on the ranch. The hard work of ranching was all I knew, and, for me, it was enough."

He paused, looking down at her tawny hair nestled against his shoulder. "Until you came along," he said softly. "At first you made me remember little Penny. With a difference, of course," he said wryly and she leaned back to look up into his eyes. "After I held you in my arms—when we danced at the Waterhole, I didn't feel very brotherly about you." Her eyes smiled at him, and her head nestled back into his shoulder. "What you made me remember was Penny's softness and her laughter. She would trade a hug for a ride on my horse. She'd sit in the saddle while I led the horse, and she'd laugh." He didn't say "like you laugh" but Dusty knew, and she smiled into his shoulder.

"Then I read your thesis about those families and generations of families living on the land." Dusty stilled, waiting breathlessly for what he would say about what she had written.

"For the first time, I began to doubt what my mother had said. All this open space wasn't empty to the people you wrote about. It was filled with life. Those people were as rooted in the land as the sagebrush and cottonwoods. But most important to them was sharing their feelings about the land with one another and with their children." His voice clouded, and he had to clear his throat before he could go on. "I've never shared the land with anyone, Dusty, but I want to share it with you." She leaned back to look at him. She could read tension in the rigid grooves of his face. "Since you started working on the ranch, even a cattle drive is different," he said, his eyes earnest. "I've never been so alive."

"Most of the time," she reminded him, "you've just been irritated."

"Yeah, that, too." He smiled, the lines of his face relaxing a bit. "I've been irritated—and worried. But, at the same time, the mountains are taller, the horses are livelier. Even the sagebrush smells good." He cupped her chin, his thumb brushing her bottom lip. "I love you, Dusty."

She traced her eyes over the face his mother called hard and ugly, and then she dropped her gaze to his powerful shoulders and the sinewy muscles of his arms. There wasn't a spare ounce on him anywhere; he was hard and tough, able to ride long hours over the most rugged country or survive the deepest bone-cold winter, but he wasn't hard like his mother meant. No, his hardness wasn't inhuman; it was the hardness of survival. He didn't live a gentle life, but what he made her feel was the gentlest, sweetest kind of loving. It had slipped inside her like the wind in aspen leaves.

Tears misted her eyes, and she smiled at him, a tremulous, glad smile. He clasped her to him, holding her against his heart. "I want you to marry me. Soon. Before my heart gives out from worrying about you."

"Marry?" she whispered against his shoulder.

"Yeah. Marry me. We could make children together and teach them to love the land. We could build a family like the ones you wrote about."

Family. The word twisted her heart. She had written about families that poured themselves into the land. Families—like hers. "Oh, no," she groaned. The last of her family had died with Blackie, and she had learned how much it hurt to have all that sharing torn out of her life. "No," she groaned again.

"That's what people who love each other do, Dusty," he said softly in her hair. "They get married. You do love me, don't you?" He looked down at her bowed head.

"Yes," she breathed, feeling his arms clutch her closer. "I love you, but..." It hurt too much to go on. Families die. Vera, Mac, Blackie. Families die. Tears spilled out from behind her tightly closed lids. How could she bear the pain of sharing so much again? Just the thought of Jake's children, children from her body, opened fresh wounds, raw wounds of grief not yet healed. "I can't explain," she whispered. "I'm sorry, I can't."

"Shh, don't cry," he whispered hoarsely, holding her tightly. "It's all right. I won't press you." He fought his impatience, sternly telling himself to be satisfied with whatever she could give him. After all, she had admitted she loved him. That had to be enough. For now.

Chapter Eleven

Later, when Jake was sitting in the chair pulling on his boots, he remembered his conversation with Gomez. Dusty was making sandwiches in the kitchen. He stopped in the doorway, not sure how to tell her about T.J., not sure even how she would react to his talking with Gomez. She might resent his butting in without telling her first.

"Dusty," he said, leaning his shoulder against the door-frame, "I rode up Bull Creek this morning."

She looked up from slicing the cheese. "All the way up to the rock slide?"

"Yeah." He shrugged.

"Thank you," she said, smiling at him.

If she isn't the damnedest woman, he thought. I expect her to jump all over me and she just smiles. "I saw Gomez." She looked up again at that. "He was tending some sheep up there." She waited for him to finish, knife suspended in space. "He mentioned something that kind of bothers me. He said T.J. was up there last week."

"That's not unusual. T.J. was born in these mountains. I wouldn't be surprised to see him anywhere. Besides, he'd want to see where Blackie was found."

"That's not what bothered Gomez. He said he used to see T.J. a lot in the mountains, but before, he always stopped to drink a cup of coffee. You know how the herders enjoy company. Gomez thought it was strange T.J. hung around in the trees and didn't come out to visit."

She put down the knife and considered what Jake had told her. She couldn't deny T.J. certainly had a grudge against Jake. But she had never known T.J. to be anything but the gentlest of men. Except recently. "No," she said finally, "I can't believe T.J. would hurt a member of my family. He was here when my mother died and when Mac died. He was devastated by Blackie's death. No, Jake, not T.J."

"Okay, you know him a lot better than I do. But I think we should mention what Gomez said to Dan Reed."

"Tell the sheriff?"

"Yes, I think we should."

"Okay. But let's wait until tomorrow. I want to look around a little first. Satisfy my curiosity." She concentrated on the sandwiches, waiting for Jake's objection. She felt his hesitation, sensed it in his stillness. "I'm glad you told me about your sister," she said, facing him, leaning her hip against the counter because she needed the support. "It helps me understand all your fussing and your coddling." Cautiously, Jake eased himself into a chair. He could feel it coming, her declaration of independence. "But it doesn't excuse it. You can't keep me caged up. I'll die that way."

He sighed, a ragged sound, and stared at his rough hands. "I know." His hands rubbed together restlessly. "Letting you loose, knowing you could be in God knows what danger will be the hardest thing I've ever had to do." He dropped his head into his hands. "I pray to God I have the courage."

She looked at his bowed head. "I have to find out the truth about Blackie's death. I can't let the mountains hide the secret from me. To live in peace I have to find out what happened. Trust me, Jake. Trust me to know what I have to do."

He looked up at her, his eyes dull with pain. "Dusty, I've never trusted anyone, man or woman, in my life."

"I know that," she said quietly. "I understand that trusting me is hard for you. But, if you love me, you have to trust me. I have to make my own decisions." She looked at him, her gaze steady. "And you have to stop keeping secrets from me. You have to trust me with all the truth."

Jake shifted uneasily under her gaze. "There's something I have to tell you. It's not anything big," he said quickly. "It's just, if you're going to talk about trust, I have to tell you about it." He let out a breath. "We had a fire in one of last year's haystacks. It did a lot of damage to one of my best hay fields, and I'll probably have to buy some hay to make up for the loss. Especially if we have a bad winter."

"When was the fire?"

"Several weeks ago."

"Oh. You didn't tell me because you didn't want me to have another reason to poke around after whoever set the fire."

"Yes."

"But you're telling me now to show me that you trust me."

"Yes," he said evenly. Then he dropped his head into his hands and sighed. "I know you're not responsible for my demons, Dusty, and you can't make them go away. But the image of you ending up like...like..." He couldn't say the words. She went to him, putting her arms around him and feeling him tremble.

"I'll be careful, Jake," she whispered. "I promise."

* * *

Jake watched her ride out to look at the broken places in the fence. He sat in his saddle and watched her until she disappeared over a rise. Then he forced himself to ride in the opposite direction. He hoped to hell that cutting out bulls would keep his mind off what she could be doing.

Since Jake had told her exactly where to look, the patches in the fence weren't hard to find. She looked down the fence line, but Jake and Hooter had already checked all the way to the road, trying to run down how the thief had transported the cattle. They'd found nothing. Not a tire track. Not even a cow-pie. Dusty decided she would make her way up into the mountains, riding along Big Piney Creek.

Big Piney roared and twisted down from the mountains in giant ess-curves that looped in on themselves forming a wide swath of thick willows. Dusty rode on the outer edge of the willows, heading upstream. The slopes of the mountains stretched out on all sides of her, rolling away in convoluted wrinkles. The peaks themselves stayed hidden behind their lesser hills. The immensity of the land overwhelmed her. The high country was so large, so riddled with canyons and creeks and deep stands of timber. So many places to hide. So many places that might not see a human being all year long.

She stopped where a rivulet of gushing water crossed under True Blue's feet. She looked up for the source of the water. There were so many of these springs, erupting high up on a slope. Many of them came out of small canyons, sharp walls rising above a vee of mossy green. Above her, the clusters of trees leveled off and rose again, rising like steps up the slope. Curious about this particularly lively ribbon of water, she headed True upward toward the source. She went in and out of trees, crossing tiny meadows rich with a rainbow of wildflowers and entering sheltering aspen with their canopy of clean green.

She felt bemused, distracted by the beauty and peace of this part of the mountains. Perhaps that's why the roll of fencing wire startled her. It sat plumply, barbs breaking the smooth roundness, like a steely cactus by the white elegance of an aspen trunk. She dismounted and walked into the trees. Immediately, she came upon a small clearing. The back walls were rock and the floor was trampled grass, closely cropped and littered with cow droppings.

"I think I better get out of here," she mumbled to herself. The sound of her own voice broke through the shock, and she felt the cold dampness of fear settle on her shoulders.

Urging True Blue to go as fast as she dared, she made it all the way down the slope. When she reached the willows of Big Piney Creek, she stopped to breathe in gulps of air. She had to get down to the ranch to alert someone to what she had found.

A flash of movement in a stand of trees ahead of her caught her eye just before she saw the flare of a rifle shot. The bullet tunneled through the air straight for True's head. The terrified horse reared wildly at the explosion of air so close to his nostrils. Seized by panic, Dusty lost her balance in the saddle for the first time in her life.

That was the last thing she knew before she fell to the rocky ground.

Ol' Yeller had just cornered a particularly stubborn bull when Jake's restless worry broke through all his defenses. Jake stared into the hot eyes of the frustrated bull, and a chill crept down his backbone. That damn woman was going to head up into the mountains—alone. Once she left the perimeters of his land and entered public land, he'd never be able to find her. He had to get to her before she got herself too far into the vast terrain, too lost in the forest for him to help her.

Yeller snorted in exasperation because Jake didn't let him follow through with the bull. Like the excellent cow horse he was, Yeller had no appreciation for anything that kept him from outwitting a bull. He balked when Jake gave him the signal to stop, but he did what Jake said even if his rider had gone suddenly crazy.

Damn, Jake cursed to himself, now she's made my horse doubt me.

He barely said anything at all to Hooter before he took off in a cloud of dust, scattering the cows unlucky enough to be nearby. Puzzled at one more strange piece of behavior, Hooter watched his departing boss and shook his head in wonder.

"What's got into him?" Ollie asked, pulling up beside his father.

"Well, now, I'm not sure," his father drawled, "but I'd say it probably has something to do with a little cowgirl we both know. There's no animal in this world more foolish than a cowboy in love."

At the north fence, Jake crossed Big Piney Creek and searched along the bank for evidence of Dusty's horse. When he squeezed through a notch between two low hills, he almost turned back, but he thought maybe Dusty had taken the high ground on the shoulder of the hill. The creek bed had widened into the broad ess-curves of its basin before he found anything reliable, a definite trail coming off the shoulder of the hill and following the edge of the wide swath of willows.

He was looking back toward the brow of the hill when the rifle shot cracked the air like a single blast of thunder. For one eternally long second, he couldn't move. He and Yeller were like one statue leaning in the direction of the shot but unable to move toward it. In that ghastly space of frozen time, he told himself the sound could be all kinds of things, things not related to Dusty. Some greenhorn playing at target practice. A seismic crew setting off a blast of dynamite.

But he knew. Down deep he knew that what had frightened him since the day Gomez found Blackie had finally happened.

Yeller seemed to know, as well. Suddenly, the big horse strained with his urgency to cover the distance between him and the hollow echo of the shot. Horse and rider climbed steep rises and fought their way around downed trees and slid down rocky inclines. The distance seemed interminable. Now and again, Jake picked up Dusty's trail, but there was no sign of the distinctive gray-blue horse or its tawny-haired rider.

He had just emerged from the gloom of lodgepole pine that covered a cutaway rise in the creek bank when he spotted True Blue. Down below him, Dusty's horse stood with his backside pushed into the sheltering willows and shifted nervously from foot to foot. His rein ends trailed the ground, and the sweat-stained leather of his saddle sat empty.

Jake's heart banged against his ribs as he and Yeller covered the ground to the frightened horse. When they reached him, True skittered away from them, his eyes blank and his ears flat against his head.

"Whoa there, True," Jake crooned in a cracked, dry voice. He dismounted and approached the horse slowly. "Shh, boy, hold still now," he said, stroking the horse's neck and searching frantically for some sign of blood. "Where is she, True? Where is she, dammit?"

True snorted and tossed his head, twitching his ears but keeping them flattened back. Jake's eyes followed the direction of the horse's head, searching the boulder-strewn slope that rose beside the willows. He spotted what looked to be a hat in the weeds by a chalky boulder.

He moved around the horse, fighting the slow motion of his panic-stricken limbs. Then he saw her, lying as still as a stone between two low-lying boulders. He would never know how he managed to get to the deathly stillness of her

202 HIGH COUNTRY COWBOY

body. One second he was standing by True Blue's head and the next he was up the slope and kneeling by Dusty. She was curled on her side, her head resting on a flat rock as if she were sleeping in her own bed. The loose rocks by her head were stained with blood.

"God, no," he pleaded. "Dusty, please, no." His eyes searched her for some sign of a gunshot wound. His throat closed, choking him and seizing his chest in a fist of agony. He touched her cheek with trembling fingers.

Just beyond the tips of his fingers, one set of long suntipped eyelashes fluttered. Then fluttered again.

"Dusty," he breathed, pressing anxious fingers along the edge of her jaw to search for a pulse. Finding a steady, strong beat with the pad of his middle finger, he bent his head and closed his eyes with relief. "Dusty," he breathed again, unaware of the tears that slipped from beneath his closed lids and slid over his hard cheeks.

Her eyebrows furrowed together in pain and she moaned, a low growl of sound. Her shoulders straightened and pushed her over on her back. "Don't move, sweetheart," he whispered urgently. "Please don't move. Be very still."

He could see the cut on her forehead. It was caked with blood and grit. He couldn't tell if it resulted from a bullet wound or from hitting the loose rocks when she fell off her horse. He moved his hands over her arms and legs, searching for broken bones. Everything seemed whole and miraculously sound. Burying his face in one hand, he gripped the jean-clad muscle of her calf with the other, gratefully relishing the resilience of her flesh.

"Thank God," he said into his hand, before swiping at the unaccountable tears that streamed down his cheeks.

"I fell," she groaned, stretching out the words woozily. Both of her hands clutched at her head.

"Don't move," he said quickly, grasping her wrists and gently lowering them. He cupped her cheek in his big hand.

"Don't move, sweetheart. Stay very still. Can you hear me?"

"J-Jake?" she mumbled, squinting her eyes to focus on him. "Where am I?"

"It's okay, sweetheart. Close your eyes. You hit your head." He passed his hand gently over her eyes to encourage the lids to close. A head injury might give her trouble with her eyes. "Do you remember what happened? How did you fall?"

"What…you d-doing here? You playing…m-mother hen again?" She licked her dry lips. Her voice sounded woozy but definitely irritated. Jake chuckled thankfully at the irritation. "Get me water," she demanded.

"Promise me you won't move while I get the canteen from your saddlebag."

"What?" she said, rolling her head on the stone.

"Don't move, Dusty," he said sternly.

"You don't have to bark at me," she complained.

"Like hell," he growled. Trying to be as quick as possible, he loped down to the horses. But, before he could get back to her, she pushed herself up on her elbows, rotating her shoulders. "I said, don't move," he shouted, coming back with the canteen.

"I heard you," she said, taking the canteen from him when he tried to pour some water in her mouth. "Watch out. You're going…get me wet. I c-can do it."

"Dusty," he said tightly, taking off his hat and wiping his sleeve across his face. He put his hat back on firmly and clenched his teeth against railing at her.

She squinted at him with a grin. "Call me sweetheart again. That sounded b-better." She shoved herself into a sitting position and then dropped her head into her hands. "God, my head hurts."

He rubbed his eyes tiredly and took the canteen from her. When she tried to move again, he helped her lean against a boulder, lifting her as gently as he could, then keeping his hands on her shoulders until he was sure she wouldn't try to rise. She lolled her head back on the grainy surface of the rock.

Her fingers found the wound. She held her hand out in front of her and squinted at it. "I'm bleeding."

"Yes, you damn well are."

"You're cursing at me."

He sighed. "Have some pity on me, sweetheart. Do what I tell you for once. Don't move."

She tried to smile at the endearment and he cupped her cheek again. When she turned her head just enough to kiss his hand, the simple gesture took his breath away. She had such power over him. She held his soul. He had just come through an eternity of fearing her dead and lost to him, the longest hell he had ever known. Heaven was feeling her kiss, a soft wetness, on his worn hand.

"Dusty, do you remember what happened? What made you fall?"

"There was a rifle shot," she said, opening her eyes carefully. "Is True Blue all right?" She pushed at the ground, trying to get up. Jake pushed her against the rock with firm hands.

"True is fine. He's a little nervous but the shot missed him. It missed both of you, thank God," he said. "Did you see where the shot came from?"

"Those trees back there. The pines."

"Right by the creek?" He looked across the boulder-strewn clearing to the trees where he had been only a few minutes before.

"No, up a ways, back toward the bluff." She indicated the rock wall that rose up amid the trees, jutting out into the place where the pines changed to aspen. She moved only her hand in that direction, not wanting to increase the pain in her head by trying to see the spot. "I saw the flash when the rifle went off. I couldn't see who was doing the shooting. True reared up. It wasn't his fault," she added in a hurry to vindicate the horse. "I think the bullet must have gone right by his head. I was afraid it hit him. Anyway, I fell out of the saddle." She slumped wearily against the rock, rolling her head slowly. "Whoever shot the rifle must be long gone. You could go see if he left anything behind," she suggested.

"All I care about now is getting you to a doctor." He took the kerchief from around his neck and wet it with some of the water. He dabbed carefully at the wound on her forehead. She was going to have quite a lump, and she probably had sustained some concussion. It was a good sign she could remember what happened.

"Jake," she said, recalling something else she'd seen, "back in those aspen over there, I found where somebody has been holding some cattle. It's a tiny place, not big enough for more than two at a time. But I saw a roll of barbed wire and, way back up there, there's a niche in the wall and that's where cattle have been."

Jake closed his eyes. "Trust you to stumble on something you shouldn't have. No wonder you were shot at."

"Jake," she said, clutching his sleeve, "you've got to go back up there and see what you think. But first, go find out if the guy who shot at me left something that could identify him."

"No, Dusty, you were unconscious when I found you. I'm getting you to a doctor as quickly as I can."

"Listen to me, Jake." She shook his sleeve. "The guy who stole your cows was in those trees. He shot at me. You have to look for him."

"Dammit, I don't care about the damn cows. You're all I care about. Now, shut up while I try to carry you down to the horses."

She pushed at him when he tried to slip his arm behind her shoulders. "But he'll get so far away, you won't be able to catch him."

"I said, shut up. I don't care if I catch him or not."

She pushed at him again. "Jake, I don't want to move my head. It hurts too much."

"I'll help you, sweetheart," he said, slipping his hand behind her head. "Now don't move. Let me lift your head." Slowly, he lifted her head and cradled it against his shoulder. He paused. "How's that? Can you hold it there?"

"I think so. Jake," she said, stretching her arm around his neck as he scooped her up, "this would be nice if my head didn't hurt so much. Maybe we could do it again when I feel better."

"Count on it, kid," he smiled at her. "I have a threshold I want to carry you over."

She swatted him weakly. "You're taking advantage of my injury."

He stopped beside Yeller. "Do you think you can sit on the saddle while I climb up behind you?"

"No, Jake, let me ride True back to the ranch."

"Don't argue with me, Dusty. I'm carrying you back to the ranch in my arms."

"But Yeller is going to hate me if you make him carry both of us one more time."

"That horse couldn't hate you any more than I could."

"Yeah," she said as he lifted her onto the saddle, holding both her legs on one side to keep her from sitting astride. "You're two of a kind. Yeller likes my massages and you like my—"

"Hush," he interrupted, swinging up behind her. He lifted her over his thighs, cradling her head again and holding her in place with a circling arm. "I guess you're going to be okay. You're getting outrageous again."

She started to laugh and then pressed her hand to her head. "O-o-o, don't make me laugh. It hurts."

He batted her hand away. "Don't touch it. Your hand is filthy. You'll get more dirt in the wound."

"Jake, what about True?" Her hand pushed against his shoulder. "I'm not going to leave him up here. We don't know if whoever shot at me is still around or not. Something could happen to True.''

"Okay. I'll use my rope to put him on a lead.''

"He won't like that. It'll hurt his pride.''

"Dammit, Dusty, stop worrying about the horse and think about me. I need to hold you right now.'' His arm around her shoulders tightened, and his other hand pressed her cheek to his chest. His breath brushed over her forehead like a kiss. "I thought for the longest minutes of my life you were dead. Now I have to convince myself you're not, that I can breathe again.'' He shifted her more securely on his lap and reached for his rope. "Stay as still as possible while I work a loop over True's head and secure his reins.''

Dusty looped her arms around Jake, holding him tightly, both to reduce the jar of the ride on her head and to hold to herself the raw emotion of his concern for her. Later, she told herself, hold all this sweetness for later when you can enjoy it.

Hooter had just gotten back to ranch headquarters when he saw them coming and rode out to meet them. Jake sat hunched in the saddle, the curve of his body protective around Dusty. He had tied off True Blue and looped his own reins around the saddle horn to use both arms to hold her. Yeller was on his own, leading them back to the ranch and safety. Even with the protective coddling, the pain had washed Dusty's cheeks with tears, soaking into Jake's shirt, as well.

Jake barely looked up at Hooter's approach, and Dusty kept her eyes tightly closed. Hooter took over True Blue's lead.

"What the hell happened?'' Hooter demanded. "That's a nasty-looking cut on her forehead.''

"She fell off her horse,'' Jake answered. Jake kept his attention focused on Dusty. His voice was low, so low Hooter had to strain to hear him.

"She fell off her horse? Off True Blue?" Hooter blared. "I don't believe it." Dusty flinched at the sudden loud noise.

Jake cut his eyes at Hooter. "Keep your voice down," he warned. Then he added, "Somebody shot at her."

"My God," exclaimed Hooter in his growly version of a whisper. "Was she hit? Is that what bloodied her forehead?"

"I don't think so. I think she hit her head on some loose rocks. The bullet must've been closer to True Blue, from the way he was acting. I think he almost bolted and ran away. When I found him, he was still nervous. He acted like he was in shock."

"You think whoever shot at Dusty could be our cattle thief?"

"Probably. Dusty found some barbed wire and a place where somebody penned up some cattle." Hooter whistled through his teeth. "I want you to take Jeep and Carl and go up there and look around. I'll tell you where we were. You should have just enough time to get there and back before dark."

"Sure. I'll take Ollie, too. We won't have much time."

"Why don't you leave True with me and take off right now?" Hooter nodded. "It's up Big Piney Creek beyond the narrows. Follow the—"

"No," Dusty said weakly, her voice muffled by Jake's shirt.

"What is it, sweetheart?" Jake said instantly. Hooter's eyes widened at the endearment.

"Can't...all go," she said haltingly, eyes tightly shut. "Somebody...take care...of True and Yeller."

"Oh, Lord," Jake said between clenched teeth.

"She's Blackie's daughter, Jake," Hooter said, grinning. "You'd have to shoot her for sure before she'd forget the horses. I always said Blackie's horses were pampered. Now, yours are."

"Okay," Jake said, resigned, "leave Ollie at the barn to take care of Yeller when we get in. You go ahead with True and leave him with Ollie, too. Satisfied?" he asked Dusty.

"Okay," she said, trying to grin.

Jake gave directions to Hooter, telling him to look for evidence of the rifle shot in the pines, maybe a casing or something, and to send someone up into the aspen to find the cattle pen. He told Hooter not to waste any time and to leave the high country before the men were caught in the dark.

At ranch headquarters, Jake instructed Ollie to call the clinic and the sheriff, in that order. After a jarring ride into Big Piney, he protectively unloaded his pain-racked cargo at the small clinic. Then, holding Dusty huddled in his arms, he stormed past the sheriff, who leaned against his truck outside, and Ruth, who paced the tiny waiting room. Ruth hovered all the way to an examination room before standing off to the side, her arms folded across her chest and her mouth firmly shut.

Doc Brophy shuffled into the room and started poking and prodding. Jake answered his questions before Dusty could make the effort. At last, the doctor straightened up and patted Dusty's shoulder affectionately. "Well, Dusty, I guess you escape with a beauty of a headache."

"Can you give her something for the pain?" Jake asked.

The doctor blinked at him thoughtfully and drawled, "Yes, I can. I plan to do that. But first, tell me what I'm supposed to do with Dan Reed. I think the sheriff has some questions he wants to ask her."

"Damn his questions," Jake snapped. "She's in pain." Dusty slipped her hand over Jake's fist and gave him a wobbly smile. "It's okay," she said. "I've made it this far. I can hold out a little longer."

"Why don't I give you some pills to swallow?" the doctor offered. "You can answer his questions while they take effect. Okay?"

"Sure," she said.

Jake held her head while she swallowed the pills, abruptly pushing away the doctor's hands. "Tell Reed," he said, "to come in here to ask his questions. Let's get it over with."

The doctor nodded and left to do Jake's bidding. Ruth snorted in the background but refrained from saying anything.

The sheriff entered the small room, eyeing each person in turn from under the brim of his hat, first Ruth, who rated a nod, then Jake, who got a hard-eyed glare, and then Dusty. He cocked his head at her, settled onto one leg and took a deep breath. "Okay, let's have it. What happened?"

Jake insisted on telling the story. He told the sheriff to listen to him first and ask Dusty questions later. The sheriff crossed his arms above his paunch and let Jake have his way.

When Jake finished, Reed looked pointedly from Jake to Dusty. "Now," he said, "tell me about that fencing you saw. Was it rusted?"

Dusty squeezed Jake's hand reassuringly. "It looked new to me. Shiny."

"What kind? Barbed wire?"

"Yes, barbed wire."

"Uh-huh," the sheriff mused out loud, twisting his mouth. "Now, tell me about those cattle signs. How recent?"

"Very recent. Flies were still buzzing the piles."

"My guess is," the sheriff said, "they won't use that place no more. Not if they know you found it. Too many other places to hide cows up there." He hitched up his pants. "Now, about that rifle shot. You sure that's what it was?"

"I heard it myself," Jake said from a stiff jaw.

"Uh-huh." He gave Jake a hard look, then turned to Dusty, "Say you saw where the shot came from?" he asked.

"Yes. It came from some pines."

"Not the same place where you found the cow signs?"

"No."

"Uh-huh. 'Course, the shot could've had nothing to do with the rustlers. Could've been some poacher. Might've mistook you for a trophy deer."

"You know very well it was no poacher," Jake said, exasperated with the sheriff's stubborn contrariness.

Reed hooked his thumbs in his belt. "Don't know nothing 'til I look into it."

Jake sighed. "There's something else. I talked with Gomez early this morning." The morning seemed an eternity ago. So much had happened since. He told Reed briefly about Gomez's observations of T.J. As he expected, the sheriff seemed less than impressed.

"T.J.?" the sheriff scoffed. "Naw, T.J. is nothing but harmless. Harmless ol' man with nothing left but eating money, a beat-up ol' truck and a ramshackle place. Sure, he don't like you none, Valiteros, but that description fits a lot of folks around here."

"Jake," Dusty said tentatively, "I can't believe T.J. would shoot at me. He would never want to hurt me."

"T.J. shoot at Dusty?" Ruth spoke up. "That's ridiculous."

The sheriff snorted, "If he did, he sure as hell wouldn't miss. T.J.'s a dead shot."

Ruth nodded curtly. "That's for sure."

Reed jerked his hat down on his forehead. "Anything else I need to know?"

"No, nothing," Jake answered.

"Uh-huh. Here's what I'll do about this. It's too late to get up Big Piney Creek today. That'll have to wait for the morning. Manure won't go away overnight, anyhow. Anything else, Hooter'll probably find today. I'll be out to your place early tomorrow, Valiteros, and you can lead me up to this cattle pen and shooting range. In the meantime, you better convince this young lady to stay put. Quit snooping around getting herself into trouble."

"I'm with you there," Ruth said.

Jake tried to keep from smiling at the indignant expression on Dusty's face. "Shh," he warned her, "you can tell Reed what you think of his advice when you feel better."

The sheriff snorted and started for the door. Jake stopped him.

"Just a minute," Jake said sternly. "I'd appreciate it if you'd at least look in on T.J. I know you and Dusty and Ruth—" he looked wryly at Ruth "—think he's harmless, but I'm not so sure. It wouldn't hurt to check him out."

"Listen here, Valiteros. I got too much to do to waste time poking around out at T.J.'s. But since I know you won't let it rest until I do, I tell you what.... When we get back from upcountry tomorrow, I'll take myself a drive over to see T.J. Will that satisfy you?"

"I guess it'll have to."

"Good. Tell Hooter to fix me up with a mount tomorrow morning. My deputy, too. Now, all of you, go home and give me some rest." He stomped out the door, his heavy footsteps echoing in the empty hallway.

Ruth recrossed her arms over an indrawn breath. "The very idea. I think it's a crime to suspect poor ol' T.J.," she chided Jake. "Whoever heard of such a thing? You just don't understand what our family means to T.J."

"Don't, Ruth," Dusty pleaded.

"Okay, honey," Ruth said, stepping up to stroke Dusty's hair back from the fresh bandage on her forehead. "I'll hush. I know Dan Reed wouldn't hurt ol' T.J., anyhow."

"Excuse me," the doctor interrupted. "If the sheriff is finished with his business, Dusty, I'd like to know if the medicine is working. You feeling those pills yet?"

"Yes." Dusty smiled weakly. "I'm getting nicely drowsy."

"That's good. Now, what are we going to do with you for the night? I'd like to keep you for observation, just to be sure. But we're not equipped for that. So maybe Ruth here'll take over."

Dusty felt Jake stiffen.

Ruth said quickly, "Of course, I will, Doc. Dusty's my niece," she added for Jake's benefit. "That's why Doc's nurse called me when she heard Dusty was coming in. I'll take Dusty home with me. Got my truck right outside."

"Good," said the doctor, nodding.

"No," said Jake in a voice like cold steel. "When Dusty leaves here, she goes home with me. I'll take care of her."

"No, you don't," Ruth protested vehemently. "Why, she's weak as a kitten. You can't take care of her."

"I can and I will." Jake fixed Ruth with his blue granite stare. "Nobody takes care of Dusty but me."

"Haven't you done enough?" Ruth seethed. "This whole town is boiling with talk. Dirty talk. You're going to make it worse. You ruin her name and get her shot at, too. It's time her family stepped in and stopped you."

"No, Ruth," Dusty said as she grabbed her aunt's arm. "Please don't say any more." She forced her eyes to focus on Jake. The creases in his cheeks were deeper, harder, and he avoided looking at her. If she hadn't known him better, she would say he looked defeated. She felt the sting of tears at the idea of a defeated Jake.

"I'm sorry, Ruth," she said gently. "Jake's right. I have to go with him. Don't worry. You go home and cook supper for Ed. I'll be fine."

Jake didn't wait any longer. He scooped up Dusty, holding her tightly in his arms, and headed for the front door of the clinic and his truck outside. Ruth sputtered after them, but she had no more effect on Jake than a pesky horsefly. He paused only to grab pills from Doc Brophy and to listen to Doc's shouted instructions.

Chapter Twelve

Jake drove slowly, carefully avoiding all the bumps he could, toward his big house. He carried Dusty upstairs, despite her protests to let her walk this time, and laid her on his bed, pushing her hands away when she tried to undress herself. After fighting the fear of losing her, he needed the reassurance of seeing her lying on his bed with the walls of his house around her. Tension made his fingers awkward, as they worked at her buttons and zippers. But even in his clumsiness, he touched her almost reverently. His flesh cherished hers with every touch.

When he had stripped her of all her clothes, he sat down beside her on the edge of the bed. She lay still as he stroked her skin from her shoulders down. His eyes kissed her: her breasts, her stomach, the hollows of her hips, her thighs, her calves. Finally, he brought his eyes back to hers. She was surprised to see the deep blue of his eyes shimmering with tears.

She reached up to hold his face with both hands and urged him down to touch him with her lips. She kissed his hard cheeks, the bridge of his nose and his eyelids. Then she wrapped her arms around him and held him to her. She rocked him gently in her arms, loving the dampness where he buried his face in the curve of her shoulder.

"You know," she said quietly in his ear, "before I go completely to sleep, I sure would like a bath."

"I think I can manage that," he said, chuckling roughly. "Don't move. Stay in bed while I run some water in the tub."

"Okay," she said softly.

While she soaked in the tub, Jake called Gaylene. He asked her to drive over to Dusty's place to get clothes and whatever else she thought Dusty might need. Gaylene was delighted to be of help. Jake grimaced at her enthusiasm, knowing she would share every detail with everyone she could reach by phone and a few she couldn't.

"I'll leave right this minute, Jake," she burbled into the phone.

"Thanks, Gaylene." Jake sighed resignedly. "Let me speak to Hooter before you run out the door."

Hooter reported that there was no sign of a bullet, just some trampled undergrowth in the pines. He'd brought down the roll of barbed wire Dusty found. Jake said he'd take a look at it in the morning before riding back up the creek with the sheriff.

Coming back to Dusty, Jake lifted her out of the tub and wrapped her in an enormous towel. Sitting with her on his lap on the closed toilet seat, he dried her.

"Who were you talking to on the phone?"

"You can't be too sleepy if you heard me on the phone."

"Jake, who was it?"

"I sent Gaylene to your house to get some things."

"Jake, you didn't." Dusty looked horrified. "That woman will tell every single person in the county."

He shrugged. "She already knows enough to make a good story." He rested his hands on her hips. "Come to think of it, she's probably doing me a favor by telling everybody she knows. I want them to know. I want everybody in the state to know you're here with me." He looked at her evenly. "And you're going to go on living here with me."

"Are you taking advantage of me when I'm injured?"

"Dusty," he said, his eyes bleak, "any other time you're spitting at me like an angry bobcat. I have to take my chances when I can."

She looped her arms around his neck and nestled her head on his shoulder. "Is it so important to you to have me live here?"

"Yes," he breathed.

"Let me think about it," she whispered. "Right now I could use another one of those pills."

"Your head is hurting again," he said, scooping her up and taking her into the bedroom.

"Yes," she said.

Later, he sat beside her until she slept soundly. She looked like a little girl when she slept, long golden lashes on her cheek, a sprinkling of freckles across her nose, the soft pinkness of her lower lip. Tomorrow, when she woke up, she'd be a stubborn woman again, but, after the terror he had been through, she belonged to him, now and forever. He had no intention of ever letting her go.

At the head of the stairs, Dusty faced the amethyst light of dawn that swam through the windows flanking the fireplace. Such gentle light, she thought, for such a hard day. The mountains across the valley to the east floated in the distant morning mist. Innocent-looking mountains, hiding their depth and their secrets. Life surrounded by mountains strained with complexity; mere survival was daunting to a weak soul.

Wind howled around the corners of the house, telling its tale of mountain secrets. In the night, clouds had gathered and boomed with thunder. Even in her drug-induced sleep, she had heard, and she had tossed uneasily. Jake took her in his arms and soothed her back into a healing rest. He feathered kisses around the bandage on her forehead and held her in the shelter of his body. Listening to the sharp voice of the morning's wind, she remembered and shivered at the cool absence of his arms.

"What are you doing out of bed?"

His low-pitched growl jerked her attention to the foot of the stairs. He stood with one boot on the bottom step and a mug of coffee in his hand. Steam rose up invitingly from the warm liquid in the cool morning air.

She descended the stairs without answering, drawn to him by the memory of his comfort in the middle of the night. On the bottom step, she paused to turn her gaze away from him and out the tall windows.

"The wind is fierce this morning," she said softly, cocking her head to hear its high whine.

"You need to rest, Dusty. Doc Brophy said for you to stay in bed today."

She moved into the lee of the leg he propped on the bottom step and circled his waist, moving her arms under his denim jacket and snuggling into the hollow of his shoulder. The jacket probably meant he was on his way out the door when he heard her on the stairs. A few more minutes and she would have escaped his interrogation, but she would have also missed touching him.

She smiled musingly and kissed the warm skin just above the chambray collar of his shirt. One arm held her loosely, and he rubbed his jaw against the coarse silk of her hair.

"Do I have to carry you back upstairs and tie you to the bed?" he asked stubbornly.

"Why don't you just share your coffee?"

Stepping back, she took the mug in both her hands and breathed in the warm steam. She walked around him and into the kitchen. He followed reluctantly.

"Okay," he said. "I'll fix you some breakfast. And then back to bed. No nonsense, Dusty. You'll make your head worse if you don't behave yourself."

She sat on one of the tall stools at the counter and watched him while he cooked some breakfast for her. She knew the less she said, the better. The constant drone of her headache protested against an argument. And she knew Jake would give her one if she let on how determined she was to get out of the house as soon as possible.

Jake would spend the morning poking around with the sheriff up Big Piney Creek. But, once they came back to the ranch, the sheriff had promised to check up on T.J. She couldn't let that happen before she saw T.J. herself to prepare him for Reed's questions. Blackie would want her to look after the old man.

After she cleaned her plate and downed her coffee, Jake said, "Now. Back to bed so I can get out of here."

"No, Jake. I'm going to ride over to T.J.'s place."

"You're going to what?" Jake glared at her, the narrow slits of his eyes glittering. "Of all the harebrained ideas . . . Why, dammit?" He slammed his fist beside her plate, making the silverware tremble nervously.

"Look," she said reasonably, "I've known T.J. all my life. When my mother died, he came to the house and took care of the horses and saw to the cattle. He did that for weeks because Blackie was too distraught to see to things himself. Then when Mac was killed in the car accident, T.J. came again to take care of things." She rested her hand on Jake's fist. "He's like a part of my family, Jake. I can't let the sheriff just show up at his place and start asking questions."

"Then wait for us to get back down from Big Piney Creek. Rest this morning and drive over there when the sheriff goes. I'll go with you."

"That won't help, Jake." She slipped off the stool and poured herself another cup of coffee. "You saw T.J. at the rodeo. I'm worried about him." She handed the mug to Jake, but he put it down on the counter, slopping some of the coffee over the rim. "He seemed so agitated. Not like himself at all."

She searched for some way to explain to Jake about T.J., some way that didn't make Jake more suspicious but helped him understand how much T.J. needed her, since she was the last of her family.

"He blames you for Blackie's losing the ranch. He thinks it's your fault."

"I guess he blames me for Blackie's death, as well."

"Yes, he does."

"Lord," he said, turning away from her.

"I'm sorry," she said, resting her aching head against the tense muscle in his upper arm. "T.J. has a tough time thinking things through. He feels a lot of resentment, and, now that Blackie's gone, he feels grief, too."

"You know as well as I do," he said wearily, "that he's not the only one who blames me for Blackie's death."

"I don't believe anyone but T.J. really takes that idea seriously. The others resent you and this ranch, but they don't really think Blackie's death was your fault. T.J. can't cope as well as most people. He's confused and very unhappy. I think maybe I can help him."

He put his arm around her and gathered her to him. "What about your head?" he said, tilting her chin up with his index finger. "I can see you're still in pain. How are you going to cope with that?"

"I'll take some aspirin."

"You're a stubborn woman, you know that?"

"Yeah, that's why you love me." She grinned.

"God, yes." He touched his lips to hers, letting himself take a slow kiss, tasting the bittersweet pleasure of loving a difficult woman. He lifted his head and studied the white patch of bandage on her forehead. "Don't ride True. Do that much for me. Take my pickup, instead. It'll be easier on your head."

"It's a deal," she said, winding her arms around his neck for another kiss.

When Dusty pulled up in front of T.J.'s house an hour later, the wind was still blowing, whipping up the dirt of the double-track road that led to the mouth of the canyon where T.J. lived. She climbed out of Jake's truck and looked around. She had been here many times with Blackie, but never alone.

The small cinder-block house faced the rolling emptiness of sagebrush hills. From behind the house came the sound of a stream, its gurgling noise hollow in the wind. Upstream, toward the head of a box canyon, trees, a mix of aspen and evergreen, twisted up along the streambed until they broadened out in the core of the canyon.

She rapped on the peeling wood of the front door. The plank shook with her knock, rattling in its frame. Not much help in keeping out the cold of winter, she mused. No one answered her knock, not a sound, except the wind against her ears. She looked across the empty yard at the shed that served as stable for T.J.'s horse. The door stood open, a sure sign that T.J. was somewhere on horseback. His battered old truck was tucked in beside the shed, the rusty tailgate snug against its unpainted wood.

She remembered a canyon trail that began behind the shed. It led over a knoll before dipping down to the stream and following it into the trees. She and Mac had fished the stream when they were kids. Heading for the trail, she saw the fence, new wire crudely sagging between hastily planted posts. Why would T.J. want to fence in his canyon? He hated fences.

A wooden gate broke the fence, one end of the gate held up by the gnarled cedar tree that had always marked the beginning of the trail. Past the gate and the cedar tree, Dusty climbed up the steep knoll to the twin cedars that stood on either side of the trail at the top. Stopping to catch her breath, she looked down the other side.

Down below, a cow and her calf grazed idly along the edge of the trees. Standing there with the sough of the wind whispering in her ear, Dusty shuddered at the dread approach of fear. The cow's brand was partially hidden in the rough hair of her hide, but Dusty could nearly make out the vague shape of a diamond. She knew even before she made her way down the slope toward the cow. She knew the cow bore the brand of the Diamond V, Jake's brand.

The cow bawled at her approach, and the calf flashed frightened eyes, skittering away into the trees. Before it disappeared, Dusty saw the calf was a slick, untouched by the spring branding. It had been taken from its home range before branding, a convenient condition for a cattle thief.

Dusty was still staring at the unmistakable brand on the cow when a horse snorted behind her, near the spot where the trail entered the trees. She turned her head slowly, in a daze of disbelief, her eyes coming to rest on the horse and rider facing her from the trail.

First she saw T.J.'s bloodshot eyes, anguish sitting on his face as tangibly as the brand on the hide of the cow. The stubble of his chin quivered; in fact, his whole face quivered, but his hand was steady. Then she saw the rifle. It was pointed in her direction, the long black barrel a single O that floated dizzily before her eyes.

Jake and Hooter sat their horses by the north fence and waited while the sheriff and his deputy poked around the creek bank trying to find evidence that someone had driven cattle through there. Neither Jake nor Hooter wasted the time. There was plenty evidence of cattle in the whole area; any fool knew that.

The sheriff, too, finally gave up and pulled up beside Jake. "Okay, let's get on with it. Looks like I've got a long day ahead of me," he said with exaggerated weariness. "That is, if you still insist I go bother poor ol' T.J. I'd say the last thing that ol' man needs is to have me poke around in his business."

Hooter pulled his horse around beside the sheriff. "What's this about T.J.?"

"Your boss here has got some burr under his saddle that makes him suspect ol' T.J. of stealing cattle."

"Why T.J., Jake?"

Jake shrugged, "Just something the sheepherder Gomez said that me wonder. Dusty's convinced T.J.'s harmless."

"Dusty's probably right, I guess. T.J.'s harmless enough, but he is a character." Hooter chuckled. "A couple of weeks ago, I saw him scooting down the road to his place in that beat-up ol' pickup of his. He was carrying a load of hay in the back, and he was flat making that pickup rattle he was going so fast."

"A load of hay?" Jake asked, going very still.

"Now don't get any ideas, Valiteros," the sheriff said, spitting tobacco juice into the dirt. "Just 'cause he had a load of hay don't mean he's got animals. Why, knowing T.J., he probably wanted to dam up that spring back behind his place to make a swimming hole or something."

"Yeah," said Hooter, "that'd be just like him. When I saw him with the hay, I thought it was something like that. Anyway, I didn't give it another thought until the rodeo the other day when I was talking to some of the other ranchers around here." He shook his head, his big-crowned hat bobbing with his chuckles. "I was asking if any of them had lost any cattle lately. When I collared Tom Watson and Ed

Taylor talking together, Tom laughed at me about the cattle but he said he sure wished somebody would tell him how to keep T.J. from stealing last year's hay. Ed got all bothered with that. He said he'd been losing hay, too. He didn't have any idea it could be T.J. He'd been blaming the elk.''

"You mean, they were losing a lot of hay?" Jake demanded. Even the sheriff was interested enough to stop chewing his fresh plug of tobacco.

"Must have been quite a lot. Ed cussed himself for not figuring it out. He said Ruth would have a fit when she heard about it. Claimed he'd seen T.J. carrying hay by his place two or three times recently, but just didn't make the connection. Anyway, he promised Tom Watson that he and Ruth would go over to T.J.'s to see what they could do.'' Hooter shook his head again. "That T.J., ain't he a character?''

"Hooter," Jake said, his voice icy steel, "the only reason T.J. would need that much hay is to feed stock."

"Everybody knows the only stock T.J.'s got is that rangy ol' horse of his," said Hooter. Then Hooter's eyes widened above his wide moustache. "You know, his canyon would sure be a good place to keep stock if a body wanted to hide 'em or something.''

Jake turned narrowed eyes on Reed. His gaze had the same sharp edge as the wind that made them turn up their coat collars. "You said T.J. is a good shot?"

"The best. He's spent his whole life hunting these mountains.''

"Maybe," said Jake, "whoever shot at Dusty didn't intend to hit her. Maybe the shot was a warning."

"Could be," acknowledged the sheriff. "I sure don't think T.J. would want to hurt Dusty, her being Blackie's kid.''

Jake's blood felt like it had turned to ice. "Dusty went over to see T.J. this morning. She took my truck."

"Good God A'mighty," exclaimed the sheriff, "that little girl is determined to get herself into trouble."

"Hooter, I want you and the sheriff to go back to ranch headquarters as fast as you can," Jake said with a kind of unreal calm. "Take the sheriff's vehicle over to T.J.'s. Don't waste any time. I can make it out there faster on Yeller." He patted Yeller's neck and backed him away from the others. Yeller, reacting to Jake's tension, tossed his head and shifted impatiently. "Get a move on," Jake shouted. "Don't just stand around here gawking. Get to Dusty as fast as you can."

The sheriff yelled at his deputy, who was still rooting around in the willows, and Jake lit out along the fence, horse and rider concentrated on getting through the difficult sagebrush as quickly as possible. They headed toward the road that ran along the edge of Jake's property, easier footing for a fast ride. The road curved around long miles of pastures and grazing land before Jake and Yeller could pick up a side road that wound toward T.J.'s canyon.

In the solidity of the silence that surrounded Dusty like a shroud, one sound lay heavily on her ears, a whining, tortured sound, like the voice of the wind, but the wind couldn't reach down in the canyon. The grief-stricken keening came, instead, from the man who held the rifle.

The throbbing in her head brought up both hands to clutch the bandage. The pain and the rough gauze under her fingers broke through her trance. Forcing her eyes to look upward, she slowly took in the reality of the rifle and the man who held it.

"T.J.?" she said in a croak that pushed its way through a throat, suddenly parched. "What are you doing? You're aiming a rifle at me. No, T.J."

The keening wailed higher, like wind driven over a taut wire being stretched to the breaking point.

"Do you know me, T.J.?" she pleaded. "It's Dusty. You don't want to hurt me. I know you'd never hurt me."

Across his watery eyes, he rubbed the soiled sleeve of his undershirt, sticking out from under plaid flannel, and the wail became a blubbering sob. Dusty stepped forward, one hand outstretched toward the familiar figure from her childhood.

The explosion of the bullet that burst through the air over her head stopped her. The sobbing ceased. T.J.'s eyes stared at her, the stare dazed and wild. The end of the rifle barrel wagged slightly as if to bat away the wisp of smoke left by the bullet. Then it jerked insistently in the direction of the trail back over the grassy knoll.

Dusty obeyed the silent communication and led the way back up the trail. She pushed the red sheen of pain ahead of her, each step like walking further into a nightmare. She stumbled on loose rocks, falling forward, unable to break her fall. The rocks scraped her cheek and the palms of her hands. The horse and rider stopped behind her, neither moving toward her nor urging her to her feet. But the keening began again.

Reeling up the knoll and down again, she reached the gate before she realized it. The gate cut into her midriff, her breath coming out in a gasp. She fumbled for the loop of wire that held it shut, unfastening the wire with numb fingers. The gate yawned open on creaking hinges and swung away from her, idly coming to rest on a patch of grass behind the shed.

She stumbled through the opening, her glance catching on Jake's truck, sitting by itself on the far side of the cinder-block house. The chance for escape flashed through the throbbing in her head. Turning her head ever so slightly in T.J.'s direction, she saw him dismounting behind her. She edged toward the truck, gradually gaining speed, until the thunder of a second bullet brought her to an instantaneous halt in the middle of the open yard.

She pulled herself around to face him, trying to judge what he could be thinking. His hand was rock steady on the rifle, trained by years of practice to handle a firearm with utmost control. In awful contrast, his face twitched and his eyes leaked tears that washed over the stubble of his beard.

She knew he had one more bullet in the rifle, one more bullet in a rifle that carried the force to rip apart the body of a large elk. She retained enough of a grip on herself to realize the extreme danger of such a rifle in the hands of someone as disturbed as T.J. appeared to be. She forced herself to stand perfectly still.

"I didn't mean nothin' by it," T.J. wailed.

The high-pitched rawness of his voice made Dusty wince. His eyes roved wildly over the tops of the trees behind his house and up into the boiling clouds of the now-threatening sky. Dusty didn't make the mistake of moving again. She realized that he would respond with the swift reflexes of a cornered animal.

"I tole you, I tole you," he wailed.

"What did you tell me?" she whispered, trying to keep her voice even and low.

He didn't appear to hear her. His eyes kept up their wild search, as if he were trying to find someone in the sky, someone who wasn't there, someone he had searched for before.

"You my bes' friend. I know it," he said, sobbing. "I didn't wanna hurt you none. I couldn't help it. You seen too much. You knowed it." He raked his sleeve across his eyes again. "You my bes' friend."

The pain knifed through Dusty's head, grating like a blade with a dull edge. T.J. killed Blackie. Blackie had seen the stolen cattle and T.J. killed him because of what he had seen.

"You hid that glove from me, I knowed you did," T.J. mumbled to the ground at his feet. "I looked and looked for it. I cain't find it nowhere."

"Did you look up Bull Creek for it, T.J.?" Dusty asked softly.

T.J. looked startled for a second as if he had forgotten she was there. Slowly, his eyes focused on her. He nodded, sobbing again. "I looked ever'where. I rode clean up to where I lef'..." His voice trailed off into broken sobs.

"I wanted to keep Blackie's gloves. Keep sumpthin' that belonged to my bes' friend. I looked ever'where for it."

"Did you lose only one of the gloves, T.J.?" Dusty asked, being careful to remain still.

His eyes narrowed. "You stole it," he said. "You stole th' only one of Blackie's gloves I got lef'. Didn't you?" He stepped toward her, the rifle barrel inches from her face.

"No, T.J.," she said, trying to hold his eyes on hers. "I didn't steal the glove. It's okay for you to have it. I don't even know where it is."

"You git in th' house. I'll see if you stole it." He nudged her with the rifle, pushing her toward the house.

Her mind frantically searched for some way to stay outside the tiny house. She thought she had a better chance of getting away from him if she could remain out in the open. She measured the distance to the woodpile and the ax leaning against it. Too far and T.J. was too close. Even the truck was too far away. She'd never make it.

"Git," T.J. said, pushing the cold rifle barrel against her shoulder blade. He clamped his big hand on her shoulder, shoving her forward. She twisted instinctively at the force of his grip, but he increased the pressure, shoving her relentlessly in front of him. At the rickety steps, his grip lifted her toward the peeling door, shoving her against it, the force of her body thrusting it open.

The dim interior had the coolness of a cave. There were high narrow windows in the thick walls of the one room, but only at the front and the back. What appeared to be the kitchen area, an old wood stove and a shelf counter with a sink, lined the back wall. An oilcloth-covered table took up the center of the room. She could remember being inside these shabby quarters only once or twice in her life.

She stumbled inside, her forward movement projecting her into a straight-back chair that stood beside the table. The big hand jerked her back, forcing her to sit on the rumpled cot against the front wall. Above her head, T.J. rooted through a collection of junk on the windowsill until he pulled out a length of rope.

With surprising dexterity, he forced her arms behind her back, tying her hands together with the length of rope. As she felt the rope tighten on her wrists, she gazed dumbly at the coils of thicker rope that hung from pegs on the side wall. Hysteria bubbled up in her throat. A childhood memory. Blackie laughing at T.J.'s collection of rope. T.J. saying, never know when you're gonna need a good piece of rope.

"That'll hold you," he said. "Sit right there and don't you move." He touched her bandage with a grimy finger. "I shot at ya yest'dy, but I din hit ya."

"No," she said, forcing down the fear at his touch. "I hit my head on some rocks. Did you try to shoot me, T.J.?"

"Naw," he shook his shaggy head, "naw, I jist wanted to skeer ya off, is all. I din wanna hafta shoot ya, li'l Dusty."

He slumped into the chair, facing her with the rifle across his knees. He looked past her to the corner that served as the head of the makeshift bed. Steeling herself to remain calm, she followed his gaze, her breath catching at what she saw. There, on the uncovered ticking of a pillow, lay Blackie's glove, the mate of the one she had found in the trees above Bull Creek.

"You cain't have it," T.J. roared, his voice loud in the small space. "You don't deserve it nohow. I seen you. You done took up with that no-good crook." His eyes hardened, flashing at her in the near darkness. "But I knowed how to git him. He put his cows on my place, the land he stoled from my fam'ly. He put up fences. He fenced all the pasture, but I knowed what to do to fences."

His voice changed to pleading. "I warned you. I tole you to go away. I knowed you'd git hurt. You're Blackie's girl." He sobbed. "You want the glove. But you cain't have it." He wiped his eyes. "It's all I got lef'."

Fear rose in her throat like bile, but she had to ask. She had to know. "T.J., what happened to Blackie? Please tell me." His sobs became the wail she had heard on the trail. "I need to know, T.J. Tell me what happened to my father," she insisted as firmly as she dared.

He stared at the butt of his rifle, rubbing it with his big paw of a hand. He rubbed vigorously as if he were trying to get it clean. "He seen the cows. Blackie seen the cows. He wuz standin' there lookin' at 'em."

He rolled his tortured eyes to the ceiling. "I come up behin' 'im. I had my rifle, but I couldn't shoot. He wuz Blackie. I cudden shoot Blackie." He wailed, "I din mean to hurt 'im. I jist hadda knock 'im out."

He raised the rifle in both hands, making a club of the butt. When his hands were above his head, sobs overtook him again. He brought the rifle back to his knees with such force that Dusty jumped. "I shook and shook 'im, but he don't move," he wailed. "I hit too hard."

One hand opened palm up on the rifle barrel. He looked at it helplessly, shaking his head at his own strength. Dusty's tears spilled over onto her cheeks, silent tears for the story she had to hear.

Then the words spilled out, stuttering over one another. "I din know whut to do. I wanted to bury 'im because he wuz my friend. But I din want somebody to come lookin' for him. So I fixed it so he'd be foun'. I tied 'im to his horse and rode crost the mountains. I rode most th' night. I took Blackie up Bull Creek. Nobody went up there 'til the snow melts. 'Cept Blackie. I knowed he done it. So I took 'im. He'd a liked that, being lef' up in th' mountains. I knowed he would. I lef' his horse down in th' trees. Keep 'im out of th' weather.''

The words stopped. His breath rasped loudly, long watery sounds. Dusty's body curved over her lap, tears making wet stains on the dark denim. In the distance, thunder rolled around the mountaintops.

Closely following the thunder came the rapid staccato of a horse's hooves, growing louder, nearer. Dusty stilled, listening. T.J. rose from the chair in slow motion and moved to the head of the bed. Propping one knee on the bed, he raised the flimsy curtain that covered the window and looked out. Dusty stared at his big paw of a hand and the gauziness of the curtain. She fought another surge of hysteria at the absurdity of the contrast.

T.J. jumped back from the window and looked at her wildly. He jerked her up and pushed her to the floor by the table. "Don't move." He cracked the door and sighted the rifle through the opening.

"Who's out there?" she asked desperately.

"Shut up," T.J. hissed, "or I'll shoot 'im where he stands."

There was only one person it could be. Jake.

Chapter Thirteen

Jake dismounted by his truck, touching it like a talisman. Let Dusty be okay. Out of the corner of his eye, he saw the door open, and the end of the rifle barrel protrude, a stiff black snake stuck through the opening. Jake's ears strained to hear something, anything that might tell him whether Dusty was alive or not. Nothing, not a sound. Only a rumble of thunder in the distance.

He kept his eyes down, afraid if he looked up he'd force a confrontation, force the old man to shoot at him. He considered frantically what would be his best protection from the rifle. T.J.'s horse stood across the yard. If he could make it to the horse, he might use the horse's body as shelter. T.J. wouldn't take the chance of shooting his own horse. The yard was wide. Jake knew he had to be quick, but he had to take the risk.

Hunkered down to make himself a smaller target, Jake ran across the yard. T.J. took aim behind the door. Before he could finish sighting in, Dusty pulled up her legs and launched herself at T.J. She hit him along his right side, making his aim go wild. The bullet blasted from the rifle and skimmed the top of the cedar tree by the gate.

T.J.'s horse reared, frightened by the explosion of the bullet and the crouched figure running toward her. Jake grabbed the reins and danced away from the horse's hooves. He and the horse struggled, Jake crooning to the frightened animal and cautiously approaching her left withers.

T.J. pushed Dusty off his bulk, cursing at her. The edge of the bed struck her midsection, momentarily taking her breath. T.J. regained his footing and shoved fresh bullets into the rifle. He jerked her up in front of him and used her as a shield as he stepped outside.

Jake stood by the walleyed mare, stroking her neck and crooning to her flattened ears. He kept up the stroking even when his heart pounded at the sight of Dusty being pushed out the door, T.J. and the rifle close behind.

A big hand circled her upper arm and the rifle barrel lay alongside her head as she descended the steps. The hand halted her only a few feet into the yard. Jake, his face rigid, watched carefully by the horse. The horse still eyed him uncertainly, ears flat, but she didn't shy away.

T.J.'s voice boomed across the yard, "Git away from my horse."

"You won't make it, T.J.," Jake answered. "The sheriff's on his way."

T.J.'s grip tightened on her arm. "Then, if I gotta die, I might's well take you with me. I guess I can save this here girl of Blackie's from th' likes of you. Git away from th' horse."

"Let Dusty drive the truck out of here. Me for her, even swap."

The throbbing pain in Dusty's head combined with the awful fear excited by the rifle, cold and deadly, next to her ear. Pain and fear swam around her in a choking red cloud that cut off her air and closed around her heart. She heard

Jake from across the yard like a voice out of a fog, distorted by her cloud of dread yet as familiar as the sharp edge of grief. Jake Valiteros would die, killed by the same rifle that killed her father, the same rifle that rested with burning coldness on her shoulder. Jake, her lover, her mountain cowboy, would die, like Mac had died, like Blackie had died.

"You won't move, guess I'll jist have to take a chance." T.J. moved the rifle to use Dusty's shoulder as a gun rest. Panic shrieking through her head, she jerked herself out of the way.

"No," she screamed at T.J. Although she wrenched desperately at his grip on her arm, she couldn't dislodge it. He had strength of iron. Jake lurched toward her, then held himself back. He knew helplessly that he would only place her in greater danger. Dusty jammed her shoulder into T.J.'s chest, holding it there.

"Listen to me, T.J.," she whispered, forcing the words from her dry throat, the rough hoarseness brittle with terror. "You owe me, T.J. You killed Blackie, you killed my father. You owe me."

T.J. stared steadily at Jake, but his chin quivered and the hand on the rifle that now was pressed across Dusty's midsection relaxed a bit. Dusty glued her shoulder to the middle of his chest.

"Blackie's dead, T.J. I lost my father. Don't make me lose Jake, too." When T.J.'s eyes narrowed at the mention of Jake, Dusty panicked, but she knew she had to talk fast. How could she get to him? How could she keep him from killing Jake? "He wants to marry me, T.J. Think about it. He wants to marry Blackie's daughter. Blackie's grandchildren will inherit all of Jake's land. All of it for Blackie's grandchildren." T.J. let out a short, sobbing breath. "Blackie's dead, but the land will belong to him, anyway. You have to let Jake live because of Blackie's grandchildren. If he dies, there's no way for the land to belong to Blackie again." T.J.'s red-rimmed eyes bore into her, eyes suffused in agony. Tears seeped into the seams of his cheeks. "Blackie will win, after all, T.J. It'll be his grandchildren that take over. Blackie's blood." Her throat felt raw, the words like red-hot brands searing her from the inside. The words were lies, lies meant to save Jake's life, but lies, nevertheless. She could never marry Jake, bear his children. Despair gripped her, locking her in a torment of grief, the despair of death pouring out of T.J.'s crazed eyes. Jake would die—please, God, not today, not this minute, but someday. He would die, like Mac had died, like Blackie had died.

T.J. wept, great broken, gasping sobs, "I didn't mean to hurt Blackie." The hot blast of his breath on her face brought tears of grief and fear from her own eyes. She forced herself to stay rigid against his chest.

"Blackie wuz my bes' friend."

"I know, T.J.," she said hoarsely, straining to concentrate. "You loved Blackie, and Blackie loved you. You have to do something for Blackie. You have to think about what Blackie would want you to do."

"I loved Blackie. He wuz my bes' friend."

"T.J., Blackie had a plan. He wanted Jake to take over his ranch. He wanted me to marry Jake."

"You lie," T.J. growled, pressing the rifle hard into her midsection.

"No, T.J.," she said, forcing down the panic that rose like bile. "Blackie never lied, and he taught me not to lie. Blackie's grandchildren, T.J., ranching Big Piney Creek. Blackie's grandchildren." The words cut like knives. They were lies, desperate lies to save Jake. There would be no family for her. Jake threatened the survival that beat through her blood, bred into her from generations of high country pioneers. She had to rid herself of the feelings that bound her to Jake, rip them out by the roots if necessary, before Jake died—like everyone else she had loved.

T.J.'s eyes crinkled into a grotesque smile that quivered on his face. "You wuz bes' rider I ever saw. Little bit of a thang, ridin' horses like a grown-up. Blackie wuz proud."

"I remember, T.J." Indecision crawled over T.J.'s ravaged face. Please, God, she prayed, don't let Jake move. Give me time. "You're going to see Blackie again someday, T.J. You know you are. He's waiting for you. Blackie wants Jake to live. You have to do this for Blackie."

T.J.'s shoulders slumped, and his grip on her arm fell away. The rifle barrel drooped toward the ground. "Oh, Blackie," he wailed. "Why'd you hafta die?" His head rolled back on his shoulders and the keening sound moaned out his open mouth.

As Dusty dropped limply to the ground, Jake crept toward them, the kneeling woman and the wailing old man. He crossed the terrible expanse of the yard, feeling the cramped tenseness that the horror of waiting had left in every muscle. When he reached them, he pushed Dusty aside and grabbed the rifle in one fluid movement. The rifle slipped loose from T.J.'s fingers without a struggle.

The loss of the rifle jerked T.J.'s heavy arms upward. With his arms outstretched and eyes wild, he looked ready to crush Jake with the sheer bulk of his body. At that moment, the loud whine of a siren split the air. The sheriff's car bounced up the double-track road toward them, lights flashing and gaining on them rapidly.

T.J. growled, a feral sound deep in his throat, jerked his bulk around and bolted for the door of his house. He was gone so quickly that Jake had no time to react.

Jake knelt by Dusty, where she lay crumpled in the dirt. His sure fingers unbound her hands. He wrapped one strong arm around her and dragged her with him in a crouched run toward the sheriff's car as it screamed to a halt.

He pushed her against the side of the car, holding her there with his body as the sheriff and Hooter jumped out into the yard. The sheriff drew his weapon and advanced on the little house. He had almost reached the steps when one hollow blast of a gun sounded from inside. He jumped to the side of the house, out of range of a second shot, but there was only silence, long seconds of eerie silence. Suddenly, thunder cracked like a ghostly echo of the gunshot, and the wind picked up, blowing the dirt of the yard into swirls.

"Oh, T.J.," Dusty whispered against the cold metal of the car, "what have you done?"

Jake held her limp body tightly in his arms, bending his head protectively over hers. The sheriff approached the door with caution, pushed it open and jumped out of the way. After he peered around the corner, he entered the dark silence of T.J.'s cinder-block house.

"It's all over, folks," the sheriff said from the doorway. He shouted at his deputy, "Call for an ambulance." Then he mumbled, "For all the good it's gonna do, call for one, anyway."

After the sheriff emerged from the blood-splattered cave of T.J.'s house, he began firing questions at Dusty and Jake. Jake protested, but Dusty insisted she wanted to get it over with. She looked pale, chalky white, the freckles across her nose like flecks of color on the back of Early Snow. The battered innocence in her face shook him. He wanted to take her home and wrap her in his arms, lie in the center of his big bed with Dusty sheltered by his body.

Instead, she climbed into the back seat of the sheriff's car and answered questions with a deadly calm. Reed ignored Jake's angry scowl and took his time getting the sequence of events down in his scribbled notes. By the time he was satisfied, the ambulance had arrived, the light flashing but the siren eerily silent.

Strangely indifferent, Dusty didn't protest when Jake sent Hooter back on Yeller. She climbed into the passenger's side of Jake's truck and shut the door without comment. When

Jake started the engine, she said, "I want to go home." She laid her head against the headrest, her eyes closed and her forehead puckered slightly between the delicate feathers of her eyebrows. When Jake reached across the seat to touch the soiled gauze of her bandage, she straightened again, away from the caress of his fingers.

He stilled, his eyes narrowing. "That's where I'm taking you. Home."

"No," she said, her voice emotionless. "I mean my home."

His tightly controlled anger erupted, blinding him with its acid poison. He had been forced to stand by while that old man threatened Dusty with a hunting rifle, powerless to protect her, unable to do anything but watch. He had listened to her plead with T.J., trying desperately to save a life that would be worthless if anything happened to her. Then he had endured the long, excruciating interrogation, listening to her answer the sheriff's questions in a flat, expressionless voice and watching her fight the pain in her head. He had fought down the urge to bust Dan Reed in the mouth and cradle Dusty in his arms, stroking the head she held so carefully between her hands.

Gritting his teeth to control his violent reaction to her indifference, he slammed both hands against the steering wheel, triggering a loud blast of the truck horn. He looked up to see the sheriff, stopped, as he was about to enter the cinder-block house, by the unexpected noise. Reed stared at the couple in the truck with undisguised curiosity. Jake jerked the truck into gear and gunned the engine, hurtling the vehicle backward away from the little house and the sheriff's speculation. Beside him, Dusty sat in frozen stillness, staring out the passenger window.

The cab of the pickup was hollow with silence all the way from T.J.'s double-track road to Blackie's small frame house. The rain swept toward them from the mountains, its gray wall growing larger and softening the air before it with moisture as it ate up the rolling sagebrush hills. Finally, it drummed down on the metal roof and bounced off the forbidding silence inside without bringing any softening at all to his sharp-edged emptiness.

"Don't get out," she said when the truck splashed to a stop in the puddle before her front steps. "Please," she added, staring at her own hand on the door handle, "I need to be alone." Then she ran inside and slammed the door before he collected himself enough to react. He sat in the empty cab and cursed, violent, obscene curses, pouring out his frustration on the closed doors between him and the person who had become his life. Finally, he drove away.

Inside the rain-darkened house, she heard Jake's truck leave, attacking the sloppy road like a sworn enemy. She leaned against the closed door and shivered, fighting to blank out the pain and grief that threatened to overwhelm her. Tears washed down her cheeks, uncontrollable tears. Swiping with both hands at her wet cheeks, she pushed away from the door. Through the sheen of tears, Blackie's chair swam before her, Blackie's empty chair. With a moaning sob, she collapsed into it, pulling her legs under her and huddling in its worn cushions. She laid her bandaged head on the armrest and let go, weeping brokenly. Tears for Blackie and tears for the pitiful old man who killed him. Tears for the terror of seeing T.J. aim a rifle at Jake. And most of all, tears for Jake, for her desperate need to rip him out of her heart.

Gradually, she heard the rain diminish until it was only a slow drip from the edge of the porch. Thunder rumbled distantly, indicating the fury of the rain had moved on into the heart of the valley. She sighed and closed her eyes, exhausted by the horror she hadn't yet survived.

She listened to the drips as they splashed on the wooden porch floor, big angry drops throwing themselves at the wood. Then, in the distance, a truck roared up the double-track road toward the house. She heard it splash through puddles, no hesitation in its speed. It screeched to a halt at her front steps, and she braced herself. It was Jake, of course. He would come in, filling up the small room, flooding her senses. How could she survive the pain?

Long, silent, tortuous minutes, then the creak of a truck door opening. Boots splashing through a puddle. At last, the bass creak of a larger door, followed by the shuffle of a horse's hooves backing out of a trailer. She pushed herself out of the soft cushions and stumbled to the front door in time to see Jake leading True Blue across the yard. He carried her saddle propped on his hip. Even in her panic, she noticed the absence of his cowboy lurch, the purposeful evenness of his gait. When he and True Blue disappeared into the barn, she stepped onto the front porch. Seconds later, she heard him call to Sunny Boy in the corral by the barn. Sunny responded instantly, trotting gladly toward the back of the barn.

Her head pounded with uncertainty. For long minutes, she huddled wretchedly behind the curtain of drops at the porch edge. No sound, no movement from the barn. Finally, she hunched her shoulders against the pain and ran awkwardly across the yard. Slipping inside the heavy warmth of the barn, she leaned against the closed door, using its sturdiness to hold herself up. Jake stood between the two horses, facing away from her, working on the saddle on True's back. It was Blackie's saddle. Jake was lengthening the stirrup. When he walked around True to adjust the other stirrup, he raised his eyes briefly, flicking his gaze at Dusty, offering only the slightest sign of recognition.

He moved around True Blue with sureness and familiarity. Watching him hurt, wrung at her heart, because he reminded her of Blackie. He stopped now and again to speak to True in a low voice or to stroke him. True's ears cocked in Jake's direction, moving as he moved, but only the ears. Otherwise, True remained perfectly still, accepting Jake with complete trust. Just as he had accepted Blackie.

Then Jake turned to Sunny Boy, exchanging the horse's halter for a bridle. When he walked toward her to pick up the saddle blanket that rested against her saddle, she had to stop him.

"What are you doing?" she asked, her question thin as a wisp of smoke.

Again those narrow eyes flicked in her direction, only a pause before striding back to Sunny Boy. "I'm saddling a couple of horses. What does it look like I'm doing?" he mumbled, intent on settling the blanket smoothly.

"Why?" Then she pleaded, "Please, go away, Jake. Leave me alone."

His face was chiseled stone when he picked up the saddle, hefting it back to the horse. "Shut up, Dusty," he growled. "You're going riding with me. I'm getting you on horseback, then you'll feel more like yourself."

"No, Jake, I can't."

He paused in adjusting the saddle to look at her. "Shut up, I said." He returned his attention to his job. "You can and you will. You're going to ride Sunny Boy. He needs the workout." He patted Sunny and reached for the cinch. "I've decided you and I are going to take up team roping. Sunny's a talented roping horse, and you're going to use that talent."

"No," she groaned. She clutched her pounding head with both hands. He wasn't listening to her. "Please, Jake, try to understand. T.J. almost killed you. He killed Blackie and he almost killed you, too." She sank to her knees on the dirt floor, unable to stand any longer. "I survived Blackie's death," she whispered, "but I couldn't survive yours. So much death. My mother, Mac, Blackie. I can't take anymore." He came to her, rushing across the dirt floor. She looked up and pleaded, "Please, Jake, not your death, too. Something will happen to you, just like it did to everyone else in my family, and I can't survive that. Please, let me live in peace."

"Get up, Dusty." He grasped her by the arms and hauled her up against him. "Lean on me. I'll help you."

"No, don't." She shook her head, defying the pounding inside it.

Jake held her head still, halting the painful movement. "You're wrong, Dusty. You can survive anything. You're strong like Blackie." She tried to pull away, but he held her, wrapping an arm around her and gripping the back of her head with his other hand. "Don't tell me you're not strong. I won't believe it. I won't let you crawl into yourself and shut me out. That's what my father did. He lost his daughter, my little sister," he said, his voice cracking, "and he lost his wife. Then he drowned himself in bitterness." He pressed her head against his shoulder. "He shut me out, and my mother ran away. She let death and the fear of death crush her, rob her of everything. She was weak, but you're not, Dusty. You're going to live—like Blackie lived. Blackie lost his Vera, but he went on loving his children. Remember that, Dusty. Blackie lost Vera, but he survived."

He gripped her upper arms and stood her on her own feet. "Look at me," he ordered. She slowly raised her chin until her eyes, cloudy with fear, met his. "Even after Mac died," he said, "Blackie survived—because he loved you."

She clutched Jake's shirt. "But Blackie sold my ranch."

He folded her in his arms, holding her in his warmth. "Yeah, he did." He rubbed his lips across the bandage on her forehead. "Even that shows how much he loved you, Dusty. He was wrong, but he did it to help you. He could see the ranch wasn't making it, financially, and he was worried you'd be stuck with debts and not much else. Besides, he thought you were making a life for yourself at the university. He thought all he could offer you was money, money from the sale of the ranch." He leaned his cheek against her hair. "It hurt him to sell the ranch."

"I know," she admitted. "He told me. He said he couldn't tell me about selling because it hurt too much to talk about it."

"He wanted to do the best for you, Dusty, because he loved you. Sometimes it's hard to know what the best really is."

"He said we could use the money to buy breeding stock. He'd always wanted to raise Appaloosas." Jake stroked her hair. "Now that I know what happened to him, how he died, I can get on with his plans. I can raise his Appaloosas." That much, raising Blackie's horses, didn't bring any pain.

"Yes." Jake smiled softly into her hair. "You can breed Appaloosas for you and quarter horses for me. You can surround yourself with horses." He tipped her chin so he could look into her eyes, distressed to see that her eyes were like two bruises in her chalky face. "But first you're going to marry me."

"Jake, try to understand," she said desperately, trembling with the urgency of her struggle. "You're too close, almost like you're inside of me. If I lost you, if something happened to you..." The words trailed off into shudders that she willed away, closing her hands in hard fists. "I've been getting by, getting through the days until I knew what happened to Blackie. But now I know, and the loss of Blackie..." She rolled her forehead against the firm plane of his chest. "It hurts so much. All of my family gone, chipped away from me piece by piece." She raised her tear-filled eyes to plead with him. "If I lost you, there wouldn't be enough of me left to live."

"I know, sweetheart," he murmured, his rough fingertips tracing her eyebrows, the straight line of her nose, her full bottom lip. "I know. I feel the same way. I was so scared back there at T.J.'s, so scared. If that rifle had slipped, if T.J. had accidentally shot you, everything that matters to me would have ended." His hand clasped her chin and his eyes traveled intently over her face, as if reassuring himself. "Nothing is as necessary to me as you are, not the cattle, not even the ranch. Just you."

"It hurts so much, Jake," she moaned.

He scooped her up in his arms and carried her to a pile of fresh straw, pausing to pick up a blanket to toss on top before he lowered her on the improvised bed. She lay back limply on the blanket, too exhausted to resist the solid comfort of Jake as he lay beside her.

"Jake, the horses," she complained weakly.

"Hush," he soothed, "they're fine. I have to touch you, to know you're all right, alive and whole." Tossing his hat aside, he pulled her into the shelter of his body.

"I don't think I have any strength left, Jake." Her voice was frail and thin, unlike he had ever heard it, and her hands moved restlessly over his chest. "When you stood by T.J.'s horse, across that awful yard, I thought I could see the blood explode on your chest, see it burst out of you and cover your chest. I kept on talking and talking to T.J., but I could still see it. I could see it happening even when it didn't." She went on in that frail whisper, "When I pushed myself against his big body, when I answered the sheriff's questions, when I rode in the truck beside you. I could see the blood, your blood."

He gripped her arms and looked down into her eyes. "Look at me, Dusty. No blood. T.J. didn't shoot me. No blood." He pushed her hair back from her forehead. "Don't you see, sweetheart? We both have our demons." His eyes smiled at hers through a mist of tears. "Before you came riding that spotted horse into my branding, I was all alone and resolved to stay that way. But you wouldn't let me. No, you stirred up the branding and irritated me and—" his voice slowed "—bewitched me and made me worry. And before I could defend myself, there wasn't room in my life for anyone or anything but you." He kissed her eyes closed, nuzzling the bridge of her nose. "I've lived in a wide-awake nightmare for weeks, afraid something would happen to you, afraid something would crush the life out of you, all that shiny, brand-new life that glistens in your aspen green eyes. I've had to face my demons, sweetheart." He whispered into her ear, "You wouldn't let me keep you safe. Yesterday, I watched you ride away from me to look around for rustlers, and I walked through fire. You were alone, and there was nothing I could do to protect you. I had to let you ride out by yourself in spite of the fear that burned around me."

"You came after me, Jake," she reminded him.

"Yes, I did," he whispered into her hair. "But not to stop you, Dusty. To ride with you, to follow in your wake, because riding with you is the only way I know I'm alive." He kissed the edge of the bandage, all around it, whispering over it. "I didn't want to love you. Worrying about you brought back painful memories, of Penny's death and my mother—" he forced out the whispered words "—and my father's long, cold silences. I understand about my father now. He felt responsible for Penny's death. She died and he shriveled into a bitter, angry man." He pulled back to look at her. "He needed my mother, and she needed him. They should have faced their demons together. We'll help each other, sweetheart," he promised, slow tears slipping from his eyes. "We'll work side by side all day and hold each other at night until some of the fear goes away, but we won't ever let go of each other. We belong together."

Her fingertips brushed his tears, and she pulled him down to her to kiss the tears away. Her own tears slipped silently from the corners of her eyes, long ropes of tears sweeping into her hair. With her lips brushing his wet cheeks, she wept, acknowledging to herself that Jake's pain was as great as her own. He had built walls around himself, locking away the deep feeling that brought the pain he had known in his childhood. Without realizing what she was doing, she had cracked open his hard life and exposed the sweetness inside, the sweet gentleness he had hidden long ago before he had even known it existed. There was no turning back because she was responsible for him now. She had to face whatever terror the future brought with all the courage she had left. As she tasted his tears, she prayed, fervently and tremulously, she had courage enough.

Bending his head to accept her caressing comfort, he trailed his hands, warm and trembling ever so slightly, down the bare skin of her neck to open her shirt, pushing aside cloth to move his rough palms over the soft skin of her breasts. Behind closed lids, he pictured her familiar woman's softness, treasuring the fullness and rubbing his thumbs back and forth over the velvet of her nipples. "We're the same breed, Dusty," he whispered, cupping her breasts in his palms. "The same breed," he repeated. "Our lungs breathe the same air, thin mountain air is mother's milk to both of us." He lowered his head to kiss first one breast and then the other. "The same blood pumps through our bodies, rich, red, high country blood." He laid his cheek on her breast. "Our hearts beat out the same song."

Laying her hand on his hair, she held his head as he nestled against her in the quiet of the barn. Yes, she thought, we are the same breed. She had stood in sunset light in his living room, recognizing herself in the house he had built as well as in the man himself. She stroked Jake's mistreated hair, brushing it back from his rugged face. The two of them shared the same heritage and the same dreams. She touched his still-damp cheek. She and Jake would have the children she had told T.J. about. Their children would be mountain-born, bred on mountain wind and the violent death of light in a mountain sunset. And she would have more reason to be afraid of the hard life and its precarious survival.

He pulled back enough to open his shirt and move her hands to his chest. She closed her eyes and fell into the familiar spell of touching Jake, hair and skin and lean muscle. Struggling with boots and jeans and shirt, he stripped away her clothes and then his own. She lay back on the blanket and warmed her hands on his bare skin, on the physical presence of her hard cowboy as he pulled at boots and jeans. At last he stretched the taut maleness of his body along the firmness of hers, slipping between her supple thighs and into the moist heart of her. Slowly, so slowly. His cowboy's body moved on hers, his chest rubbed her breasts, his belly stroked hers. His voice rumbled in her ear, "Say you love me, Dusty. Say it."

"I love you, Jake," she whispered. "I love you."

"Say you'll marry me."

A quick, indrawn breath and her eyes opened, the last hesitation before the plunge, before she committed herself irrevocably to facing the terror, the star-banged terror, of loving someone more than life itself.

"Say it, Dusty." He moved inside of her, deep inside, gently prodding her. "Say you'll marry me and ride by my side for the rest of your life."

She clutched his shoulders, holding him close, as close as she could possibly get to the warm, solidness of his male body. "Yes, Jake," she whispered, pressing her lips against his ear. "Yes, I'll marry you, and I'll ride by your side, and I won't let you go as long as I live."

They moved slowly together, their hearts beating the same rhythm, and surrendered, each to the other. When the passion burst within them, they looked at each other, staring into eyes that looked at the treasure inside, each recognizing the other too deeply for words.

In the warmth of the barn, with the sound of horses' hooves shifting on the dirt floor, they lay together as their bodies grew quiet. When he felt the last of her tremors leave her, he braced himself on an elbow and smiled at her closed eyes. He opened them with brushed kisses.

"Ready for our ride?" he asked.

She rubbed her hand across his lean shoulder. He knew her so well. He had been right to bring True Blue. A ride would restore her sense of balance, chase away the shadows. She placed her hand in his. "Help me up, cowboy."

Minutes later, by the opened gate to the pasture, as she swung into her saddle on Sunny, she remembered something. "Jake," she said, looking at him on True's back by the gate, "didn't you mention something about team roping earlier?"

He shrugged, "Why not? We own talented roping horses. It makes sense to take up team roping." He grinned at her. "I think we'd make a hell of a team."

"But my roping is awful rusty," she said, riding toward him.

"So what? You can pick it up again. I figure you'll be ready by next summer when the riding clubs around here start holding their competitions." He leaned down and closed the gate behind her.

She looked at him speculatively. "Riding club competitions," she mused. "That means you'll have to associate with your neighbors, doesn't it?"

"I guess so," he said, staring at the reins in his hands.

"Oh." She smiled softly at his discomfort and decided the idea of team roping definitely had merit.

He looked up at her from beneath the brim of his hat and grinned at her self-satisfied smile. My God, he thought, she looks glorious with the sun peeking out from behind a cloud to turn her hair to gold.

"Turn around, sweetheart," he said gently. "Look at the mountains."

Obediently, she turned her horse toward the mountains, as Jake rode True Blue to her side. Immediately, she gasped, startled by the awesome beauty stretched before her. On the horizon, the afternoon light, softened by the light gray remains of rain clouds, shimmered over deep green mountainsides like jeweled mist. And, from the gray-green of the sagebrush rose the perfect arc of a rainbow, beginning at the foot of the mountains and bending its colors like a benediction high above the willows of the creek to lose itself again in sagebrush.

Jake reached out for her hand, holding it firmly between their two mounts. "What do you see?" he asked, watching the expression on her face. "I'll tell you what I see. When I look at the mountains now, I don't see them with my eyes. Because I love you, I see the high country with my heart. Before you took over my life, it was just land, good for nothing more than raising the best cattle. Now, Dusty," he said, lacing his fingers with hers, "I can't see the mountains without my love for you stirring inside me. You have become home for me, and what you love, the high country that holds your heart, holds mine, too."

Dusty leaned toward their joined hands, pressing a swift kiss on his fingers. Jake sighed, content, at the sweetness of having Dusty by his side and the feel of her kiss on his hand.

"We're lucky, Dusty, like Blackie was lucky with his jade-eyed Vera. As long as he could see the mountains, Vera was alive in his heart. That's true for us, too. As long as those mountains endure, Dusty, that's how long my love for you will endure, and when we're apart, all we have to do is look at those mountains to find each other again. Every stream, every tree, every rock, it's all the two of us together."

Dusty smiled, her heart warmed, washed clean by mountain rain and the strength of Jake's love.

* * * * *

COMING NEXT MONTH

#919 MAIL ORDER COWBOY—Patricia Coughlin
That Special Woman!
Allie Halston swore she'd conquer rigorous ranch life, even if it meant taking on all of Texas! Then she faced sexy Burn Monroe—who was more than just a cowboy with an attitude....

#920 B IS FOR BABY—Lisa Jackson
Love Letters
Beth Crandall's single passionate night with Jenner McKee had changed her life forever. Years later, an unexpected letter drew her back home, and to the man she'd never forgotten....

#921 THE GREATEST GIFT OF ALL—Penny Richards
Baron Montgomery knew determined Mallory Ryan would sacrifice anything for her young child. But when her boundless mother's love was tested, could Mallory accept his help and his promise of everlasting devotion?

#922 WHEN MORNING COMES—Christine Flynn
Driven and dedicated, Travis McCloud had sacrificed his marriage for career. Now a chance reunion with Brooke compelled him to open his heart...and to take a second chance at love.

#923 COWBOY'S KIN—Victoria Pade
A Ranching Family
Linc Heller's wild, hell-raising ways were legendary. Yet Kansas Daye wondered if becoming a father had tempered Linc—and if he was ready to step into her waiting arms.

#924 LET'S MAKE IT LEGAL—Trisha Alexander
John Appleton gave up the fast track to become Mr. Mom. Then high-powered lawyer Sydney Scott Wells stormed into his life, and John knew he'd show her the best of both worlds!

MILLION DOLLAR SWEEPSTAKES (III)

Dark secrets, dangerous desire...

Lovers DARK AND DANGEROUS

Three spine-tingling tales from the dark side of love.

This October, enter the world of shadowy romance as *Silhouette* presents the third in their annual tradition of thrilling love stories and chilling story lines. Written by three of Silhouette's top names:

LINDSAY McKENNA
LEE KARR
RACHEL LEE

Haunting a store near you this October.

Only from

V Silhouette®
™

...where passion lives.

JINGLE BELLS, WEDDING BELLS:
Silhouette's Christmas Collection for 1994

Christmas Wish List

*To beat the crowds at the malls and get the perfect present for *everyone,* even that snoopy Mrs. Smith next door!

*To get through the holiday parties without running my panty hose.

*To bake cookies, decorate the house and serve the perfect Christmas dinner—just like the women in all those magazines.

*To sit down, curl up and read my Silhouette Christmas stories!

Join *New York Times* bestselling author Nora Roberts, along with popular writers Barbara Boswell, Myrna Temte and Elizabeth August, as we celebrate the joys of Christmas—and the magic of marriage—with

JINGLE BELLS, WEDDING BELLS

Silhouette's Christmas Collection for 1994.

JBWB

BABY'S CHOICE

Join Marie Ferrarella—and not one, but two, beautiful babies—as her "Baby's Choice" series concludes in October with *BABY TIMES TWO* (SR #1037)

She hadn't thought about Chase Randolph in ages, yet now Gina Delmonico couldn't get her ex-husband out of her mind. Then fate intervened, forcing them together again. Chase, too, seemed to remember their all-too-brief marriage—especially the honeymoon. And before long, these predestined parents discovered the happiness—and the family—that had always been meant to be.

It's "Baby's Choice" when angelic babies-in-waiting select their own delivery dates, only in

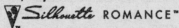

Silhouette ROMANCE™

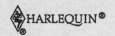 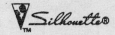

"HOORAY FOR HOLLYWOOD" SWEEPSTAKES

HERE'S HOW THE SWEEPSTAKES WORKS

OFFICIAL RULES — NO PURCHASE NECESSARY

To enter, complete an Official Entry Form or hand print on a 3" x 5" card the words "HOORAY FOR HOLLYWOOD", your name and address and mail your entry in the pre-addressed envelope (if provided) or to: "Hooray for Hollywood" Sweepstakes, P.O. Box 9076, Buffalo, NY 14269-9076 or "Hooray for Hollywood" Sweepstakes, P.O. Box 637, Fort Erie, Ontario L2A 5X3. Entries must be sent via First Class Mail and be received no later than 12/31/94. No liability is assumed for lost, late or misdirected mail.

Winners will be selected in random drawings to be conducted no later than January 31, 1995 from all eligible entries received.

Grand Prize: A 7-day/6-night trip for 2 to Los Angeles, CA including round trip air transportation from commercial airport nearest winner's residence, accommodations at the Regent Beverly Wilshire Hotel, free rental car, and $1,000 spending money. (Approximate prize value which will vary dependent upon winner's residence: $5,400.00 U.S.); 500 Second Prizes: A pair of "Hollywood Star" sunglasses (prize value: $9.95 U.S. each). Winner selection is under the supervision of D.L. Blair, Inc., an independent judging organization, whose decisions are final. Grand Prize travelers must sign and return a release of liability prior to traveling. Trip must be taken by 2/1/96 and is subject to airline schedules and accommodations availability.

Sweepstakes offer is open to residents of the U.S. (except Puerto Rico) and Canada who are 18 years of age or older, except employees and immediate family members of Harlequin Enterprises, Ltd., its affiliates, subsidiaries, and all agencies, entities or persons connected with the use, marketing or conduct of this sweepstakes. All federal, state, provincial, municipal and local laws apply. Offer void wherever prohibited by law. Taxes and/or duties are the sole responsibility of the winners. Any litigation within the province of Quebec respecting the conduct and awarding of prizes may be submitted to the Regie des loteries et courses du Quebec. All prizes will be awarded; winners will be notified by mail. No substitution of prizes are permitted. Odds of winning are dependent upon the number of eligible entries received.

Potential grand prize winner must sign and return an Affidavit of Eligibility within 30 days of notification. In the event of non-compliance within this time period, prize may be awarded to an alternate winner. Prize notification returned as undeliverable may result in the awarding of prize to an alternate winner. By acceptance of their prize, winners consent to use of their names, photographs, or likenesses for purpose of advertising, trade and promotion on behalf of Harlequin Enterprises, Ltd., without further compensation unless prohibited by law. A Canadian winner must correctly answer an arithmetical skill-testing question in order to be awarded the prize.

For a list of winners (available after 2/28/95), send a separate stamped, self-addressed envelope to: Hooray for Hollywood Sweepstakes 3252 Winners, P.O. Box 4200, Blair, NE 68009.

CBSRLS

OFFICIAL ENTRY COUPON

"Hooray for Hollywood"
SWEEPSTAKES!

Yes, I'd love to win the Grand Prize — a vacation in Hollywood — or one of 500 pairs of "sunglasses of the stars"! Please enter me in the sweepstakes!

This entry must be received by December 31, 1994.
Winners will be notified by January 31, 1995.

Name _____

Address _____ Apt. _____

City _____

State/Prov. _____ Zip/Postal Code _____

Daytime phone number _____
(area code)

Mail all entries to: Hooray for Hollywood Sweepstakes,
P.O. Box 9076, Buffalo, NY 14269-9076.
In Canada, mail to: Hooray for Hollywood Sweepstakes,
P.O. Box 637, Fort Erie, ON L2A 5X3.

KCH